The Island & Other Nightmares

M. P. Seipolt

For everyone who believed in me, including myself.

Copyright © M. P. Seipolt 2026
ISBN: 978-1-7644578-0-4

This is a work of fiction. Similarities to real people, places, or events are entirely coincidental.

Cover art by Cosmic Flame Studio

Table of Contents

The Beast of Canniswood	*7*
The Journal in the Cabin	*17*
The Island in Oswelth Cove	*21*
A Vampire's Reflection	*30*
Golden Child	*44*
In the Shadow of the Wyrm	*61*
Metal Hearts	*78*
Cheating Death	*86*
Let Me Taste You	*109*
The Tapping in the Wall	*119*
Help Wanted	*137*
Fool's Gold	*163*
Visions of the Blind	*176*
Tickets?	*191*
The Hunt	*205*

The Beast of Canniswood

I would never forget the day I found my parents dead. All memories of that day elude me, all but that vicious scene that had been seared into my mind and subconscious.

That unforgettable event was set in motion the night before when my parents failed to return from their trip into the city. Yet as I sat in our kitchen, I watched the dinner I prepared for them slowly go cold. I was a restless bundle of nerves when I eventually retired to bed for the night. I ground my teeth and clawed at my bedding until, exhausted, sleep finally overtook me.

In the early hours of the next morning, my parents were still yet to return. So I set off to find them, but not before enlisting the help of a family friend. I stopped down the end of the road and knocked upon the front door of the humble abode that stood there. My knocking must've been quite startling, for the face and tone that Mr McKinnel greeted me with when he finally opened the door.

'Nicolas? What are ye doin' bangin' on me door like that? What's got into ye?''My parents haven't returned from the city. I fear they got lost somehow. I am going into the forest to look for them but, you know these woods better than anyone. Will you come help me?' He must have seen the fear in my face for he agreed immediately and hurried to grab his coat and rifle. In case of bears or wolves, he said. Together we rushed through the streets – Mr McKinnel hobbling alongside me, as fast as his bad leg would carry him – and made our way into the woods, just as the sun was rising to welcome a new dawn.

Off the beaten path through those thick, dead woods that surrounded our humble town, I found my parent's carriage. It lay in ruins. Their corpses were scattered across the frozen dirt throughout the wreckage. The winter chill had preserved them in twisted, bloodied pieces. I hadn't eaten since the night before, but that did nothing to stop the remaining contents of my stomach to spew forth from the nausea-inducing scene. When I had set out to search that morning, I could never have imagined what I would discover. I doubt anyone but I would've been able to recognise my parents or the shredded chunks of them that were left.

One eyeball dangled from my mother's face like a squashed grape, the other was rolled back into her head so that only the white was showing; gaping wounds had been deeply clawed into her cheek; patches of her hair ripped from her scalp; one of her ears was found twenty yards away from the wreck, and her mouth hung open in a never-ending silent scream. My father's jaw, on the other hand, was only connected to the rest of his face by one side; tongue torn from his throat; his eyes bloodshot, wide, and almost falling out of his head; his nose had been shattered and no longer even resembled a nose; one of his arms had been gnawed down to the bone in places, the bones themselves even showing breaks where they had been crunched open, the marrow from within sucked out; the top of his skull had been cracked open down the middle, his brain spilled out, it reminded me of the delicious runny eggs mother would always make to go with our toast each morning; neither head was attached to its corresponding body and multiple bitemarks had been found over the both of them.

Of the horses that had drawn the carriage, there was no sign.

Mr McKinnel limped onto the scene not too long after I had come across it, the fallen leaves of autumn past crunched under his heavy boots. He found it in the same state that I had. I was on my hands and knees, sobbing hysterically when my stomach heaved, and I brought forth last night's dinner. The seasoned hunter muttered a prayer, then rushed behind a tree; not even he could hold back from vomiting at the grizzly sight. Mr McKinnel was reluctant to leave me there, but I was unable to move. He headed back to town to seek help. He led a pair of officers back to the scene. There they found me in the same spot, having cried until my throat was raw and my eyes were dry. When the officers saw the scene, more bile was freshly spilled onto the forest floor.

'Jesus Christ...' one of them muttered after they regained their composure. 'What could've done something like this Jim?'

'God... I-I don't know Bill, it ain't right whatever it is.'

The officers helped me to my feet and shepherded me away from the scene. I felt my legs moving, beyond my control. Then one of them spoke, 'Lad. Were you the first one here? Did you see anything? Do you know who these people were?'

'M-My parents,' I choked out past my sobs.

'Blazes. I'm sorry Lad. What...what were their names?' his hand on my shoulder did little to comfort me.

'Alice and Douglas Lawson.'

'And yours Lad?'

'Nicolas,' I said simply. They then turned their attention towards Mr McKinnel.

'Are you, his grandfather?'

'No, I'm just a neighbour.'

The officers continued their investigation of the scene, taking note of every gruesome detail; anything that could give them a clue as to what type of monster could do something like this.

'It's not human whatever it is, but I've never seen a cursed beast capable of such a thing,' Bill scratched at his head after the officers had stepped away again.

'We'll get the hounds over here and see if they can find any tracks or scent,' Jim responded.

Mr McKinnel stepped closer and spoke up, 'Thank ye for all ye help. I know these woods well, I hunt in 'em often, and I'm more than willin' to lend ye a hand.'

I stood there as my body trembled, and I wiped my face, 'I'm coming too then, this beast needs to be blasted to the deepest pits of hell!'

'Nicolas... no. Ye aren't in yer right mind. Ye need some rest. Go home, I'll take care of it.' Both of Mr McKinnel's hands came to rest on my shoulders before he pulled me into a hug. I gripped tightly at him as I buried my face into his shoulder.

'Promise me. Promise me you'll kill that fiendish thing!'

'I promise ye.'

The hunt was almost fruitless: the hounds unable to pick up the scent of the beast. The horses were found much further away: dead at the bottom of a cliff, having broken their harnesses and bolted. They were unharmed aside from the fatal damage the drop had done to them. The officers and Mr McKinnel were left dumbfounded by how a beast could cause such devastating wreckage and slaughter, and then just vanish. The officers assured us they wouldn't give up the hunt however, 'We'll keep searching through these woods, we'll find it,' they'd said.

I would become a recluse for some weeks after that horrid day, I only ever left home during my restless nights, hardly able to sleep anymore. I searched for the beast, but it was all in vain. I don't know what I would've done if I had found that terrible creature, but I found even less than what the official hunt had turned up. The horror of that day was inescapable. I struggled to eat, unable to bear the sight of meat. The horrendous smell would assault my senses, fill my head, and overpower the taste of the food. Ever since that day I struggled to keep any kind of food down.

Then came the night, and with it the dreams and nightmares. My brain worked overtime, imagining how the massacre might've played out. Each time it would always feel so real, like I was truly there, stuck frozen in place, watching helplessly from the sidelines. Even when I closed my eyes it brought no reprieve, it did nothing to stop the screams, not even when I covered my ears did that block out the wails of my mother and father as they were eaten alive. Even worse than these nightmares, was when the perspective of them was heavily shifted. Instead of being a helpless spectator, I would see it all from the point of view of that beast. I would be the one to carry out the slaughter in these most detestable and vile dreams.

The home that I had once loved and cherished, now felt empty and cold; the silence within, unbearable. No more family dinners, never could I see my parents dance together in front of the fireplace or hear their laughter echo down the hall. I could never tell them how much I loved them, could never feel their warmth again.

It wasn't until the new moon, weeks later, that the vile beast returned. Townsfolk began sharing frightened whispers of what they saw, silhouetted against the full moon. A hideous creature that stood tall like a man, with gangly, gnarled limbs, and jagged teeth and claws as long as knives. Others who hadn't seen it themselves insisted that they heard it late at night. That bloodcurdling, howling noise sent fear through all and robbed them of their sleep. Some reported strange behaviour in their animals at night, or that they had even gone missing. Though as no remains had been found, not even a drop of blood to indicate any attacks, it was all chalked up to these missing animals simply having run away from their homes, kennels, or enclosures.

Mr McKinnel took it upon himself to ease the fears of the people. He wandered the town at night, lantern in one hand, a loaded musket in the other, patrolling the silent, cobbled streets. Such was his selfless nature. He had no family of his own, but he cared for as many strangers as he could, befriended as many as he could, so that they might be his substitute family in the end. He'd been the only one to check up on me after the tragedy, the one who kept pushing me to try and stomach something so that I'd have the energy I needed to keep going. He was always there to talk, or just so that I wouldn't be alone, even if we sat in silence while he puffed on his pipe or cleaned his old-fashioned musket – an arduous and time-consuming task, but one that was soothing to watch. He knew the true horror; he had shared that frightening scene with me after all. He wasn't like the rest of the people who only seemed to care about the beast when it could affect them directly, who didn't care about what had happened to my family. I was reluctant to join Mr McKinnel on his patrols for this reason, I had no desire to help these selfish people or ease their troubled nights. They never helped me sleep easier or showed that they even cared about what I was going through; why would I be so kind to them? But if the beast really had returned, mayhap this was my chance to avenge my family. It was with this thought in mind, that I ventured out into the dull light of a new moon and down the road to speak with Mr McKinnel.

I met him as he stepped out of his home. He was surprised to see me, but he welcomed me with a smile.

'Nicolas? What are ye doing out so late? Is there somethin' I can help ye with?' he asked me.

'Mr McKinnel, I'm going out on patrol as well. It isn't right that you're out here on your own, and it'll be faster for us to take one half of the town each' – my voice was sterner than it ever had been when I spoke to Mr McKinnel, who had been like a grandfather to me.

'Nicolas...' – he sighed; his eyes showed his heartbreak – 'I won't let ye. I wouldn't be able to live with meself if somethin' were to happen to ye.'

I bit down on the insides of my cheeks and shook my head, 'I have to. My family must be avenged. I'm just here so that you knew what I was doing, and so that you don't go to parts of town that I've already been to.'

'Ye feel that strongly about it do ye...?' – he took his cap off and rubbed at his bald head – 'aye, I can see that ye don't mean to back down from it. Your mother would get that same look. At least come along with me instead of goin' off by yerself.'

'You'll have to cuff yourself to me if you want me going with you.'

Mr McKinnel sighed in defeat and put his cap back. He turned back inside; gesturing for me to follow.

'At least let me give ye somethin' to protect yerself with' – he shuffled across the room and down the hall. He returned shortly with an ancient looking, flintlock pistol, which he assured me would work. 'Ye know how to fire one o' these things don't ye?' I gave a nod as I took the relic from him. 'Good, now it's already loaded, but ye will only get one shot, so make sure you kill the bastard thing.'

After that he fetched another lantern for me and offered me a warmer coat; I took the lantern but declined the latter. The lantern provided me enough solace and warmth for the rest of the night on its own. I thanked him for the generosity, and then the two of us set out down the road together; when we reached a branch in the path, he once again tried coaxing me into following him. I quickly refused and started down one of the branching streets. I didn't even look back as he called out to me.

'Ye just make sure ye come back here a few hours from now! Be safe Nicolas!'

The night was quiet and calm, an occasional cloud drifted past the moon, obscuring it from view briefly and shrouding the slumbering town in darkness. The silence was only disturbed by the heels of my boots clicking along the cobbled path. I turned my gaze this way and that, shining my light upon this stone or that wall, yet the only "beasts" to be found were the alley cats of the neighbourhood, or a stray hound here and there. The only person I came across, was Miss Carla, a young woman who recently came of age and was two years my junior. She was locking up her family's shop, about to walk home; I offered to accompany her, and she seemed glad to have me along. After that we walked in silence, small talk was never my strong suit even before I'd lost my parents in such a violent way. I was happy just to be in her presence, to have her by my side. The smell of her perfume was comforting and enticing. Even just to have her there as something nice to look at; or to remind me that I wasn't alone out here was comforting enough. It also made part of me think that maybe I should've taken Mr McKinnel up on his offer to accompany him on the patrol instead. When we got to Carla's family home, she turned to me and said,

'Thank you for walking me home, Nic... I'm sorry about what happened to your family I...' she paused and wiped away a tear, 'it's horrible what happened, and I'm sorry that I haven't spoken with you since. My family and I, our door is always open to you if you need anything. Anything at all.' It took all I had to offer her a warm smile as thanks for her kind words. I stayed silent; I feared that I would break down into sobs if I opened my mouth. She returned my smile and then turned away, she thanked me once more before she stepped into her home and shut the door.

I turned away and finished the rest of my patrol. Nothing else of note happened. I found myself back at Mr McKinnel's home sometime later. I enjoyed a hot cup of tea with him, returned his lantern, then made my way back to my own home; to get what I hoped would be a dreamless sleep. Of course, I would not be so lucky this night.

The next day was quite peculiar. Mr McKinnel came to my doorstep in the late morning; of course, I let him in and prepared a cup of coffee just the way he liked it; I even gave him a plate of bread and cheese to go along with it. I set the plate down on the small stand between our seats to give the illusion it was for us both as we had a drink together, though I couldn't eat any of it. I was able to eat again by now, but coincidentally enough, meat was the only thing I could stomach. It was after we'd gotten comfortably seated and with mugs in hand that Mr McKinnel brought up why he was really here today.

'I'd like to talk to ye about what ye did or didn't see last night,' he started, 'Now I already knows what ye told me before, that nothing unusual was afoot. Ye just walked that young missy, Carla, home, and she's attested to that. But ye swear that you didn't hear anything after that or ere?'

I was puzzled. 'No, of course not. I told you last night, I neither saw, nor heard anything of the beast that is said to be lurking hereabouts.

'Now the strange thing about that is, ye see. Folks in town are still going on about them sightings, just like they was ere I started walking up and down the streets at night.' He set his drink aside and sat back, puffing on his pipe, deep in thought. His eyes studied my face, as if searching for an answer that might be hidden therein. When he spoke again, he said quietly: 'But I can see that ye speak the truth, it's just that I seen that same look on the faces of other folks 'round town too.'

We finished our coffee in silence. How could the townsfolk and I have had completely opposite experiences last night? Afterwards, I showed Mr McKinnel out with the promise that I'd see him again that night for our patrol.

That marked the beginning of a routine for me. Each night I'd join Mr McKinnel on his patrol; there were nights when we'd hear the beast, yet the townsfolk heard nothing, other nights the reverse was true, and nights where none of us heard a thing. My hunger pangs returned, not even the most tender of meat could sate them now. I was also plagued daily, with horrible nightmares. Yet there had not been another grizzly attack since the violent deaths of my beloved parents. I thought my hunger and troubled sleep a small price for peace. But peace never lasts, it must inevitably be broken.

That night began like any other. I'd gone out on over a dozen of these nightly patrols; they now felt like a normal part of life. Yet the beast that slaughtered my family continued to elude me. Some nights Carla stayed late at the store, to clean or take stock, and I would escort her home during my patrol.

On this fateful night, as that store was about to be within sight, I heard it. No, not the sounds of any beast, oh how I wish it was only the sounds of that damnable beast I heard. Instead, what I heard was that voice I had come to cherish so dearly – the voice that belonged to sweet Carla – distorted in such a way through pain and fear, that it was the most horrible, heart-shattering voice I'd ever heard. I dropped my lantern and rushed down the street, faster than I'd ever run in my life. But I wasn't fast enough. As I pounded down the hill and Miss Carla's store came in sight, I saw no beast and I no longer heard any sound, other than my own boots thudding against the cobblestones. What I did see however, was almost as bad as what I found that day my parents died. It was just as gruesome, but only half as bloody. Only one victim had been ripped apart this time.

Carla was dead, her face unrecognisable from the way it had been disfigured by that beast. I fell to my knees beside her mangled corpse – still so fresh and warm – and I howled. Tears streaked down my messy face. My arms cradled Carla's severed head to my chest; chunks of flesh had been ripped from her skull; her beautiful eyes picked clean from their sockets; her jaw was permanently contorted into the scream of her final moments; her tongue stuck out from her mauled lips; her body stiff, as if she'd been petrified in fright; one of her arms and one leg lay some feet away from the rest of her, the arm was only bone, bone that was still intact; her belly had been clawed open, entrails squeezed out of her like bloody sausages. She lay in a pool of blood, which sloshed over the pavement and flowed down the gutter. And the smell. It overpowered me, as if her viscera were stuffed directly up my nostrils and reached into the back of my throat. I could taste her, as if her raw flavour assaulted my mouth with every breath I sucked in. Drool ran down my wet, warm chin as I was slumped over, slack-jawed.

'Oh sweet God... what have ye done' – Mr McKinnel's voice seemed to come from far away, yet he stood right there in the street as I turned my head to look at him – 'Oh Carla...' he said as his pipe had fallen from his mouth, lips trembling. 'No... Nicolas. Oh God, Nicolas!' he wailed. His lantern lay discarded at his feet. Both of his hands shook as they grasped his rifle. Tears filled his eyes as he raised that trusty musket. His vision was blurred, but his target was close. I couldn't move, I couldn't even speak, my mouth was too full. Mr McKinnel hesitated – eventually he turned his gaze away from his target completely, the barrel of his weapon wobbled and lowered – but I remembered our promise,

'Promise me you'll kill that thing,' I had said.

'I promise ye,' he'd replied.

He steadied his aim again and squeezed the trigger. The shot rang out and echoed through the silent night. It was the last thing I ever heard.

The Journal in the Cabin

I'd wanted an escape, to get some time away from everything and focus on myself. I needed to find myself ... but when I found that lonesome cabin, I found so much more.

I couldn't tell how long it had been abandoned, but it was enshrouded in cobwebs. I never should've entered, but it looked like the perfect hideaway, a place forgotten by the rest of the world, a place all my own.

Inside, a nightmare had waited for centuries.

Resting on the dusty bed, was an old, crumbly skeleton. Clutched tight to its chest in two cold hands, was a journal.

I never should've opened it. After I read that first line, I couldn't put it down.

I am trapped.

Something's watching me, and I am stuck within a cage of mine own making. It was my slice of Heaven. Now it is my personal Hell. I am alone, and that *thing* knows it. It won't let me leave, and I've no way to contact help. I am writing this because I wish for whosoever happens to find it, to know

The Journal in the Cabin

what happened. If you are reading this, I am sure I will already be dead. Please. Do not let that thing trap you as well.

I've no idea how long I've been trapped. The days have blended into one. I live the same routine over and over. I wake from what little amount of tormented sleep I was fortunate enough to get, and I feel its gaze. My ever-present, omniscient warden. It hides during the day, but I know it's there, taunting me, teasing me, tricking me. It wants me to have hope, to believe that it has given up and found another, more tantalising prey, but I won't be so foolish as to go blindly running out into its domain. Sometimes the temptation is almost too much. I find myself lacing my boots twice, stuffing what I can carry into my bag, and standing in the open door, staring out at freedom. But I never take that first step, I'm sure it would be my last. I can't see it, but I know it's there, waiting. It's as if it already has its jaws around my chest, and if I willingly step out into its waiting maw, I'll never see the sun again.

I slam the door and cower in the safety of my cage—being trapped is better than what that beast will do to me. It always shows up again, sometimes right away, sometimes longer. Every time I curse myself for not having the courage to make a run for it, to chance it. Would it really be so bad if it caught me? Surely it couldn't be worse than subjecting myself to this purgatory for another day and night. But the next day it is more of the same. I am full of hope and determined to take that first step, but such foolishness is quickly pushed aside for greater reasoning, some days faster than others. Some days I never get the door open, others I never even get my shoes on before giving up. Every night I try to convince myself I made the right decision.

Its presence is oppressive, like a great shadow blotting out the sky. Its darkness has pervaded my world and will never let me out of its grasp, even when I can bathe in the light I still feel cold. I dare not look at it directly. Some days I see its silhouette standing in front of my window, towering over the cabin. I never have the willpower to raise the curtains—to look upon it, and face it directly would surely spell my doom.

> Has it been weeks? Months? Years? Or merely days? I do not know. But I do know that I cannot live like this any longer. I will not. If I cannot flee the safety of mine own cage, the trap of mine own making, then I must rid myself of the option altogether. It may sound drastic but that is what must be done, I cannot leave myself with anything to fall back on, I must thrust myself into fight or flight. I will burn this place. Burn this cage, burn this forest. I will burn this book, and I will burn that thing. If not ... I will throw myself into the flames, anything to escape this nightmare.

That was where the man's journal abruptly ended, the bottom of the final page ripped away.

After a quick search, I found the following passage on the scrap of paper that had been torn out of the journal, it was left next to the man's boots that stood abandoned by the door. It read thus:

> If you're reading this ... know that my courage failed. Shame me as a coward and never give my soul peace or rest. Pity me, fear my grizzly fate, or I'm afraid you'll soon share it. Run. It's not too late. Get out while you can. Burn it all down, with whatever remains of me. Do what I couldn't ... don't hide within the cage.

The paper dropped from my hands. I snatched my things and turned towards the door. Then I saw it. The curtains were still closed, covered in a veneer of cobwebs, but I could still see its silhouette.

`The Journal in the Cabin`

I stumbled back and my hand found the slip of paper as I braced myself. I picked it up and turned it over. On the back was an even more foreboding message. Written in a rough, violent hand, not with ink, but with blood.

Don't run. It's too late. Hide within the darkness and cling to all you have left. You're already trapped.

I'm watching.

The Island in Oswelth Cove

Oswelth was a quiet, coastal town. The cove was hemmed in from the north and south by looming mountains like iron towers. Only one winding road led in or out through the hills west of the town. In summer and springtime, it's a beautiful place. The hills and fields are covered with a rainbow of flowers, and the serene sea glistens, creeping right up to the edge of the white beaches, sweeping them clean thanks to the melt from the mountains' snowcaps. During these seasons, tourism keeps the town afloat as people from all around convene to enjoy the picturesque scenery.

In winter, it's a different story. The flowers wither and die, a white sheet of frost blankets the hills, and the sea is as dark and oppressive as the mountains. The town becomes quieter than a library; all is grey. Houses jut out sporadically, like festering growths from the narrow cobblestone streets. The dreary buildings sport slate roofs, flowers hang from window sills like corpses from branches. *some* residents prefer winter.

One morning, when a paper-thin layer of ice sealed the cove, and the sky was a grey curtain, the residents of Oswelth found something unusual in their cove. Something distressing, horrifying, and mind-boggling. It should've been impossible, and many thought it was—a new island had appeared. From thin air or the depths of the ocean, they did not know.

From the shore, the island didn't appear large, nor very wide, though it was tall. Most of its surface area was dominated by a mountain which reached half the height of those surrounding the cove. The island would've been within swimming distance if it weren't for the sea being frozen. Even so, the mayor swiftly took action and closed the beach—which had never happened before, not even in winters past when no one braved the icy depths—and docks until more could be learned about this island.

The sudden appearance disturbed the town, but the large portion of fishermen—who were the main driving force behind the town's economy during winter seasons—were more upset by the docks being closed.

One such affected family, were the Frosts. The night of the island's discovery was tense indeed within the Frost household. Mr Frost chomped his dinner so forcefully it was a wonder he didn't bite through his fork.

'What a load of trite. That bloody mayor, who's he think he is, telling everyone that they can't set sail until the *proper authorities* take a look at it? You know he had Lawerence locked up 'cause he wasn't gonna let no bleeding "island" keep him from checking his nets.'

'Really?' Mrs Frost looked up from her book, she'd been nibbling her stew as she read. '... Poor Cheryl.' Mrs Frost returned to her book.

'It's bad enough with the tourists, but now we'll have the bloody government disrupting the town, keeping everyone from their daily lives. This is prime fishing season! Doesn't that mayor know anything? He never should've been reelected, I tell ya. I'll bloody miss the migration if they drag this out long enough, and I bet this house they will, you know how those bureaucrats are, always making everything as long and complicated as they can.' Mr Frost shook his head. 'It'd be a miracle for the town to get through this without any people losing their homes. Some of them smaller boats need to have a good season *every* season, or else there won't be any fish to put on their tables.'

'I'm sure they'll figure something out, dear.' Mrs Frost had only been paying half attention throughout her husband's rant, however, one thought made her put her book down for a moment. 'It's a bit exciting though, don't you think? What with the government coming to town.'

'It's not like the bleedin' president is gonna show up on our doorstep, Jannet.'

'I know ... but still, this is big news. And not just local, or even statewide, a new island discovered off our coast, that'll be on National TV! Ooh! I wonder if we could get interviewed?'

'Tch, *the news*. I can't wait to see that circus blocking up the beach as well. There really won't be getting out of the docks if those leeches are clogging up the cove.'

'But wouldn't it be nice to see yourself on TV?'

Mrs Frost raised her book back up to shield herself from her husband's icy stare.

'I wonder what it is though. Or how it appeared. I mean, islands don't just appear, do they?' she said.

'I know what it is.'

Mrs Frost sighed. 'Oh, do you? Pray tell, what do *you* think it is, dear?' she asked the way one does when one already knows the answer.

'It's them damn red flags,' he said.

'Of course it is. You think *everything* is to do with those "damn red flags". There aren't as many fish one season—it's the red flags. There's *too many* fish the next—it's the red flags. Every flag is red with you.'

'What else can it be? You said it yourself, islands don't just pop up. It's not like they can swim around and visit any place they please. They're either there or they're not, and wherever they are, they stay there.'

'Uh-huh.' Mrs Frost tried to get back into her book to block out the incoming rant about "the enemy".

'I bet it's some kind of fancy new submarine they've come up with, make it so they can blend in with the surroundings while they spy on us.'

Mrs Frost's attempts to concentrate on her book failed. The table shuddered with the force she used to set her book down. 'And why exactly would they want to spy on us?

Nothing happens in our town, we're just a bunch of fishers and farmers.'

'Yeah, but nobody would expect them here, that's what makes it the perfect place to attack.'

'God you're an idiot sometimes. And why would they make it look like a bloody island and not an iceberg if they were trying to blend in? They've done the opposite if that's what they were trying.'

As the talk devolved into an argument about a much more boring topic, a third, unspoken party at the table shut out the elevating voices of his parents. Oscar Frost's food was practically untouched. He kept pushing a chunk of tuna around his plate with his fork. The excitement of the mysterious island had left him without any appetite.

The night faded away, the argument faded slower. As Oscar went to bed, his mind raced with thoughts of the island and what it could be.

Just after sunrise, Oscar went to the beach. He was glad his school was out for winter, he never would've been able to concentrate with this hubbub. He perched upon a hill overlooking the beach. The white sand looked like snow. The grey sea still wore an icy cover. Officials were stationed on the beach already, rolling a fence across it, drawing a line in the sand. They weren't from the government, just a few members from the town's department.

Why are they blocking off the beach? Oscar wondered. *Does the island have radiation?*

'Wow, they *are* closing up the beach.' A frumpy, overly rugged-up girl trudged over to the edge of the hill.

Oscar smiled as his neighbour sat by him. 'Hi, Leslie.'

'Hi.' She returned the smile, showing a gap where one of her front teeth refused to grow.

Quickly, the kids were drawn back to the grey-brown mass floating just at the edge of their little cove. 'What do you think it is?' Leslie asked.

'I'm still trying to figure that out.'

'You wanna know what I think? I think it's a spaceship that crash-landed, and now it's trying to blend in with the mountains while the aliens are busy making repairs so they can fly back home ... wherever that is.'

'Maybe their planet doesn't have water, and they're stealing ours,' Oscar suggested. 'Maybe they're Martians.'

'Oh my god! You're right! They're Martians coming to suck Earth as dry as Mars. Do you think that's what they did before? Maybe they're super greedy, dumb aliens, and they sucked up all their water, and that's why Mars is all rocks and dust.' She giggled and swung her legs, watching small waves crash against the island.

'Do *you* think it's aliens?' she asked.

'Hmm...' Oscar thought about it more. It could be anything. '... No. I think it's Atlantis, the drowned city, resurfaced after countless years! A city full of treasures and wonders beyond our imagination. Now it's just waiting for someone brave enough to explore it.'

'Whoa...' Leslie stared at the island, dreams of gold glittered in her amazed eyes. 'But... if it's Atlantis, and it was at the bottom of the ocean for all those years, then wouldn't the people have turned into mutant fish monsters? After all that time, they finally figured out a way to return to the surface so they could take their revenge on the people who abandoned them and left them to drown and rot!' She gasped and shivered.

Oscar chuckled. 'Wow. Did you get that from a movie or something?'

'N-No, that's what I just thought of.' She pouted a bit.

'Maybe you should make a movie then, or write a book. You always come up with awesome stories.' Oscar's hand rested atop Leslie's.

'R-Really?' She blushed.

He nodded. 'Really, really.'

She smiled that same gap-toothed smile, her cheeks still burning red. 'Well, if I did make that story, I know the main character would have to be an adventurer as smart and brave as you.'

It was Oscar's turn to blush. He looked away as Leslie giggled. They kept holding each other's hand and sitting there for a while longer. Eventually, Leslie's mother called for her and she had to leave, but Oscar remained and wondered about the island some more.

That night, Oscar dreamed of the island.

If it was a stranded alien ship, he pictured a hollowed-out centre, the rough, rocky exterior a facade, whilst underneath was shiny polished metal, and bright, blinking lights. There were more switches and buttons than anyone could find a use for, and the Martians! He tried to come up with what they would look like, but his mind's eye was bombarded with the generic, grey-skinned alien with a bulging head, long limbs, and huge blank eyes. Even though he knew they wouldn't look like that, he couldn't come up with anything else. *Leslie would be able to come up with really cool aliens.* But what if they weren't Martians? What if they were aliens from somewhere else, and Mars was the last planet they'd sucked all the water from and now it was Earth's time?

Or, what if it was the golden city of Atlantis that was waiting inside the outer shell of that mountain? If there were vengeful Atlanteans ready to wage war on the air-breathing surface dwellers, would they ambush him in the night and drag him to the bottom of the black sea?

Or what if it was an entirely new island, one no man had ever set foot on? It could have its own wonders and secrets to be discovered, new kinds of animals and plants and everything. Unicorns, dinosaurs, and gems more brilliant than diamonds. Anything could be possible, and it was right there for the taking, waiting for someone brave enough.

He didn't see Leslie the next day, but even without her, he sat on the hill, island-gazing until it was time for dinner.

'That idiot still has the docks on lockdown,' Mr Frost said. 'I saw others complaining at Town Hall today, though it'll take some work to drill the message through that thick skull of his.'

'Mhm, that's good, dear.' Mrs Frost was already onto another book.

'But, that stubborn, brainless mayor, he's still going on about "the proper authorities". He said it'll be *five. bleeding. days.* until they get here. I mean, five more days of this? People really will starve! Is he trying to kill 'em? Maybe we should take his food and money away for a week and see how he likes that!' The table rattled after Mr Frost smashed his fist on it.

Mrs Frost scowled at him over the top of her book. 'Well, I hope those families were responsible enough to keep money tucked away for occasions like this. We were.'

'Y-Yeah, well ... still, it's not bleeding right.' Mr Frost went back to chomping on his dinner.

All this talk about the island told Oscar one thing. He *needed* to explore it, no matter what.

A good hour after his parents had gone to bed and the pillow-side arguing died down, Oscar crept out of bed. He covered himself from head to toe in his warmest clothes, then slunk out of the house.

The moon shone in the cloudless sky, a bright eye in the darkness of space. Oscar's breath fogged up in front of him, but that, and the gently lulling waves were the only movement in the silent town. He marched towards the docks. The gravel road crunching underfoot sounded like explosions to him.

No one else was at the docks. The major vessels were tied and anchored down, the smaller ships too. Standing at the end of the dock, Oscar peered into the black, shimmering water. Stretching along the width of the cove, just beneath the waves, he could see a net blocking off the cove. But, this would only stop the larger boats, it wouldn't have any effect on say, a row boat, like the emergency boat they had on the family ship.

He approached *The Ice Queen*. It was tied down and anchored like all the others, but it was close enough to step aboard. He did so and went right for the emergency raft, his heart slamming against his ribcage. He unravelled the ropes tying the tiny craft down, and gave it a shove overboard. He watched it plunge onto the sea ten feet below with a heavy splash. He took up a nearby oar, and looked back towards home. Nothing had stirred. He looked to the island, a darker mass against the shadows of the night. This was it, there was no turning back. He leapt over the railing and landed in the row boat with a thud.

After regaining his footing, he pushed off, and began his voyage to the island. It was a tiring, gruelling task. There were multiple instances where he thought of turning back, but he pushed onward, unrelenting. The island looming larger before him was the perfect motivation. Even when he felt as if his arms would fall off, he kept paddling.

When the island was only a few hundred metres away, he was assaulted with the most foul smell to ever infest his nostrils. It was even worse than the time he found a rotting fish in his locker, or those unfortunate mornings when he had to use the bathroom after his father. But even the island's horrid stench couldn't dissuade him.

The rowboat crunched to a halt against the island's shore. He forgot all about his exhaustion, the exhilaration of discovery coursed through him like fire. He hopped over the side of the boat but paused immediately; the land was not at all like he imagined. Instead of the solid, rough rock it looked like, or even the sinking feeling of sand, the ground was soft and slightly spongey under his feet.

He dragged the boat higher onto this bumpy, uneven land, and investigated further. He slipped a glove off and touched the ground. He recoiled instantly, almost tumbling over the boat. The ground had a familiar but absurd sensation—it felt like fish scales. His heart raced for altogether different reasons now. He placed his hand on another patch of ground nearby and dragged it back and forth. He winced and recoiled again, this time, a crimson slash welled up across his grubby palm where he'd cut himself on a barnacle.

He looked around. The island was covered in large patches of barnacles, reeds were strung from some of these patches, as well as hanging off bumps and outcroppings. Lichen and moss grew in some parts as well. It was unlike any place he had ever seen. Oscar pressed onwards. He strode directly towards the peak, though up close, it wasn't much of a mountain, but a large, sloping hill. It was still a fair way up, and the stench worsened the higher he climbed.

The sun crested over the horizon. Oscar stood at the top of the rise and froze. His face transformed into a mask of terror, and his soul tore from his body momentarily. The truth of the island was staring him in the face and it was much more horrible than he or even Leslie could've ever imagined.

It was no island at all. He now knew why the ground *felt* like scales, because they *were* scales. He wasn't standing on a mountain, or land of any kind. He was standing on the corpse of a gargantuan beast from the darkest depths of a watery hell. Even now his feet were sinking into its decomposing eyeball. And now that he saw the side of the "island" that was shielded from the town's cove, facing out to sea, he saw the worst thing of all.

This beast, as massive as it was, had been bitten in half.

A Vampire's Reflection

Before I start my tale, I must confess, I am not human. I am a vampire, at least that's what my kind has come to be known as. Yes, the immortal, blood-sucking, garlic-averse, creature of the night that burns to ash if touched by sunlight. The kind you see in plenty of your stories. Though I will say, I'd rather die ... again, than sleep in a coffin, and silver actually goes quite well with the old pale complexion. And no, I cannot turn myself into a bat of any kind. However, there was one more detail you mortals have figured out about us—our reflections are non-existent. Not in any picture, mirror, or liquid's surface, will our countenance be reflected. That is why what I tell you now is distressing me so. For as long as I can remember, for the centuries of my unlife, I have never been able to view myself. I have solely relied on other people's interpretations and descriptions of my appearance, and those of portraits painted by far more talented hands than mine, even after all my years of practice. When I awoke last morning and ventured to my sitting room to enjoy a cup of tea, as I do every morning, I was deeply disturbed to find my reflection, staring back at me in the floor-to-ceiling mirror that takes up the centre of one of my sitting room walls.

So shocked was I, that I felt as if my heart had resumed beating for a moment. Once I had gotten over my shock, I observed the reflection, treating it as if it were some newly discovered creature and I was the first explorer to have ever come into contact with it. Despite my trepidation, the reflection acted exactly as it was supposed to, if what the mortals said could be trusted. It was just a mirrored version of myself, replicating my movements perfectly—it inspected me as closely as I inspected it.

It was a harrowing experience, and one that I couldn't quite understand. I had to know if any of my associates knew of phenomena like this happening to any of our kind before, and what it meant. I resolved to go and speak with my closest friend, a lady by the name of Stephanie, a vampire only a few decades my elder—a relatively small age gap amongst our kind. However, when I turned to leave, I noticed the reflection did not move, it was still looking at me, staring intently. I turned my head to get a better look, to make sure I wasn't just seeing things, and I confirmed my reflection was indeed watching me. It stood front on, shoulders sagged, staring at me with a blank face. It was indescribably eerie, and I don't doubt it would've scared me to death if I wasn't already dead. I bolted from the room and my home as quickly as my feet could carry me. Thankfully it was night, and the cool embrace of the moonlight was much healthier for my well-being than the destructive power of the sun. I rushed to Stephanie's abode on the other side of town, praying to anything that would listen for her to be home.

Thankfully, she was, and accepted me into her house graciously, albeit surprised and confused—it was very uncharacteristic of me to show up unannounced. We sat down in her living room. Black and purple curtains adorned every wall, making the spacious room snug and homely. I refused her offer of tea and biscuits, I was in no mood to play at mortality and feast on such empty calories.

'What is the matter with you?' she said to me, an airy laugh curling her lips into a beautiful, ruby-coloured smile.

'Have you ever heard of a vampire acquiring a reflection?' I said.

'What?' She was baffled by my question, rightfully so, it was an absurd thing to ask.

I explained my situation and encounter with the reflection to the best of my abilities, yet she did not believe me. I could tell she thought me mad, because even as she humoured me and treated the subject seriously, her coy smile never once left.

'Unfortunately, dear friend, I do not recall ever hearing about *any* vampire who saw their reflection, at least not after they had lost their mortality, if they ever had such a curse to begin with.' She paused to sip her chamomile, then said, 'Furthermore, I've heard no tales from *anyone* about a reflection ever moving with a mind of its own. It defeats the whole purpose of a reflection if it's not *reflecting* you, don't you think?'

'That may be so,' I said, 'but that still doesn't change what I saw—'

'What you think you saw.'

'I'm not lying to you.'

'I never accused you of that, I merely suggested that what you think you saw, and what occurred are two different things.'

'Well, if you don't believe me, then you can come and see for yourself.'

I couldn't be angry with her, I must've sounded ridiculous. A vampire with a reflection? Ludicrous! Even more so if that reflection didn't do a good job of reflecting. Nevertheless, she agreed to accompany me and see this reflection herself. She must've thought it would put my mind at ease, perhaps she was curious. However, when we returned and I once again stood before the mirror, there was no reflection for either myself or Stephanie, only our surroundings.

Stephanie stifled a chortle, then said: 'Have you been feeding on drunkards again? Or are you just trying to make a fool of me?'

I turned my nose up, offended that she would even suggest I'd stoop so low to a foolish prank like this. 'It was there, believe me or don't, but don't accuse me of playing childish games.'

'Maybe your eyes played tricks on you; maybe it was just a dream. Whatever you saw, it's not there now, and maybe it never was. Best to forget about this.' She patted me on the back, rather condescendingly, though I'm sure she didn't mean it like that. She informed me she would be at her home if I needed her for anything else, and with that, she left.

The reflection didn't reappear after I saw her out, and I started to believe that it was a fantasy. Vampires aren't supposed to have reflections, it just isn't possible. It is another of our curses, as real and potent as our sensitivity to the sun—to put it lightly. I turned in for the day, hoping to put this mess behind me.

When I awoke the next night, I went about my usual hygiene routine. I showered first. After drying off, I began to shave. As I stared into the mirror above my bathroom sink, I found no reflection staring back at me, just the blank tiles behind me. I was convinced yesterday's insanity had passed.

Now, whilst some think vampires groom each other in pairs—and whilst some may do, I will not speak on their behalf—I *absolutely* do not. I won't reduce myself to such an embarrassing act, especially when one can just *feel* the hairs on their face. But, I still looked into the mirror as I did so, because it sat above the sink, and once again, it was installed by the time I procured the house.

As I was finishing my shave, I rinsed my face in the sink. When I stood up and looked upon the mirror once more, I found myself staring back. I jumped and dropped my razor from the shock. I ducked down and quickly picked it back up. I rose slowly, peeking over the sink, hoping that what I'd seen was a trick, a deception I played upon myself because I was thinking so hard about the reflection from yesterday. Chillingly, that was not the case. The reflection was pressed right up against the mirror, their face almost touching it as they stared down at me.

I set the razor upon the edge of the sink and took a step back, wanting more distance between myself and that horrid thing in the mirror. The reflection placed their palm against the mirror's surface, and once more beckoned for me to do the same.

I refused, then said: 'What in the cold, dark hells, do you want, fiend?'

The reflection tilted their head in confusion. Their lips moved, but I heard no sound, not even the distorted warblings of a voice. There was only silence.

Next, I said: 'One moment.' However, as I went to leave, the reflection smashed a fist against the mirror. Despite the violent motion, there was still no sound, and no reverberation like one would expect. Nevertheless, I was frozen in shock. I watched as the irritated reflection looked all about its surroundings, then its eyes latched onto the razor upon the sink. It snatched the object up in a hurry and ferociously cracked it open, freeing the blade.

'Wait!' My pleas fell upon my ears only. As I reached towards the mirror, the reflection paused, razor lifted to their face.

When I made no further movement forward, the reflection bared their fangs at me and then dragged the blade across the flesh of their cheek. I felt the burn across my own and with a hiss, I threw myself out of the room. The cut suddenly stopped and the path it was carving towards my eye ended.

I touched my face, blood clung to my fingertips after I pulled my hand away. The pain wasn't an illusion, it was a real injury that had been inflicted upon me, and it wasn't just the large mirror in the living room that housed the reflection now.

I risked one more peek into the bathroom and found the reflection staring at me again, its face against the mirror, bleeding cheek visibly squished against the glass. At the flash of the razor, I quickly slammed the door and pressed myself against it, as if the reflection would somehow leap into my world and try to break the door down.

I stayed locked away in my room that night, not even daring to risk passing through the living room and in sight of the large mirror it housed. I stayed far away from them until the next night came to be; no more cuts had appeared on my body. I resolved to communicate with this reflection and find out who or what they were, and what they wanted from me. I marched into the living room, armed with a blank scrapbook and a pen. If verbal communication was impossible between us, then I would have to try my luck with the written word.

I found the reflection waiting for me, sitting on the coffee table. When I entered the room, it rose and approached the mirror, slamming its palm against it. I already knew what it wanted, but I was going to figure out why. I quickly wrote out my question in large, bold, letters—it pained me almost as much as the cut upon my face to write in such a thick, simple hand—then I showed the page to the mirror.

My question read thus: 'Why do you want me to touch the mirror?'

I saw the reflection's eyes read through the question. Then they went back through the words. Again and again, the reflection read the question, and I began to worry that the fiend was illiterate and whilst it could mimic my appearance, it couldn't mimic my intelligence. After the fifth or so attempt at reading the question they gave up, looking quite confused and angered. However, instead of taking out that anger on anything, they looked around, presumably for their own pen and paper upon which they could attempt to communicate. Curiously, they did not have a scrapbook or pen of their own. I set the utensils upon the coffee table and stepped away. After a few seconds, I saw them materialise in the mirror. The reflection snatched them up in that hurried, feral way of theirs and then turned away to scribble something onto the page.

I didn't have high hopes, and was ready to mark this down as another failed attempt at communication, my mind already occupied with trying to formulate the next suggestion. However, the reflection was finished sooner than I expected, though when it showed its own page, my worst fears were realised; their writing was completely illegible.

I despaired and slumped upon the sofa, my head in my hands. After a moment's contemplation, something struck me as odd. I looked at the mirror again, the reflection still stood there, angrily gesturing with their scribbled page. But they weren't messy, unthinking scribbles of an idiot, or one who had no idea how words and letters worked. No, there was structure, and form, and even a neat hand—as neat a replica of such blocky lettering could be—the language was just one I didn't comprehend. I stared harder and longer.

Suddenly, I felt as if I were the fool. Those were real words, and the language was none other than English. The letters and words were simply back to front, and even upside down. They were mirrored in multiple ways, but after inspecting them for long enough, I saw that they read: 'I don't understand.'

I picked up my pen again, but hesitated. The reflection set aside their paper, watching intently as I very carefully, and painfully slowly, wrote out my message in the reversed, upside-down, mirrored style.

What I had written was a message explaining my findings and telling the reflection how we must write so that the words will be legible to the other when showing our messages. They had no struggle reading this message, and after a moment, began writing another of their own, this one taking much more effort and time than the last, despite being smaller and simpler. Their message read: 'Like this?'

A breakthrough, at last! And now that a line of communication had been opened, the reflection seemed much more docile and willing to talk rather than getting right to that awful cutting business. I conveyed that it had indeed worked and I understood the reflection, then began writing my question out again, this time back to front. The reflection read it easily this time, then sat in thought ... for too long. I could tell they were trying to come up with a false answer, one that would satisfy me whilst hiding their real motives behind wanting me to touch the mirror. Eventually, they wrote down: 'Easier to show. Touch the mirror.' They showed this answer with a smile, standing close to the mirror, the page and their hand pressed against it.

I refused. Their smile dropped into a hideous scowl as soon as I shook my head. I wrote to them: 'Tell me the truth and I'll consider what you ask.'

Again the reflection took their time to think. In the end, they came up with nothing. Growling, they showed their next message; it wasn't an answer, and instead only read: 'Touch the mirror. *Now!*'

I sighed to myself and picked up the pen again. I decided to pursue a different line of questions. If they wouldn't tell me what they truly wanted, I'd see if they were more open about sharing what they truly were.

I wrote: 'What are you?'

This gave the reflection a chuckle and seemed to put them in a brighter mood, though their answer baffled me. 'I am you,' the reflection wrote back.

I stewed on this for some time, pacing around the room as I thought the answer and its implications over. Of course, the reflection would say it was me. Technically, even if it was just a reflection, somehow returned to me, but distorted and given a mind of its own, it would still be a reflection of *me*. If it was a demon or some other creature the mortals see as myth, then of course it would use this lie. I decided to play into its answer and accept it for now, wishing to see where this led. I wrote: 'Reflections don't work like this. Vampires aren't even supposed to have them.'

Anger flared on the reflection's face as they read my passage. Their fangs flashed before they picked up their pen. They stabbed the page and carved words into it. With a jagged, furious hand they wrote: 'Not reflection. *I am you!*'

Again I was baffled, yet they wrote with such conviction, and they had reacted with true anger and disdain for my equating them as a mere reflection, as if it was an insult that had harmed them. I was convinced by their words even if I didn't know how such a thing could be possible. I was so confused and dumbstruck by the revelation, I defaulted to my original line of questioning and wrote: 'What do you want?' Perhaps I hoped their recent openness would lead them to divulge their true intentions; after all, why would one lie to oneself?

The reflection's anger subsided, but not by much. And despite their revelations, they would not give me an answer to their motivations. Instead, they wrote: 'Touch the mirror.'

Again, I refused with a shake of my head. The reflection exploded with anger, they threw their book and pen against the mirror. I stepped away, hastily writing but they were not looking, nor did I get to finish my message. As they paced around, their eyes locked onto the glass coffee table. They reared back and smashed a fist through the glass, pain stabbed my hand and I dropped my pen. I noticed, however, that *my* table remained whole, despite its reflection having been obliterated. The reflection snatched one of the dozens of broken shards from the table and even as its edges cut into our palms, brought it up to their cheek. I rushed for the exit, though before I could make it out of the room, and out of sight of that cursed mirror, I felt the burn of a new wound being carved into my cheek. I dived out of the room and into the hall, panting heavily as I pressed flat against the wall. The burning had stopped; the wound wasn't growing further. I closed my eyes and recovered my breath and strength. A fiendish reflection was living in my mirrors and trying to kill me, and I had no idea what to do.

I needed to speak with Stephanie again.

I fled my home using one of the windows, like some kind of vagrant. I rushed across the city and towards Stephanie's abode, thankfully, she was still in for the night. She let me in, but her distress at my appearance and the wounds marring my features was apparent. 'What in the hells has happened to you?'

I told her that we could sit down and I would explain, though I also asked kindly for a morsel of blood, not having fed in several nights.

We sat down with our cups of red, and we stayed in silence. Stephanie kept a constant, worried eye on me, like my face would burst into a thousand cuts at any second. Eventually, I began to explain, and recounted my latest encounters with the reflection.

At first, she didn't believe me. Perhaps it was too insane a story to believe. 'You're making a fool of me, and I really don't like it. Even going so far as to cut yourself on purpose, or did you nick yourself while shaving and come up with this grandiose story to try and trick me? I've told you I'd be more than happy to groom you, but you just won't let me!'

I sighed and slumped back in the deep, comfortable sofa chair. I neither had the heart nor the will to argue with her at that moment. I weakly shook my head and pleaded with her. 'It's the truth. I know it sounds absurd but when has reality been anything less? Look at us, are we not absurd to the mortals? My dear lady, you needn't believe my story, but please believe me.'

She softened at my words and sat back down. She put her trust in me and wished to see this vile reflection herself. I worried for a moment but she insisted, she also insisted that she bandage my wounds before we leave. After she dressed the cuts along my cheek and deep red scratches over my hand, we swiftly travelled back to my home. Before I welcomed her inside, I stopped her and devised a plan. She would wait outside, then, when I had the reflection, I would signal her and she would enter to witness it with her own eyes before it could vanish. She accepted my request and waited in the cold a while longer.

I tried to keep things brief. I stomped through the house, towards the living room. The reflected world was empty of life, though the broken coffee table was still there, its pieces scattered across the wooden floorboards. I stood defiantly in front of the mirror, and after a few moments, the reflection reappeared, pacing into view. It went right over to its discarded scrapbook and tore out a page, slamming it against the mirror. The note, of course, read: 'Touch the mirror.'

I looked around and found my own scrapbook and pen, lying on the floor where I had dropped them. I plucked them up, and simply wrote: 'Why?'

The reflection snarled like a beast and hammered their demand against the mirror once more, refusing to explain themselves, just as I refused to give in to their demands.

I shook my head and turned away. With my face hidden, I signalled Stephanie and bade her enter, knowing the reflection would not be able to hear, and would have no chance to vanish before she arrived. I glanced at her as she strolled into the room and froze under the arched entranceway.

'What the fuck is that?' she said, unable to contain her vulgarity due to her shock, no doubt. 'It's true but… it's not even… oh God! It's moving!'

I turned my head back to see how the reflection had reacted to the intrusion. It was highly panicked, looking as if they were a child whose parents had caught them up past their bedtime. Their eyes were bloodshot and wide, almost popping out of their skull. Stephanie stepped further into the room, looking more closely at the reflection. Curiously, no reflection of her appeared.

My reflection soon overcame their shock, and went back to their demands of me, yet when I still refused, they went for another shard. I quickly darted out of the room and bade Stephanie to remain and watch the fiend. When I was out of the room and beyond the reach of the reflection; when I was safe, I called back to Stephanie again and asked her to explain what was happening, if she could still see the reflection or not.

She said: 'It...It vanished. Even though it was pressed right up against the glass, it suddenly disappeared when you left the room.'

I waited a full minute before I approached the archway and poked my head into the room. I looked at the mirror, but saw no reflection staring back at me.

'It's still gone,' Stephanie said. Even when I emerged fully into the room and strode right up to the mirror, the reflection did not return.

'Evidentally, they are quite shy around others... maybe they cannot conjure themselves when there are others around,' I said.

Stephanie shook her head, she couldn't believe it. We sat down again and confided in each other how bizarre this whole situation was. Stephanie asked how it all started, and I explained once again that it had happened out of the blue, one day it was just ... there. I did not remember doing anything to trigger such an oddity. I asked her if she had ever heard of anything like this happening before.

She said: 'No, never.' She apologised for not being of more help, though I assured her that she had nothing to apologise for. After a long silence, she spoke again, and dove into the realm of speculation. 'It isn't exactly to do with us, but I have heard some mortals theorise that mirrors aren't reflections at all, but are, in fact, portals to another world... I always thought such a fantasy was preposterous but maybe...maybe it is true. After all, are we not preposterous to the mortals, as you said?'

I pondered this belief. A portal into another world, it sounded too magical to believe, but in a world with demons, angels, vampires, werewolves, etcetera, was there anything that could be considered "too magical" for reality?

Eventually, the reflection returned, and I leapt from my chair with a start. It was not alone this time—it had dragged along a reflection of Stephanie.

'Wh-What the fuck is this now?' Stephanie cried.

The hands of her reflection were bound in coarse, thick rope, though it looked much more ghoulish than my own reflection did. Whereas my reflection was a one-to-one copy, down to every last detail, Stephanie's—whilst wearing the same outfit and having the same rough features—appeared much more ghastly and decrepit. Their hair was so thin and frail it was almost falling out, their cheeks were hollow, their skin grey and even more lifeless, and their eyes were so sunken it was a wonder they didn't disappear into their body completely.

Before we could recover from our shock, my reflection demanded I touch the mirror. However, this time when I refused, they already had a shard stashed away in their sleeve, they quickly brandished it, and as I turned to the exit, I heard a sharp cry from Stephanie. It was her pale cheek that now bore a crimson slash across it.

I froze. In the mirror, the shard dripped with blood. My reflection grinned wickedly, eyes locked on me, whilst Stephanie's stared deadpanned, not reacting to the wound carved into its face.

'Run!' I shouted and urged Stephanie to the archway, but she didn't move. My reflection pressed the glass shard against the neck of Stephanie's. Tears trickled down Stephanie's face. I turned to the mirror and pleaded with my reflection to let her go. I fell to my knees. I scrambled to my pen and then the nearest page, urgently writing a message that I would touch the mirror only if the reflection let Stephanie go and explained why it wanted me to do so.

The reflection—whilst never moving the shard away from the throat of Stephanie's zombie-like reflection—began to write again. Their eyes constantly darted back to us to make sure we didn't run whilst it was otherwise occupied. We took no chances and stayed right where we were.

The first message the reflection wrote was directed to Stephanie, demanding she look away. At her hesitation, the shard dug into her throat more. A pinprick of blood seeped out of her neck and trickled down. She slowly turned away, shaking as she stood with her back to me and the mirror.

The reflection resumed writing. They wrote for a long time, and I knew they were explaining everything about their situation, why they were doing this, and what they wanted from me.

A Vampire's Reflection

As I read the long message, my already cold, dead heart was stabbed through with ice, and fell to the floor, shattering infinitely. I only had a breath to come to terms with the situation, there was no time to hesitate with Stephanie's life on the line. I simply nodded in agreement, and shuffled towards the mirror, as one shuffles to the gallows.

The reflection's hand was already waiting for mine against the mirror, a grin as ravenous as a shark's took up the majority of their face. When our hands touched—and I truly did feel the warmth and spark of another person's touch instead of the coldness of the mirror—there was a rush of air. The light from my world vanished, and it was as if I was flipped inside out, upside down, and then back to normal again all in the same instant.

I was in my living room, the same living room, yet it was different. It was darker, as if everything was veiled in shadow, and it was all the wrong way round. Everything was back to front, flipped right to left, and upside down. When I turned around to face the mirror it was as if the floor under me was a rolling sea, I almost lost my footing. I saw the mirror, though it seemed so much smaller in this strange world, and I saw Stephanie on the other side—the *real* Stephanie. The zombified mimic stood beside me, looking truly dead on its feet. There was also *me*, standing in the mirror, standing next to Stephanie, comforting her.

Even though I saw their lips moving, I heard no sound. I tried to scream but found I had no voice. I tried to move towards the mirror but left was right and up was down. I stumbled to the ground.

After I crashed to the cold, hard floor, it took some time just to look *up*. I saw Stephanie looking at *me* with disgust, fear, and a smidge of pity, all while she took comfort in the arms of the reflection. They turned away, and the reflection started to guide her out of the room.

With one last look back at me, he grinned like a Cheshire cat who had all the cream in the world to himself. I screamed a silent scream, and as the two walked out of my sight, the light left the mirror, and the tiny frame showcasing my old world went black, leaving me in this abyss.

* * *

The reporter sat back in his seat. His notepad rested on the table before him, the current page empty, the story's climax had been too captivating. He stared at the vampire sitting opposite him. 'Wow.' Was all he could say.

'Quite the story, isn't it? All true, mind you.'

'Ah, y-yes it's, incredible. I can't thank you enough for sharing your story with me.' The reporter stood, offering a hand to the vampire. The vampire raised from his seat and accepted the handshake. A puzzled look flitted across the reporter's face. 'I do just have one question, if you may.'

'Please, go right ahead.'

The air suddenly felt cold and dry, reporter wet his lips before he spoke. 'If that's the end of your story, how did you manage to escape the mirrored world?'

The vampire didn't release the reporter's hand. He tilted his head, fangs poking out of his mouth as he smiled coyly. 'Whatever do you mean? I just told you how I managed to free myself from that eternal nightmare.'

Golden Child

Carlo pushed open the heavy, shimmering gate at the bottom of the drive that wound up the imposing hillside. A manor crowned the hill, its tall, marble pillars, gold-trimmed windows, and angled, royal blue roof crafted a regal image. Even the hill was strong and noble with thick hedges lining the opaline drive, and strong, proud oaks along the hillside. The weather had been good to the gardens, even as summer drifted by, they were still proudly showing off the growth they'd had from the bountiful spring. Flowers adorned the hill in neat rows starting halfway up, growing brighter in colour the closer they got to the house.

Conversely, Carlo was a battered and downtrodden stain upon the pristine hill as he limped up it. His hair stuck to his dirty face in thick black clumps, at least that way, it hid some of the bruises. It didn't hide the shallow cut across his pale cheek, right along his prominent cheekbone. His clothes as well, were stained grey and brown with the grit and grime of the town, and had a few new tears.

Carlo reached the imposing front doors, and grasped the lion-head knocker. The heavy knocks echoed through the manor like a tomb. It didn't take long before a man answered the door. Everything about the man was tall and long, his arms and legs, his torso, even his face and the nose he looked down at Carlo with. The man's slicked-back hair shone in the faint orange light of the entryway, and a neat moustache rested atop his thin, pink lips; his lips curled with disgust as he examined Carlo.

Carlo wore a fake smile as he said: 'Father.'

'You're a disgrace, Carlo.' Father slammed the door shut.

Carlo's smile vanished. His lips trembled with rage. He thought about turning around and trudging back down the hill, but the door was soon reopened. A woman stood there now, Carlo's mother. Her wavy brown hair framed her face beautifully and drew attention to her large, green eyes and pert, ruby lips. She gasped loudly upon seeing Carlo, trembling hands over her chest. She hugged Carlo to her bosom and dragged him inside, shutting the door firmly behind them. 'How many times have I told you to stop hanging around those brutes?' She stroked his head frantically, sobbing. 'My poor baby.'

'I'm not a baby,' Carlo protested. He couldn't squirm free from her iron grasp, and she dragged him to the sitting room, where Father was, nose buried in the day's paper.

The inside of the manor was as grand as the outside, though more cluttered. Leaving the gleaming, tiled floors of the entryway, the sitting room had dark, wooden floorboards, covered in a richly-coloured cashmere rug Mother had custom-made. The walls were adorned with paintings of all kinds: a visage of a boat withstanding the raging sea, Mediterranean landscapes in the glory of the rising sun, an image of their house and hill, and a family portrait. Shelves overflowing with books filled the spaces between each painting, each tome heavy with dust, as was much of the furniture.

Carlo's mother sat him in front of a large gold-framed mirror, and started cleaning him up as best she could. 'How terrible the state of the college must be if they're producing violent savages that would beat on a boy half their size and age,' she said.

Carlo rolled his eyes at her exaggeration.

'I doubt those "savages" would pay him any mind if he didn't always instigate things ... the little shit.'

'Roger!' Mother trembled with rage as she glared at her husband. She cradled Carlo's head against her chest, covering his ears. 'Don't listen to him, baby boy. You're a wonderful little angel, Mummy knows it. You've never done anything to those horrible bullies.' She wet a thumb and brushed it over his cut, wiping away the dirt around it. 'Mummy will fix you up and make you beautiful again.'

Carlo slapped her hand away. Mother gasped loudly, holding her hand as if he'd stabbed it. Carlo stomped out of the room and up the stairs. 'I'm not a baby!'

Father stood from his chair. 'Well then, if you're so grown, perhaps it's time you started acting like a man instead of some unruly beast!' He strode to the bottom of the stairs. 'You should worry less about winning fights, and think of getting a job!'

Carlo slammed his bedroom door shut. He threw off his filthy clothes and crawled under his covers, where he remained for the rest of the night.

Downstairs, Mother curled up in her chair, sobbing. 'Where did I go wrong? What happened to my precious baby?'

Father returned to his chair. 'Oh stop crying, Marilyn. Get a hold of yourself.'

'It's all *your* fault, Roger. You're too hard on poor Carlo. He's a victim.'

'A victim of you, perhaps.' He reopened the paper.

She scowled at him but said nothing more. She snatched up her magazine and left to read it in the kitchen. As she read further, a curious advertisement caught her eye. 'Lifelike puppets? How bizarre.' Entranced, she read more.

At breakfast, Carlo struggled to eat his oatmeal in peace, Mother still fussing over him. She couldn't even wait to let him finish eating before she started brushing his hair. He lifted another spoonful to his mouth when her brush yanked his head back. 'Ah!' His oatmeal splattered on the table. He whipped round to face her. 'Mum!'

'Sorry, darling, your beautiful hair is just so knotted today. Look forward, please.'

'I'm trying to eat,' he grumbled. Though before he turned back to his food, he saw something which nearly caused him to double take—Mother plucked a strand of his hair from the brush and pocketed it. His brow furrowed in confusion as he continued eating, and, thankfully, the brushing became much gentler and smoother.

Her cloying fussiness didn't stop even after she finished brushing his hair, and he rose from the table. When he was dressing himself for the day she was still worrying over him. 'Mum! Get out of my room, I need to change.' She was even stranger than before; now she had a measuring tape. 'And stop measuring me, what are you doing?' He backed away, pushing her off.

'Oh just hold still, Carlo. Mummy only needs a minute. It's for a surprise.'

'No!' He backed further away from her and her measuring tape. 'Get out!'

She huffed but relented and left his room. When he had finished dressing, and came downstairs, he saw her removing his solo portrait from the hallway wall. Surely *that* was a bit of an overreaction just because he wouldn't let her measure or dress him.

'Ah, Carlo. Good morning,' Father said. Mother passed them in the hall, portrait under her arm. Father paid her no mind, his eyes never leaving Carlo; he had a concerning smile.

'Good morning, Father.' Carlo looked Father over, adjusting the final button on his shirt.

'I have good news today—you'll like this—you won't be attending school today.'

Carlo's eyes brightened. As he realised something *this* good could never happen, his father explained the catch.

'Instead, I've scheduled an orientation for you at the local printing press, don't worry about directions, I'll drop you off personally so that you can't miss it.'

Carlo knew he meant, "so you can't skip it".

'You know, the owner of the town's paper is actually an old friend of mine, and he's been very helpful setting this all up. ... You best not disappoint me today.'

'No, Father.'

'Hm, very good. Now, have you eaten already?'

'Yes, Father.'

'Rightio, then we best be off without delay.' Father turned. Carlo followed him to the dining room where he retrieved his cap, driving gloves, and cane. As they headed for the front door, they passed the kitchen, and Carlo looked in, seeing another strange act from his mother—she put his clump of hair into an envelope.

Carlo followed Father into the garage and the two entered Father's prized Bentley. Carlo sat next to him, staring back at the garage door, brow wrinkling with concern. 'Is Mother acting strange?'

'When isn't that woman acting strange? If you mean stranger than usual, I've noticed no such thing.'

'She hasn't said anything about ... I don't know, ordering a new outfit for me? There isn't a friend's wedding coming up, is there?'

'Not that I've heard. ... Though she was talking about ordering a puppet of some sort last night, stupid woman, who has the time to play with puppets.'

'A puppet?' Carlo frowned, looking back at the house, trying to piece together how a new fascination with puppets related to her strange behaviour that morning.

The printing press's building was on the outskirts of town, so the drive wasn't long at all. When Father parked outside of the large, brick building, he didn't bother getting out of the car. 'Need I remind you, Carlo, you are not to make a fool of me in front of my old partner. Do you understand?'

Carlo didn't look at him. 'Yes, Father.'

'Good. Go now, and don't disappoint me. Your behaviour directly reflects our parental proficiency. I'm off to check on the factory. I'll be working late, so you'll need to find your own way home.'

Carlo sighed but got out of the car. Father drove off. Carlo turned and waved goodbye, smiling woodenly while he watched the Bentley disappear around the corner. 'That's right, go fuck your whores and say you're "working".'

Carlo stepped into the building and was met with a rather bland, sterile lobby that would've looked more appropriate in a hospital. There was an elevator in front of him, and a reception desk to the left. A woman sat behind the desk. Her eyes were tired and her smile was rehearsed. 'Can I help you?' she asked.

He explained who he was and why he was there. At the mention of his family name "Weathers" her expression brightened and she told him to take a seat. The chair was uncomfortable no matter which way Carlo sat in it, but thankfully it wasn't long before the elevator opened with a piercing ding. A pudgy little man waddled out, gut bulging between his suspenders. Mr Ingles was not a pretty man, his pencil-thin moustache looked out of place above his thick jowls, and his greasy, thinning combover did nothing to hide his growing bald spot. His eyes lit up upon finding Carlo, and he hurried over, shaking Carlo's hand vigorously. Mr Ingles stumbled over himself as he told Carlo how he'd heard many great tales about him from Carlo's father. Carlo begrudgingly accepted the handshake, feeling the grease rub off onto his palm from Mr Ingles' hand. When he was freed and Mr Ingles's back was turned, Carlo wiped his hand off on his trousers.

Carlo followed Mr Ingles into the elevator, and one short trip later they stepped onto the main floor. It was a wide, open space, crammed full of tiny cubicles which were crammed with people, like pigs in a trailer. Each individual was hard at work within their cubicle. Chatter was practically non-existent, and the only noises were the occasional cough undercutting the incessant scratching of pencils across paper. Looking around, the people themselves were as grey and drab as the building. Carlo suppressed a shudder.

Mr Ingles clapped a hand on Carlo's shoulder and showed him around the floor, telling him all the lies Carlo's father had fed him. Lies like how Carlo was a great worker, so creative and flamboyant, how he was so determined to be the next big writer. Vapid, empty lies about the son Father wanted Carlo to be.

Carlo was shown all around the building, even down into its bowels to see the massive printing press that was like a great grumbling slug spread throughout the basement. The tour ended where it began, and Mr Ingles turned to Carlo with an expectant, smug smile.

'What do you think, young Carlo? Wouldn't you love to be part of the team?'

Carlo stared the pudgy man straight in the eye. 'I'd rather be locked in a closet all day than be enslaved to a snobbish, brown-nosed twat, in this lifeless hell-hole.'

Mr Ingles trembled, his face swelling, reddening. 'Y-You impudent brat! H-How dare you!' Spittle flung from his quivering mouth. 'Your father will hear of this!'

'Don't care.' Carlo turned and left, making sure to knock a stack of papers off someone's desk on his way out. Walking out of the building, he breathed in the heavy city air, then followed his feet to the local cinema. Carlo's favourite thing about the cinema, and one of the only benefits he noticed from being a nobleman's son, was that the staff didn't dare kick him out if he stayed for another movie after the one he paid for was finished. With one ticket, he could see all the shows he wanted. Nor did they think about stopping him from watching something that would've been seen as inappropriate for his age.

In the cinema, time flew by unnoticed. Carlo wasn't sure how much time had passed when his father plucked him out of his seat and started dragging him out of the cinema by the arm.

'I hand you a golden opportunity on a golden platter and *this* is how you repay me? By making me look a foolish, horrible father, then spending the rest of the day rotting your brain with that ... that filth?!'

'You are a horrible father!' Carlo yanked free as they reached the lobby.

Father whirled around and struck him across the face. Carlo fell to the popcorn-smelling carpet. He held his stinging cheek, the mark already beginning to darken. He didn't resist when Father heaved him back up and to the car.

When they arrived home, Mother came rushing over. 'Did you find him? Is he okay?' She almost fell over when she saw Carlo's face, a dark bruise now marring his cheek. 'What happened?!'

Father ignored her, ushering Carlo upstairs. He continued to ignore her even when she berated him for his rough treatment of their baby. He threw open Carlo's door and flung him inside. 'You *will* go back to the paper tomorrow, you *will* apologise to Mr Ingles, and you *will* be a good employee ... or you *will* be thrown onto the streets, like the ungrateful mutt you're being.' Without waiting for a response, Father shut the door.

'Ohh, my poor baby. Did you have to be so cruel?' Mother whined.

Father scoffed, heading past her and back downstairs. 'Your poor baby is growing into a dangerous and worthless thug. It's hard to believe such a horrific child could be *my* offspring.'

'How *dare* you.' As she followed him downstairs, the shouting faded until Carlo could no longer hear them. He could imagine the screaming match ongoing beneath him. He curled up on his bed, stewing in his anger. If anyone should be screaming and shouting and stomping, it should be him. He should run away, that would show them. He'd bet they'd start treating him more kindly if they thought they lost him. It'd be easy too, he'd run and they'd never find him, not until he wanted them.

He decided against it, at least for tonight, and instead drifted off to sleep.

He was awoken in the morning by his mother's squeals. He fell out of bed with a thud and a groan. Another squeal bounced around the house. As Carlo regathered his wits, he wasn't in a rush to check on what his mother was screaming about, it didn't sound like a "I'm getting murdered" scream. But when he was descending the staircase, and saw some burly men walk out the door, he second-guessed his earlier assumption. He moved with more urgency and turned into the sitting room, which the men had left. He saw his mother bouncing up and down like a giddy schoolgirl, in front of a large, rectangular crate.

'What's this?' Carlo asked.

'Oh, Carlo, go and get your father.' Without waiting for him to leave, she shouted: 'Roger! Get the crowbar.'

Father entered the room shortly after, empty-handed. He looked the crate up and down, then turned and walked right back out. 'You bought it, you open it.'

'Ugh, pig.' Mother shook her head. 'I can't wait to have some proper help around here. Carlo, be a dear and open the crate for Mummy.'

Carlo sighed but didn't see any way to avoid this chore without getting screamed at. He stepped up to the crate, forgoing the crowbar, and started pulling at the lid. Despite his mother's concerns, he continued straining until a wood panel broke away. With the first one out of the way, the rest came off quickly, and when the front side was fully opened, he staggered back, unable to believe his eyes.

Polystyrene poured onto the floor. Standing upright in the crate, was a replica of Carlo. A life-size puppet, made mostly of wood but with some metal. It even had hair ... real hair. Mother looked inside the box and squealed again, clapping happily. 'It's here! Ohh isn't it exciting?'

'Wh-What the hell is it?'

'Language,' she snapped, her smile vanishing for a moment. 'Can't you see? It's the latest innovation in puppetry! A mimic. It should even...' She reached into the box and hauled the puppet out, keeping it on its feet. She turned it around, revealing a winder on its back. 'Ah! There it is. You can wind it up to make it move. I even got to pick what personality I wanted for it.'

'Personality?' Carlo grew increasingly confused with every second. He couldn't tear his eyes away as his mother wound the puppet up. The winder clicked, and Mother stepped back. Wooden, blue eyes snapped open. Carlo jumped back with a gasp.

The puppet looked towards Mother and opened its mouth. 'Hello ... Mummy.' Its voice was monotone, inhuman, and was like electricity crackling through Carlo's skin.

'What the fuck,' Carlo whispered.

The puppet's head snapped towards the sound. The unblinking eyes stared deep into Carlo's.

'Language!' Mother growled, harsher than her earlier reprimand. She turned to the puppet, gushing over it. 'Ohh it's really here, it's really real! Look at it.' She caressed the puppet's face.

Father pulled Carlo from the room; the puppet never stopped staring at him. 'Hurry up and get dressed. I'm taking you to the paper. You *will* do your work there today.'

Carlo was eager to leave the house, and that vile puppet behind.

Father didn't just drop Carlo off outside of the press this time, instead, he walked Carlo into the building and handed him off to Mr Ingles directly. Mr Ingles was all smiles whilst Father was there, chumming it up with his old college buddy, but as soon as Father left, the smile dropped and the thinly veiled wrath burst to the forefront. Carlo was worked to the bone that day. Fetching coffees and lunch, cleaning and tidying people's cubicles, even their shit ... literally—Mr Ingles forced him to clean the toilets at one point. There were multiple instances where Carl thought about running away, whenever another order was barked at him he thought about responding with a "fuck you" instead of a "yes, sir", or even throwing their stupid bitter coffees right in their faces, but he didn't. Father's threats from the previous night stayed his hand and tongue.

Promised threats weren't the only thing gnawing at Carlo's mind throughout the day, intermittently he would be reminded of that creepy puppet. If he caught his reflection in a mirror or window, he'd have to stop and double-check that it wasn't a wooden face staring back at him. *Just why would Mother buy such a thing? Why was it so real?*

Finally, Carlo was freed from his work. Father picked him up and brought him back home. Carlo was exhausted, and could only answer his father's questions with grunts and half nods, though Father smiled widely, pleased with the day's results.

Returning home, they entered and were hit with a welcoming, savoury aroma filling the house. It originated from the kitchen. Carlo sought it out, his nose and stomach leading his feet, though whatever happiness at the thought of a filling meal was quickly replaced with dread when he saw what was occurring in the kitchen. The puppet was helping Mother with supper, she'd even dressed it up in a rosy pink apron, and put a matching headband on it to keep its hair back. Worse than that, it was even dressed differently. It was an obscene, ill-fitting outfit, because it was one Carlo had worn when he was six. Mother had dressed the thing in a puffy dress shirt and pantaloons that should've been burned rather than kept all these years. Mother hummed and swayed her hips as she worked, smiling more genuinely and warmly than Carlo had seen in years.

'You two make quite the pair, don't you?' Father said. Carlo jumped at the voice, not hearing Father walk up behind him. Mother and puppet looked over, the puppet with wooden eyes only for Carlo.

'Oh it's just a dream to have such a useful and eager little helper in the kitchen,' Mother said. 'Dinner will be ready in no time.'

'Hm, very well. Now, be a dear and get me a drink while you're at it.' Father strode back into the sitting room where his chair and paper were waiting for him.

Mother huffed and turned up her nose, going back to her cooking, but the puppet tore its gaze away from Carlo and moved to the cupboard, retrieving Father's brandy, just as he asked. With a bottle and glass, it walked out of the kitchen. Carlo jumped out of the way but never took his eyes off it. The puppet went directly to Father and poured him a glass before setting the bottle and drink down on the side table. 'Here ... Sir.'

Father looked up from the paper, a smile touching his lips. 'You are a helpful thing, aren't you?'

'Thank ... you.'

'If you want to be truly helpful, polish my shoes too.'

'Yes ... Sir.' Stiffly, the puppet turned and ventured to the entryway to retrieve Father's shoes. Carlo shuddered as he watched it disappear through the doorway.

When dinner was served and the family ate, the puppet's disturbing actions continued. It hovered just in the other room, cleaning up in the kitchen. Carlo caught glimpses of it passing by the doorway, and of those glimpses, there was more than one occasion where it was staring back at him. When he put his head down and focused on his meal, it frightened him half to death by appearing beside him, it hadn't made a sound. It held a knife in one hand as it loomed over him. Carlo's fist tightened around his own knife, much smaller in comparison to the one the puppet held, but the puppet wasn't looking at him, its attention was fixed on his parents.

'Would ... you ... like ... some ... wine? ... Mummy? ... Sir?' it asked in its jagged, broken voice.

Carlo noticed the wine bottle in its other hand. It used the knife to pop the cork even before it received an answer. Mother giggled. 'Aren't you the sweetest! Yes, dear, Mummy would *love* some wine. Thank you so much.' Her lashes fluttered as she held out her glass.

Even Father smiled and held out his glass for the puppet to pour into. 'My, this thing is an upstanding helper.'

'Don't call it a thing,' Mother snapped.

'Yes, alright, well, I was just saying that maybe *somebody* could learn a thing or two from this puppet.' He wasn't even subtle with the glance he gave Carlo.

Carlo rose from his seat, the chair falling back with a clatter. 'I'm going to my room,' he said. He wiped his mouth and stormed out of the room whilst the puppet picked up his chair then cleared his plate from the table.

Carlo threw himself into bed and under the covers. Sleep was hard to come by with the puppet still fresh in his mind.

Carlo roused in the middle of the night, head still clouded with sleep, he was unsure why he had woken; the sound of something scraping along wood, was that a dream? He sat up, looking around the dark room, peering at shadows and shapes he thought were odd. After a minute, he resolved that's all they were, just shadows. His eyes still leaden with sleep, he laid back down, closing them.

A short time later, when he was only half in the grip of sleep, he woke again, this time feeling something heavy sag the foot of his mattress. His eyes snapped open and even in the dark, he saw the puppet's face looming over him. He shrieked like a babe and shot up so violently he almost headbutted the puppet. He blindly groped the bedside table until he latched onto his small lantern. He smashed it over the puppet's head and sent it crashing to the floor with a heavy thud. Carlo leapt from his bed and across the room to the unlit fireplace, snatching an iron poker from the chilled coals.

The puppet stood, its face heavily scratched as moonlight shone through the curtains, but other than that it was unscathed. Before either it or Carlo could move, Mother and Father burst into the room. Mother shrieked, but Carlo's relief flipped into confusion as she rushed to the puppet. 'No no no no, oh no what happened to my beautiful baby.' She cradled its head, sobbing as she fussed over its scratched face.

'Hello? I'm here, and I'm fine, no thanks to whatever that *thing* was trying to do to me in my sleep.' Carlo gestured at the puppet with his poker.

'Put that thing down!' Father snapped before snatching the poker from Carlo's grasp. 'What are you even do—' His eyes fell on the shattered lantern. 'Foolish boy!' He slapped Carlo across the face. Mother didn't even flinch, she never even looked his way or said a word, still occupied with the puppet. 'Is this it, hm? Is this your attempt at revenge for me making you work at the paper? Trying to destroy the new helper we just spent more than a good few pennies on?'

Carlo stepped back, his parents' reactions were more stunning than any physical blow could be. His astonishment quickly turned to rage. 'Seriously? You care more about that stupid hunk of wood than your son!? Fine! Have it, I don't care.' He stormed out of the room. His fury wasn't enough to carry him out of the house, but he stomped to the opposite wing and locked himself into one of the guest rooms, barricading himself in for the night. He was undisturbed, no one even tried to enter. He knew as much because he didn't sleep a wink more that night.

He rose early and went downstairs before anyone else. He made his own breakfast, simple buttered toast, and he ate by himself. As he did so, his parents, and the puppet came downstairs as well. They paid Carlo no mind—only the puppet looked his way, Carlo stared back.

Carlo's parents didn't even say a word to him before he left. He headed out earlier than he needed, even so, he still went to the press. He was so confused, the past couple of days had been a blur, his life had turned upside down so suddenly. At least he could think at the press.

His workload was more of the same it had been the previous day, though Carlo was still afforded a lunch break. This day, when he was sent out to gather all the sandwiches and coffees he could carry, he passed the cafe, and instead returned home. When he arrived, instead of entering, he lurked throughout the gardens like some kind of burglar casing a joint. He crept along the walls and peered into the open windows. In the sitting room, he found them. His blood ran cold as he watched Mother and the puppet.

She was brushing its hair, a bandage now covering the scratches on its cheek. And she was humming. It was a different tune than last night, it was a tune that Carlo hadn't heard since he was a much younger child, one that caused tender memories of happier, easier days to flare in him.

The memories were shattered when he heard the puppet say: 'I ... love ... Mummy.'

The puppet's voice was different. It was still broken but Carlo could've sworn ... *Impossible.* He never wanted to hear that voice again in fear it would realise his worst nightmares.

But Mother on the other hand couldn't be any more ecstatic. 'Wh-What did you just say?' She stopped brushing, bending down with her ear to the puppet's mouth.

'I ... love ... Mummy.'

Carlo had to grip the windowsill just to stay upright, he'd almost fainted. That voice. It was the strained, jagged puppet voice, but it was now eerily similar to his own.

'Mommy loves you too, Carlo.'

The words were an assault on Carlo's mind. He stepped away from the window, unable to bear it any further. A twig cracked underfoot. The puppet's head snapped around like an owl's. Carlo ducked down and slammed against the wall, flattening against it as much as possible. The puppet stalked over to the window and peered out. Carlo's heart tried to jump out of his body as the puppet craned its neck down and stared him directly in the eye.

'What is it, Carlo?' Mother asks.

'Nothing ... Mummy. A rat.'

'Eugh, horrid little things. I'll have to see about getting an exterminator. If you find one, there's bound to be more. Leave it alone for now, Carlo and come back to Mummy.'

The puppet closed the window and returned to Mother. Carlo bolted from the garden. His heart raced him down the hill. He didn't stop running until he was in the centre of town. He wandered thoughtlessly. When night fell, his tired feet and empty stomach led him back home.

He entered and was greeted by another heavenly aroma, but only that. He shambled to the dining room. The family was already at the table, even the puppet was sitting down, parked right between Mother and Father, a plate of—untouched—food before it. Mother and Father looked up when Carlo entered, but they made no comment on his late appearance, nor did they ask where he had been that day.

'I left the newspaper early today,' he said.

'So you did,' Father replied. There wasn't even a hint of anger or disappointment in his voice.

Carlo was growing increasingly baffled. He stepped behind the puppet, looking down at the uneaten food. 'Move.' He ordered.

The puppet went to rise, but Mother placed a hand on its lap and held it in its seat. 'How rude!'

Father stood, his chair scraping along the floor. 'I'm sorry, you think you deserve supper after skipping out on work? Go to your room, and let that be a lesson for you.'

Carlo scoffed. His disbelief stripped all appropriate words from him. He shook his head and walked out.

While leaving, he heard the puppet say: 'He ... needs ... supper.'

'Oh, no, he'll be fine one night. If he wanted food he should've thought of that before being such a rotten boy. I'm just sorry your brother is such a terrible role model. I wish he could be more like *you*, Carlo,' she said.

Carlo stopped outside the door. Father spoke next and said: 'Yes, you're a wonderful child. That boy won't get *anywhere* unless he starts acting more like you ... Son.'

Something inside Carlo snapped. He turned from the stairway and slunk around to the kitchen instead. He swiped the largest knife, then returned to the entryway, taking a lantern from the wall by the door. He checked it had enough oil, then he returned to the guest room he had commandeered. He'd wait until everyone went to sleep, then he'd destroy that vile puppet. He had to. It had to be controlling his parents somehow, some kind of brainwashing or hypnotism. If he killed it, everything would go back to normal.

Midnight came and went, only then did Carlo move to enact his plan. With knife in hand, he snuck through the dark halls. He kept the lantern mostly shuttered, casting only a thin ray of light before him as he stalked through the house. He went downstairs, checking through the lower rooms first, but he didn't find the puppet in the kitchen, dining or sitting room, nor any of the storage rooms. He tried the basement and wine cellar next, but still, there was no sign of the puppet. 'It couldn't be...' Irate, but with a clear idea where the puppet could be, he marched to the second floor. If it wasn't anywhere else, it *had* to be in his bed. The nerve. *Sleeping in my room, in my bed. I hope it's comfy because it'll be your tomb, you stupid block of wood.* He pushed his door open as quietly as an ant, as slowly and patiently as a snail. Millimetre by millimetre, minute by minute the door opened further until Carlo was able to fit his head, and the lantern inside the room. It was pitch black inside, the curtains drawn tight. Carlo shone the slim beam of lantern light over his bed, tracing a thick lump in the covers. He didn't know if the puppet truly slept, surely it couldn't, not like a real boy anyway, but it couldn't last forever, it had to rest sometime.

This rest you won't ever wake from. He shoved the door open and pounced onto the bed, stabbing wildly with his knife, plunging it into the mound repeatedly, savagely. ... He struck only pillows and feathers, rather than wood and metal.

Carlo knelt on the bed, straddling the victim of his stabbing. He pulled back the covers and found only extra pillows and sheets instead of the puppet. His confusion was broken when the closet door behind him creaked open. He whirled around just as the puppet lunged for him. The bed bounced roughly under them, but didn't buck them off. The lantern spilt from Carlo's grip and to the floor but didn't break. The puppet clasped an iron hand over Carlo's mouth, holding his jaw like a vice. Its other hand controlled Carlo's knife hand, like a shackle around his wrist.

Carlo thrashed uselessly, unable to throw the puppet off. He stretched and strained, but the lantern was just out of reach on the floor, his fingers only able to graze against the rusted metal.

Pain shot through Carlo's arm as the puppet snapped his wrist, his bones crumbling like a cracker. Carlo's screams were stifled by the oppressive palm over his mouth. The puppet slowly picked up the knife that had fallen from Carlo's grip, his hand now hanging limply.

Carlo kicked and screamed as the puppet leered. But the puppet didn't strike right away. It first said: 'I'm better. ... but I can't be ... a *real* son ... for Mummy ... and Father ... not like ... you. ... You *real*. ... Real hands.' The puppet pushed Carlo's limp hand around with the flat of the knife. '...Real skin.' It traced the knife along Carlo's arm. Carlo wrenched away, cutting himself. The puppet looked at the blood that trickled along the knife's edge. '...Real blood. ... Real heart.' The puppet stood the tip of the knife over Carlo's chest. Carlo froze, his heart did too, fearing one of its frantic beats would thrust it up into the knife. The knife moved up to Carlo's throat. '...Real voice. ...Real eyes.' The puppet tightened its grip on the knife, bringing the tip right to Carlo's socket, starting to slip it in just under his eyeball.

Carlo's screaming and thrashing renewed but the hand was like a dozen pillows over his face, and the puppet was a mountain on his chest. His teeth scratched and bit into the wooden palm as he struggled with every ounce of his life.

* * *

Mother stood in the sitting room. The fire blazed within the hearth to fight off winter's chill and warm her back. Carlo sat before her in a low back chair from the dining room, he was as still as a statue as she brushed his hair. She hummed her sweet lullaby, and Carlo hummed with her.

'There! All done,' she said with a flourish before stepping back.

Carlo stood and turned to her. 'Thank you, Mummy.'

Her heart gushed for her perfect baby boy. She opened her arms wide. 'Mummy loves you *so* much, my sweet.'

'I love you too, Mummy.' He hugged her tight.

She sighed, relaxing completely against his strong, sturdy body. He pressed her as close to him as he could. She shut her eyes, listening to their hearts beating in unison.

In the Shadow of the Wyrm

As the sun fell ever closer to the horizon, a scarlet hew stretched across the sky. The towering fortress of black rock—known as Mount Dormorh, home to the ancient dragon Numador—loomed above what few clouds there were. The mountain's dreaded shadow fell upon the quiet town of Lihdor. Lihdor was a secluded place that saw few visitors, but currently, was host to a party of five adventurers. These adventurers, however, weren't met with any welcome, even when they approached stalls to browse the wares on offer or tried to ask the locals for directions, they were received coldly and with few words.

After the party had wandered through Lihdor for some time and got a layout of the land, they noticed the town had become deadly silent now that the sky darkened. They walked the now empty streets, still yet to find an inn, and from the fearful looks gazing out from the houses they passed—before the shutters quickly clattered closed—it was unlikely a local would give them any guidance.

'Something tells me we're disliked by the townsfolk,' Horace said. The knight wore no helm, his shaggy mane of red hair blew freely in the wind. A thick, matching beard covered the lower half of his face, and the middle-aged man was clad in steel from the neck down. He strode along at the head of the party, a shield strapped to his back, and a longsword sheathed at his hip.

'I wonder what could've possibly made you think that, dear.' The woman beside him chuckled softly. She was Elarin, Horace's wife. Elarin was much taller than her husband, so much so that he barely made it to her shoulders. Her arms and armour matched her husband's. Pointed ears stuck out from her head of long, blonde hair, for Elarin was an elf and despite having lived for hundreds of years, her age did not show on her graceful face or in her silver eyes.

'Look, we passed a tavern a little while back, even shitty villages without inns have those. It seems these drunks must think it's more important to get their own booze rather than show any hospitality to strangers,' a lanky figure in the middle of the pack said. Everyone turned their attention towards Smeeden, the speaker. His hooded robe shrouded most of his face, but his elongated nose and ears stuck out clearly. The troll's arms hung down low, hands almost scraping the floor despite him being nearly as tall as Elarin. A wooden staff made of two branches twisted together in a helix pattern was slung across his back.

'We'll see what information we can gather from it, maybe they even have a place for us to stay,' Smeeden said.

The party agreed, and backtracked to the tavern. It was a small place, but the only building in the town that still held any life and light since the sun had set. However, the quiet chatter inside was snuffed out the moment the party entered. The lively, cosy atmosphere quickly turned cold despite the blazing fire within the hearth. All eyes were locked on the newcomers.

'I've had warmer welcomes in a necromancer's tomb,' Smeeden whispered.

They all approached the bar, and the elf on the opposite side welcomed them with a glare as she leaned against the counter.

'What do ye want?' she spat.

'What more could one want from such a fine establishment? We'd like a drink if you please, and we've plenty of coin to be spent,' a purple-skinned female said. She pushed herself to the forefront of the party and slid a few coins across the bar.

This was Umbra, a half-demon, as denoted by her strangely coloured skin along with her thick tail that dragged along the floor. Another prominent feature of her kind was their horns, but Umbra's had been smoothed down so they were hardly more than little bumps above either temple, nestled just under her boyish black hair. Umbra carried a lute across her back, the instrument magically imbued to provide much more utility than just simple entertainment. On the surface, she loosely wore a simple tunic, and a long, flowing skirt, but underneath her shirt, the faint rustling of chainmail could be heard.

The elven barkeep took the coins, still glaring and not yet moving to provide any drinks for anyone.

'And some information wouldn't hurt either. Primarily, if you could point us to the nearest inn, or somewhere, anywhere, we could spend the night,' Horace added.

'No. There's no place for folks like ye here.'

'Are you sure about that?' Horace laid a coin purse upon the bar, though the mood and expression of the elf didn't change.

'Just shut yer trap and wait for yer drinks.' The elf turned her back to them and retrieved her cheapest bottle of ale.

'Hm. Surely someone knows of a place where we may rest our weary heads for a night. We won't cause trouble and just need some sleep, I promise we don't bite,' Umbra said loudly, showing off the coin purse to the rest of the tavern.

For a time, no one answered her call, the tavern was silent; distrusting and hateful glares were directed towards the party from all corners.

'What if we don't want you here? We didn't ask you to come through our town, and we don't want you to stay!' someone shouted. 'We ain't need no adventurers and we got no place for you lot!'

Some folk quietly grumbled their agreement with this outburst, others just continued to watch in silence, their looks speaking loudly enough for them.

'Tough crowd.' Smeeden mumbled.

'Look, this is yer last warnin' 'fore I kick ye all out. Can't have ye disturbing me regulars,' the barkeep said. She slammed their drinks onto the counter. 'Take 'em, and get outta me face.'

'Thank you, we won't cause any more trouble, I'm sorry,' Elarin said. Both she and Horace offered apologetic smiles as they took their mugs, the rest of the party took their own and followed the husband and wife into an unoccupied corner of the tavern.

'To ease the tension, I'd suggest playing a song, but I'm sure they'd just throw us out 'fore I'd been singing long.'

'Something must've happened with a previous party of adventurers that came through here, something that left a rotten taste in all their mouths.' Horace sighed before he took a drink.

'Trust these shitty simpletons to take out their grievances from the past on innocent, kind-hearted folk like us,' Smeeden said, perhaps a little too loudly. 'Might as well burn down some of their houses if they're already treating us like criminals.'

'Smeeden!' Elarin shouted before covering her mouth and drooping her head. She leaned over the table, closer to Smeeden and lowered her voice to a whisper. 'You can't say something like that! Don't act like the monsters they might perceive us to be. The only way to win their trust and hospitality is to prove them wrong.'

The troll rolled his eyes before he turned his head towards the human female on his left and said, 'You're with me, right? I mean, maybe we don't have to be so overt, we could just poison their water supply.'

The woman raised a pierced brow, contemplating Smeeden's suggestion. Her name was Astrid, and she was the shortest of the lot. Her thick leather gear was dyed black, and she wore a black bandana over the lower half of her face, a dagger through a dragon's skull emblazoned upon it. She was as silent in conversation as she was deadly in battle. Before Astrid could give any answer to the question, Horace put his foot down.

'We're not poisoning their water, nor burning their houses, nothing like that. End of discussion.' He glared at Smeeden and Astrid, the latter of which looked annoyed at being lumped in with the spiteful troll.

The party didn't stay at the tavern long, only having one drink—making sure to down it rather quickly—before they left.

'Oh well, even if no one is willing to take us in, it's not the first time we've had to make camp on our own. Besides, that's always fun and cosy~' Elarin smiled around at the others as they made their way out of the little town.

So the party searched for a reasonable spot to make camp for the night. In the forest to the north of the town, surrounding the foot of Mount Dormorh, they found little shelter, as the lands near the dragon's lair were full of evidence of the dragon's wrath and destruction. What little charred and barren trees there were on that side, looked like they were lucky to be standing. Though even within these wastelands, Crows perched along the gnarled black branches of the trees, watching the party.

'A great battle must've taken place here when the dragon first made its roost in the mountain,' Horace said.

'Either that or the fat wyrm must've used these lands as a warning for what may happen if the town strikes out in open revolt,' Smeeden said. Astrid nodded in agreement with his line of thought.

'If there was a great battle once fought here, I've not heard any tales or songs of it I fear.'

With only unease and a reminder of death to be found instead of comfort, the party moved on and circled to the south. The southern forest was much more hospitable. The trees were alive and thriving, and the green foliage provided shelter from both the weather and prying eyes. They didn't delve too deep off the beaten path before setting up their camp for the night, huddling around a small fire.

'Great... we could've gotten a meal at that useless tavern before leaving, now we have to settle for... the emergency food.' Smeeden almost baulked as Elarin and Horace heated the party's dinner for the night. In the cans that roasted over the fire was what could only be called, slop. "Slop" was a brown sludgy mixture that looked like lumpy mud and tasted even worse. None of the adventurers were overly happy with having to settle for a piece of their emergency food supply that night, however, as they watched the brown sludge—which none of them quite knew what it exactly was—bubble and boil, they tried to remind themselves that it was at least nutritious.

'Mayhap you should leave your complaints in your head, for I do not see you offering to hunt down some food instead.'

Smeeden scoffed at Umbra's jest but suffered in silence for the rest of that night's meal.

'I still can't believe they didn't let us stay in the town. That's got to be the worst hospitality we've ever been shown.' Horace said, glancing beyond the trees to where the town stood in the distance.

Astrid signed that they seemed scared.

'They live in the shadow of a dragon, I'd be scared too,' Smeeden said.

'They didn't seem scared of the dragon, I think they were scared of us,' Elarin said.

'Hmmm...' Horace took his wife's hand in his own. 'When we vanquish the dragon, they'll have nothing to fear, and we'll be met with a hero's welcome upon our return.'

'Though... if those stupid peasants want no part of us, then we won't be needing to share the dragon's horde with them.'

Umbra laughed as the married couple glared at Smeeden. Astrid's eyes sparkled as she thought of the treasure trove held within that dark mountain.

It wasn't long until they were all ready for bed. Astrid took the first watch, having saved her portion of dinner for after everyone else had gone to sleep so she could eat in peace. In the morning, the others found that Astrid had stayed up all night instead of waking someone to relieve her of watch duty.

'Ugh, I don't blame you for being unable to sleep. How do those bastards even do it with that bloody mountain leering over them all the time, like some creep watching you through the night,' Smeeden said.

'Well, I'm sure you'll both rest easy tonight, once we've taken care of that dragon,' Elarin said with a smile, patting both Astrid and Smeeden on the back. After a quick breakfast—which was another round of slop, though Smeeden skipped out on eating this time around—the party set out towards Mount Dormorh. They avoided the town altogether, journeying around it, finding no need to disrupt the townsfolk any further. They left their camp-site mostly set up, in case the townsfolk were still unwelcoming towards them even after their triumphant return. As they were passing by the outskirts of the town, at the edge of the woods, Horace spotted something peculiar in the sky above the town.

'Whoa... what in the Hells is going on there?' he said as he pointed it out to the others. They stopped and looked, Astrid narrowing her tired eyes. A black cloud swirled above the centre of the town. Astrid was the first to understand its true nature. Her body stiffened and a chill ran down her spine. She tried to keep her worry hidden as she tugged on Umbra's sleeve and got the attention of the rest of the party. She told them what she knew—it was no cloud that hung above the town, but a flock of birds. The others weren't as frightened by the discovery as Astrid had been, instead, they found it intriguing more than anything else.

'How strange, I've never seen anything like that before, have you, Smeeden?' Elarin asked.

'Well no. Not such a dense gathering before, but it's not uncommon for birds to gather en masse in search of carrion at battlefields or where a heap of death awaits. So... it surely cannot be a good sign.'

Astrid nodded enthusiastically at his conclusion.

'Hm, the sight could make you sick, or it could inspire a piece of music.' The bard plucks on the strings of her lute.

'Right yes, speaking of song,' Horace said, continuing forward and hoping to change the topic, 'how 'bout you play us one? What epic have you been working up to tell of our victory over the great wyrm?'

'Oh? Well, I do have the beginnings of a ballad, for the song is not yet finished. but I suppose I can play it for you now and your input can help to make it more polished.' With that, Umbra cleared her throat, strummed the chords of her lute more melodically, and began to sing:

'In this hill lies Numador the Red,

'He filled all the lands with vile dread.

'Upon piles of gold, he made his bed,

'Until a merry band slayed him dead.

'Oh what tales will this band tell,

'Of the great beast that they did fell?

'Or the riches that made their pockets swell,

'For sending that fat wyrm straight to Hell.

'And the hearts of the people they did mend.

'For Numador's tyranny was put to end.

'A party so great has never before been penned.

'Nay, none greater than me and my dear friends.

'Those epic adventurers will go down in history,

'And this is just a small part of their grand story.

'But don't let it ever be of any mystery,

'That these adventurers were the best the world will ever see.'

Umbra trailed off into silence, a sheepish grin on her face. She kept her head down whilst the others of the party showered her with applause and praise.

They continued along their path, putting the town and the birds behind them. The trees surrounding the party lessened, and eventually, the adventurers passed through a long clearing between the two distinct forests, now entering into the graveyard of dead trees and burnt lands. As they passed by a blackened, gnarled trunk, a crow, perched on the sole-surviving branch of the dead tree, stared down at them with black eyes. The bird let out a loud caw as Smeeden met its unblinking gaze.

'Damn flying rat,' Smeeden grumbled. The bird never took its eyes off them as they passed it and continued towards the mountain.

Eventually, the dead forest faded away into a rocky plain, full of bubbling geysers that would violently erupt with a tremendous hiss and spew forth jets of steam to fill the air.

The cracked ground had swarms of insects spilling out of it, like blood from a fresh wound. These bugs would scatter and flee with every tentative step from the party. There was no cover in this final stretch to the mountain, and the looming tower of stone before them started to weigh down the adventurers' boots with fear.

'One little look out his window, and we're as good as dead. We're sitting ducks out here,' Smeeden said, putting a voice to that fear.

'Smeeden!... If you feel that way, perhaps you should sprint across these plains to draw the dragon's attention and be a distraction for us,' Elarin retorted as she looked back at him.

The troll grumbled but quietened before almost getting into a scuffle as Astrid playfully tried to shove him beyond the final trees and out into the open.

None of them wanted to be the first to take that first step out, feeling as if the dragon was waiting for someone foolish enough to present themself so that he could swoop down for a nice and easy snack.

'If we cannot go forward, we can always turn back. We'll return at dusk, and give it another crack.'

The party contemplated that option, travelling under the protection of night could provide an easier means to approach the mountain. Just as they were about to voice their opinions on the matter, Astrid stepped forth, fists clenched tightly at her sides as she stared straight ahead at the gaping maw of the cave near the mountain's peak; gold gleamed in her eyes.

'Astrid is right. We cannot turn back,' Horace said, stepping forward and taking his place at the front of the party once more. His wife soon joined his side again.

With their fear defeated—or at least pushed aside—the party continued their forward march. As they neared the base of the mountain, they heard a terrible cry overhead, and the sky was blotted black for a moment. At first, they could only imagine the worst and thought it was the great wyrm itself coming down from his lair to kill them then and there. But as their fearful eyes turned skyward, they were met with a sight that offered only a small relief—a sea of crows, flocking to the mountain. Some flew head first into the entrance of the cave, whilst others of the murder circled the jagged peak, and a considerable amount covered the dead trees the party had left behind.

'Fucking birds... they're a bad omen I tell you,' Smeeden said. The rest of the party agreed with him, however, they felt they had already passed the point of no return. If they were to turn back now, they'd never get another chance to strike down the dragon. They hurried to the base of the mountain and slammed themselves up against the sheer wall, finding small solace and comfort in the minimal shelter it provided. Their eyes turned to the path that jutted out of the mountain and wound its way up to the entrance of the cave.

Astrid shook her head; the front entrance wouldn't work, and they all knew it. She motioned for her companions to stay put as her eyes scanned the mountain wall they clung to. She pointed out a deep crevice in the wall and led the party to it.

Once they were hidden away, Elarin spoke up. 'Right. You scout out another entrance, we'll wait right here for you. Be safe.'

Astrid nodded before departing. She moved away from the mountain and slowly circled its base, eyes constantly scanning the rocky surfaces for any further openings. On the near-opposite side of the mountain, she found something—a small hole about fifteen metres up. She moved to the wall and grabbed onto one of the small, rocky outcroppings, testing it for a good handhold. Once she had found one sturdy enough to support herself, she scanned out a path up towards the hole and began her climb. It was slow going, but she eventually managed to find a safe and reliable path up to the hole, pulling herself up and in. It was a tunnel! At least she thought it was, even her trained eyes—so accustomed to the dark—could only see so far into the yawning abyss in front of her. The tunnel's walls were cramped and narrow, and the ceiling was short, even for her. Elarin and Smeeden would most likely have to hunch down quite a bit, but they could still make it through as it was now. As she tried to move further her hands and feet stuck to the floor and walls somewhat, each step took a slight bit extra effort to tug herself free, and when her limbs did come away, a slimy substance clung to her boots and hands. As she trudged further within, she noticed that the ceiling of the dark tunnel was lined with bats—they were asleep for now. Though the ceiling didn't come any lower, even with the path forward being on a slight incline, so Smeeden and Elarin would be able to make it all the way through.

Astrid travelled deeper into the abyss and came to an exit that curved upwards. She crawled up and poked her head out of the opening, peering into the darkness. She could see a deeper shade of black in front of her as her eyes further adjusted to the lack of light. There was a great mound before her, and she wasn't sure if it was the dragon or not, perhaps it could be a pile of treasure. But she was certain of one thing—she had found a way into Numador's lair.

She snuck back into the tunnel and hurriedly made her way out. She carefully climbed down to the ground and rushed to tell her companions the excellent news.

When they were all in front of the tunnel, Smeeden eyed the hole cautiously as Elarin and Horace tried the handholds Astrid had pointed out.

'Are you sure that hole will be big enough for us?' Smeeden said.

Astrid nodded emphatically.

'Be sure to lead the way, we will follow the course you lay out for us... and pray that the rock is strong enough to hold us and our armour,' Horace said to Astrid as he worriedly looked his wife over.

Astrid clambered up the mountain once again, taking her time and making sure to show off the correct path to take.

'You'll be ready to catch us with a feather fall spell, won't you, Smeeden?' Elarin asked the troll sweetly.

'Of course,' he said as he readied his staff.

Horace went up next, Elarin watched from below, ready to catch him with the help of her magical friend. But there was no need in the end, the rock held out and Horace was able to make it to the tunnel. The rest of the party came up quickly after him, having no trouble at all.

'Ugh, it's all sticky!' Smeeden complained once they had all squeezed into the tunnel.

'This wouldn't be the first hole you've been in that is tight and wet, in fact, I doubt it would even be considered the grossest you've ever met,' Umbra said.

Astrid held back laughter and then motioned to be quiet, Horace, who was right behind her, passed on the message to the others with a soft "Shh". Elarin and Smeeden did have to crouch and bend down significantly to fit into the tunnel, even Horace had to stoop his head to avoid disturbing the many bats above. But they continued forward unperturbed by their tight confines. It was only a shame that all three members at the back were the ones whose eyes were naturally able to see in such dark conditions, but as it was only a single path, there was no danger of getting lost, and it was not hard to follow and reach the end.

Astrid climbed out into the cavern first, then Horace, Elarin, Smeeden, and Umbra brought up the rear. Once out into the open space and with more freedom to move, everyone readied their weapons again and took in their surroundings before them.

'What do you see, my love?' Horace whispered to Elarin as Astrid slowly approached the dark mound.

'Oh... no Astrid, stop. That's... it's all bones,' Elarin said.

As Astrid got close, she could see for herself that the darkness began to form a shape and she was able to make out the countless burnt skulls and bones piled together in the room.

'The dragon is not here, we'll have to push deeper—' Umbra's rhyme was cut off by a heavy impact and a gargled scream. Smeeden felt a warm, thick liquid splash upon his back. He slowly turned around and came face to face with Umbra and the dragon; his wooden staff clattered to the floor.

'*Umbra!*' Elarin let out a horrified scream. Umbra had been lifted off her feet. A single, giant talon from one of Numador's hands had pierced her chest fully through and now held her aloft. Blood gushed from around the talon and flooded from her mouth, staining her purple, leathery skin. Her eyes were already devoid of both colour and life as she hung limply.

Numador stuck to the wall above the opening of the tunnel, like a spider waiting for its prey to stumble blindly into its web. The cavernous room filled with an orange glow as a great rumbling growl came from the wyrm's fiery maw.

'Get behind us!' Horace yelled as he readied his shield by his wife's side. Elarin shakily raised her own. Astrid dove behind the pile of bones, and Smeeden threw himself back into the tunnel.

Numador flung Umbra aside before dropping to the floor with a crash heavy enough to shake the mountain itself, staggering the husband and wife. Before Horace could even recover and take a step forward, Numador's tail whipped out with blinding speed, smashing straight through the husband and wife's defence and sending them flying to different corners of the room.

Horace slowly pushed himself back up to his feet, shield arm broken and hanging uselessly by his side, though he still held his sword tightly. Numador approached him and laughed off Horace's attempted attack, the weak slash not even leaving a scratch across the wyrm's scaly snout as his deep cackling echoed around the cave. The dragon opened its maw wide, a furnace burning behind rows upon rows of teeth as big as swords.

Red flames screamed forth and engulfed the armoured knight. Horace was cooked alive as his screams echoed out of the mountain and the stench of his burning flesh filled the room.

Elarin's sword and shield clanged against the stone floor, blood pouring from her head as she could only watch in horrified silence as her husband was reduced to ash; she ran.

Astrid leapt from the mound of bones, throwing herself onto the dragon's neck and stabbing down at it furiously with her daggers. The blades broke upon the armoured scales and she was quickly thrown off the beast with a simple shake of its head. She cried out as she hit the floor and rolled along it. The cracking of her ribs rang out more clearly than her mangled scream. She had lost her bandana in the tumble, revealing her deformed mouth. An old burn had melted most of the skin on one side of her jaw, the scarred tissue kept her mouth partially fused.

Numador's attention was grabbed by different screams that rang out from inside the walls of the cave—Smeeden had been beset by the awoken bats as he tried to flee through the tunnel. They gnawed and scratched at his spindly body, teeth and claws gashing his arms as he covered his head and tried to push through the blockade of winged demons.

Numador smashed his thick tail against the wall of the cavern, just above the tunnel's entrance. The mountain shook once more and the tunnel began to cave in upon itself. Rocks crumbled down from above, squashing bats underneath them and raining upon Smeeden, forcing the troll to his knees. He was so close; he could see the light, the exit, safety, life. It was all right there before his eyes. He reached out. His hand felt the fresh air of the outside world, just before the tunnel fully collapsed and crushed him under the weight of the entire mountain. He would be entombed there forever, leaving only one hand and arm partially exposed for the crows to pick clean as they pleased.

When the rumbling stopped, Numador looked around the cavern again—he was alone. Astrid had fled as well.

'An elf can't die like this! No no no, we're supposed to be immortal! Ohh, I don't care about treasure, I don't care about revenge, I just want to live! That's right, that's right. What's a human to an elf? He was going to die anyways. But not me. No! Not an elf. Never!' Elarin laughed to herself as tears washed down her face. She ran through the maze-like lair faster than her legs had ever carried her before, and eventually, through luck or fate, she reached the exit. She sprinted out of the mouth of the cave and didn't stop running, thundering down the mountain and following the road's many twists and turns.

Astrid shambled through the corridors and rooms of the cave, one hand clutching at her ribs, as the other helped support her against the near wall. Her breaths came out short and raspy, she knew that one of her lungs had to have been punctured in her earlier fall. She was desperate to find an exit, any exit to get out of this dark Hell. There was no light anywhere within the mountain, so she didn't even know if she was blindly stumbling around in circles or not. She couldn't hold back her tears anymore and let them flow freely as she cried. She stumbled to the floor and was about to give up and curl into a ball to accept her death when she saw a ray of light—her last beacon of hope.

She pushed herself back up and hurried over to the light above, the wall sloped upwards towards this tiny opening and she scrambled up to it. It was too small for her to climb through, but she frantically started digging, clawing, and pulling at the rock, doing anything in her power to tear that hole open just a little bit further. She pulled with all her might, teeth grinding together roughly as she bit back the pain screaming at her from her ribs, and then, the rock came free. It broke away from the wall with such force that it sent Astrid tumbling back down the slope. When she opened her eyes and looked up again, she saw the ray of light had expanded considerably, but as her eyes followed its downward trajectory, she also saw what it was now shining upon—gold.

She looked along the floor, following the trail of glimmering coins which soon turned from a light scattering across the floor to an entire ocean. Jewels and gems were sprinkled throughout this golden ocean, great statues and sculptures jutted out from it. It was more wealth than she had ever seen in her life or even thought possible. This room was a never-ending treasure trove that went even further beyond what her eyes could see. It'd be such a waste to have come all this way and to have sacrificed so much without even taking a pinch of it.

As if in a trance, captivated by a dragon horde greater than even legends foretold of, she shuffled into the golden sea and raked in as much of the riches as she could pile into her arms. So enamoured she was, that she didn't even notice the rumbling growl behind her nor did she fear the orange glow behind her that caused the gold and jewels to sparkle and shine in front of her, like the most beautiful dancing light she had ever witnessed.

***

Elarin had made it down the mountain. Elated, she fell to her hands and knees, still sobbing, but now with joy as she praised the gods. 'I'm free... I'm free...'

She looked up and saw a mob of villagers in front of her. She looked around at all the gaunt faces, pale with terror, finding her luck to be unbelievable now that helping hands had been delivered right into her lap during her time of need. 'I-It's not safe! Quickly. Help me back to the village before the dragon emerges!'

The villagers did not move, staring at her as she staggered to her feet.

'Wh-What are you waiting for? We must hurry! I... can't you see I need medical attention?' She walked up to the front of the crowd, grabbing onto the shirt of the woman nearest to her. 'Take me to your healer, now!'

Elarin was shoved away by multiple hands. She slipped back and landed on one knee.

'What are you—'

Thwack! A meaty fist smashed into her face and sent her reeling to the ground. Before she even knew what was happening, they swarmed her. The villagers piled on top of her, hitting and scratching at her, pulling and tearing at her armour and body.

'For the dragon. For the lord. No help. We didn't help. Not with us, not with us. Don't punish us for their sins. Don't punish us for their sins!' They all muttered and chanted, voices shaking with terror.

'Feed the sinner to the dragon lord! An offering so that we may be spared his wrath!' one shrieked out.

Elarin wailed louder than a banshee as she desperately tried to fight them off, but even for a trained warrior like her—especially one unarmed like her—there were just too many of them. They ripped her armour from her, no matter how many she beat away there were always two more pairs of hands to replace them, clawing and tearing at her body. Eventually, she was ripped apart, still screaming until her last breath. Every man, woman, and child of Lihdor would carry their pound of Elarin's flesh back up the mountain as an offering to Numador so that the great wyrm would know they had no part in the adventurers' foolish plan to overthrow the dragon lord and steal his treasure. After all, the town was his most prized possession.

Metal Hearts

Sara scanned the treetop. She stared at the dense branches individually. Once she was certain no birds nested, nor any critter resided, inside the great tree, she smiled and lowered her axe from her shoulder.

With one hand, she felt the bark of the trunk. Fingers traced over the ridges and grooves of the aged wood. She closed her eyes and stood there awhile, envisioning the tree's life from sapling until now. She was not sorry for what she had to do, it was simply natural for this world.

Natural. What a strange concept.

She stepped back and readied the hefty axe. The sharp head gleamed in the sun before her first swing.

The solid "thok" axe meeting tree rung rhythmically throughout the forest. Felling the tree would be long work, though not necessarily hard for Sara. She was built strong and sturdy, tall for a female, and her slender frame was deceiving when it came to how powerful she was. After all, she was not human, only a machine built to resemble her organic creators.

Even so, she still needed to take the life from this tree and use it as fuel to continue not just her own "life" but Zane's as well. Their internal heating and cooling system needed outside assistance to maintain their operational temperature in extreme weather conditions, much like the conditions of the snowy, winter nights they now had to endure; they still needed food to power themselves; and they still needed to melt down water to keep their coolant levels optimal.

Her thoughts drifted as she swung the axe in her unwavering rhythm. Zane would still be gathering more food for quite some time. If he was unsuccessful, they'd be out of food after today's meals. Their supply of ice and Frostsalt was dwindling too. *A trek up the mountain would be nice. Perhaps we shall journey together at dawn.*

She swung her axe one last time. A distinct crack resonated from within the tree. She removed her axe from the trunk and stepped closer. She gave the tree a soft, guiding push, sending it crashing, safely, to the earth.

Her metallic body did not produce sweat, though she knew her interior cooling was pushing its limits to keep her from overheating. But her task was not yet done. She still had to clean the trunk of its branches, trimming them away before she could further break the trunk down into logs that would be suitable for firewood.

As she went about these tasks, she thought about what meal she would replenish her energy with today. Another stew would work wonders. It was efficient, and still left room for plenty of flavour. Sara often wondered if her artificial tastebuds actually worked, or if she was simply triggering a built-in program that *told* her what reaction to have.

We should still have some Meleagris Gallopavo. She had to remind herself that it was "unnatural" to refer to things by the names listed in her database. *Turkey. Humans call them turkeys. Think human. Be human.*

When she was done cutting up the tree into lengths of firewood, she set her axe down and hauled a few chunks of wood towards her and Zane's quaint cabin. She stared longingly at the treeline to the south of their home, where Zane had ventured earlier. Oh, how she wished he would return quickly.

A wolf's howl startled her. She almost dropped the wood. Her eyes darted towards the direction of the noise. South. Sparks erupted inside her head; her gears ground together rapidly. *Zane will be fine. He can handle himself.* She turned away, trusting that he would be fine, though that didn't stop the sparks or the grinding. *I must need maintenance. When Zane returns, I must ask him to perform diagnostics.*

She brought the logs inside, and started a fire under the chimney. A single strike of her forearm against the flint was all it took for the kindling to alight. She carefully fed the flames until they were a suitable size and heat for cooking.

She hoped Zane would be home when the meal was done. The howl echoed in her head and she turned her gaze out of the window, a frown on her face. She hoped he would be alright.

She placed a small chunk of Frostsalt into the pot, and the icy blue, crystalline rock slowly melted. Sara crushed some sweet berries and added their juice to the sparkling liquid forming at the bottom of the pot.

Frostsalt. Zane had found it at the top of the mountain, and that was why they had decided to settle in this place. They had named it such because of its resemblance to ice crystals, and also because of the salty flavour it produced when added to food. The structural makeup of the ore was similar to their cores, and they found that the essence inside, when melted down and ingested, was an incredible fuel source. It easily maintained them on its own and eliminated the necessity for food. ...Yet... it felt wrong to survive without food. To go without eating ... was it unnatural? Even for machines like them, Sara felt a strange desire to consume, and this desire grew harder to ignore the more it lingered. The same could be said for cooking. Whilst there were no dangers in eating raw meat for the machines, such food did not satisfy that innate craving she felt.

A defect that was built into us so that we mimic humanity more closely? Sara did not have the answers herself, and now that they had fled The Organisation, she would most likely never have them.

She shook her head and continued cooking. *No more distractions.* She added more ice to melt down and complete the stock, before sprinkling in some herbs and then finally adding the meat of the turkey. *Yes. I'm sure this will be perfect. Zane will enjoy the taste, and it'll re-energise him when he returns.*

However, when the stew finished cooking, Sara was still alone. She grew increasingly worried. She paced back and forth by the window looking out upon the southern forest. Her eyes constantly darted out to the darkening woods, searching for any sign of her companion. She saw none.

The two bowls of stew sat on a small, round table, having long since gone cold.

Had the wolf gotten to Zane? Why had she heard that howl earlier? There had never been one so close to their home before. Her chest wound itself tighter as she winced, and gripped the windowsill so hard the wood chipped. He was alone out there. Alone and without any food. She hoped he had found some form of energy during his hunt, otherwise, he wouldn't last the night.

She waited by the window, unable to calm herself as she resumed pacing back and forth, even if it was a waste of energy, she couldn't sit still, she had to move, lest she goes mad. *He is alone. ... And so am I.*

When the sun set upon the world and the forest was shrouded in near darkness, there was still no sign of Zane. *I have to find him.* The pressure inside her alleviated slightly as she came to this decision. She would find him, and bring him back home. Everything would be alright.

First, she replenished her energy. Her levels were getting low, and there was no point in her wandering out there and getting into trouble herself. She devoured her bowl of stew, opening her gullet wide and gulping it down without chewing. Her internal acids would dissolve it down and convert it to the necessary fuel, chunks and all.

She took the last of the Frostsalt with her, a fist-sized chunk that glowed a faint blue in the moonlight. It would more than replenish Zane's reserves if he needed it. But they would *need* to go for more in the morning. She stepped out of their home and retrieved her axe, bringing it along as she marched into the woods. Her jaw was set tightly with determination. Her bright eyes illuminated the path before her.

Not long into her journey, she heard another howl, this one much closer, much louder. She increased her pace, gripping her axe so tightly the shaft started to splinter in her hand. Alarms blared in her head as her body heated up exponentially. Her energy output was so high she was shaking. *I have to find him!*

She feared the worst. An image of his broken body, torn to shreds, with gaping, smoking wounds flashed through her head. Surely a wolf's sharp claws and teeth could rip even their metal bodies apart. Zane's eyes were black and dull, his unresponsive body damaged beyond repair ... he died alone ... and she would too.

She panted, inhaling more oxygen than her body could use, further straining her internal systems which worked harder to expunge the excess. She broke into a jog. Her head whipped side to side as she scanned every nook and cranny of the forest for Zane.

'Zaaaaaane!'

There was no answer.

A stray wolf was not the only danger, not the only fear that worried her. What if he had been exploring a new part of the woods? This land was still so unfamiliar to them. He could have gotten lost. He could have fallen down a ridge and broken something vital, leaving him immobilised and helpless—how long could he have been waiting for her to find him, calling out for her to save him until he ran out of power? She clutched her chest. Her jog turned into a sprint as she called for him again.

There was no answer.

If it was not a wolf, or getting lost, or falling and damaging something, perhaps he had already run out of energy, having lost track of time and how far he had gone. He hadn't eaten before leaving that morning, maybe his energy was lower than anticipated and now he was stuck somewhere, motionless and unable to answer her no matter how loud she cried for him. He would freeze overnight, his joints seizing up, his wires closing in on themselves, filling with ice ... she may never be able to revive him even if she refuelled him with all the Frostsalt in the world.

She screamed even louder, pushing her speakers to their limits. '*Zaaaaaaaaaaaaaaaaaaaaaaaane!*'

Silence continued to be her only answer.

Or, worst of all, what if The Organisation's Hunters had found him? The Hunters were the reason they had to flee in the first place, why they had to abandon their home, abandon their world. They were why their creator was killed. The machines were to be decommissioned—destroyed—and neither Sara nor Zane knew why, they had never been given time for an explanation before The Hunters attacked and they were forced to run. Now she could only imagine Hunters had finally found them. They ambushed Zane when he was least suspecting it and left him a pile of scrap. His core would be smashed to bits. He'd be broken beyond recognition, even to her.

As she continued panickedly scanning the forest, she came across a splatter of blood, and a scene of obvious struggle and violence with broken branches and crushed shrubbery. Her eyes widened. Without scanning thoroughly, there was no way to tell if the blood was synthetic like hers and Zane's, or if it belonged to a living creature. She didn't have time for such a procedure. '*Zane!?*'

She stumbled over a root sticking out of the ground and crashed to the leafy floor. She lay face down in the dirt, her body feeling like it was trying to collapse in on itself, her limbs spasming as she envisioned more and more ways that Zane had died. Images of his motionless, unsalvageable corpse flooded her vision.

'*Aaaahhhhhhh!*' She bolted upright with a piercing wail, birds and wildlife scattering away from the sky-splitting shriek. Her speakers broke through the limiters placed on them. '*ZAAAAAAAAAaAAAaAAaAAaAAAaAAAaAaAAAANE!*' Her circuits felt like they were on fire. Her head felt like it would split open at any moment. She feared her core would explode.

If Zane was gone. Then what was the point? She slumped against the ground, sobbing loudly. Her systems plummeted and her output crashed towards shutdown.

'Sara?' His ghost was talking to her. The memory of Zane had come back to haunt her for failing him. 'Sara?! Are you alright?' His voice was as clear as day and snapped Sara out of her psychosis. She looked around wildly.

'Z-Zane? Where are you?'

'Over here. Can you see the mouth of the den?' His voice echoed. A light flashed from the entrance of a small cave burrowing into a rocky outcropping near a gentle stream.

'I see it!' Sara scrambled to her feet and rushed towards the light, expecting to find Zane in need of urgent repair. What she found, was much more surprising.

Zane sat in the middle of the small den. His bow, and quiver of arrows were set aside as he cradled a skinny fawn in his arms. He was feeding some berries out of the palm of his hand to the fawn. A heavily injured doe sat near Zane, though she bristled and screamed when Sara barged into the den.

'Whoa, easy now,' Zane said softly. 'It's okay, she's a friend too.' The doe eased back down. He looked up at Sara, his eyes sparkling. 'Hey. What are you doing out here?'

'Z-Zane... don't you realise how long you've been gone! I-I was so worried about you ... you never came home ... the blood outside ...' She looked at the doe again. The doe had multiple, deep gashes across her belly, and even a few bite marks along her flanks and legs.

Zane set the fawn aside, leaving the remaining berries in front of its nose before he stood. His gaze turned to the entrance of the den, looking out at the darkness beyond. 'Oh. I suppose I lost track of time. Sorry. When I was gathering food, I heard these horrible sounds. When I investigated, I saw a wolf attacking this deer. I scared the wolf off and then tried to help the doe as best I could.' He looked at the doe and fawn. 'I couldn't just leave them. I'm sorry I—'

Sara hugged him tight, almost crushing him in her grasp. She was much taller than him, and his face was pressed tightly against her chest as her arms wrapped around his neck. She sobbed and pressed her head down on his. 'I was so scared ... I thought I had lost you. That you had been damaged and couldn't get back home. That you had been killed by that wolf, or that Hunters had found you. I thought you had left me ... I thought I was alone.'

Zane hugged back, patting her back as she sobbed against him. Soon he began to laugh.

'Wh-What's so funny? Why are you laughing?' Sara leaned away, looking down at him.

'Hahaha. I'm sorry, I'm sorry.' He grinned up at her. 'It's just too funny.'

She looked confused.

'Of course, I would never leave you. Don't be ridiculous. I'm sorry if you were scared. But I'm not going anywhere. No matter what happens to us, I will *never* leave you. *Ever*.'

Sara's face scrunched up more, lips trembling. 'Zane...' her voice warbled before she started crying and once more crushed him against her chest.

He laughed again and let her hug him for as long as she needed to calm down.

After she had recovered, he ingested some of the Frostsalt, noting that his power levels had lowered more than he realised. He also apologised for not finding any further food as he had gotten distracted.

Sara looked at the injured doe. 'Will she survive?'

'I think so. But I think she'll need help.'

Sara nodded. 'We can come back tomorrow. Together, and look after them.'

Zane grinned. 'That sounds like a great idea. For now, we should get back home. We could both do with some rest.'

'Okay. Oh, and when we get home, could you perform a diagnostics report on me? I think my internal systems were malfunctioning slightly today.' Sara took his hand.

Zane's smile only grew as he squeezed her hand. 'Sure. I'm sure you're perfectly fine.'

The two of them returned home to their cosy cabin at the foot of the mountain.

Cheating Death

Mary's lonely footsteps echoed throughout the empty halls she patrolled. Overnight, the morgue may as well have been a graveyard—the dead were her only company. She passed by the "meat locker" as she called it. It was a grim place, walls packed full of corpses, others laid out on cold tables, left to thaw overnight like frozen chicken.

Do they taste like chicken? Mary shook the intrusive thought out of her head, delving deeper into such a topic, she couldn't imagine any other taste for human flesh than the most rotten hunk of meat possible. Might as well eat garbage. She stepped into the room, her torch lighting her way. She scanned the doors lining the far wall, a filing cabinet of death. She approached the wall, her morbid curiosity getting the better of her as she took hold of a handle, slowly sliding a drawer out. It opened silently, revealing naked, pale flesh laid upon a tray. There was nothing spectacular about the male, he was the most average man Mary'd seen. If anything was surprising, it was the fact that he was quite young, in his 30s Mary guessed, and she couldn't see any wound which would've led him here. *Hardly any older than me. Unlucky bastard.* She slammed the drawer shut.

Her head snapped towards the door, torch flashing out into the hall. Had she heard another thud out there? Or was it merely an echo? Or maybe nothing at all ... Mary decided it was the latter, mentally chiding herself for being so jumpy. There was no one in here but her and the dead.

Her eyes scanned the room again. This time her gaze fell upon the shape of a body hidden beneath a plain white sheet. Another male with a gunshot wound to his head lay beside the covered body. She approached the covered corpse—her new object of fascination—swiped the sheet away, and gasped.

Now *this* was a beautiful corpse.

'What a tragedy.' She pulled the sheet entirely out of the way, letting it crumple to the floor as she looked over every inch of the female body now revealed. Her light shone against the dark, ebony skin, so smooth and free of imperfections. She let her hand rest upon the woman's thigh, such a soft and tender feel. Mary licked her lips. Her eyes slowly travelled up the woman's body from foot to head, taking in the details of the toe tag first. Jane Doe—an unknown. How curious. Her legs were long and shapely, her thighs and hips just plump enough for Mary's liking. 'What a tragedy indeed.' Her hand glided along the woman's torso, rubbing over the hump of her belly, one that would've been good cushioning for cuddles. Her hand didn't stop there and continued up to the woman's breasts. She cupped one—it filled her palm and then some—and gave it a gentle squeeze. Perfectly full and round, with large, dark nipples. 'A shame I'll never know how sensitive these nipples were.'

Her eyes were drawn to the middle of the woman's chest. 'Huh...' What she found there was strange—a necklace hung from the woman's neck. Usually, any belongings a person came in with were removed and set aside in a different container, where they'd be used later while preparing them for their funeral if the next of kin wished it so. But for some reason, this woman still had a pendant or... it looked more like an amulet to Mary, as fantastical as that sounded. She'd never seen anything quite like it. A strange, opalescent gemstone of purple, red, black, blue, and gold, hung from a necklace of delicate, black pearls. The stone was shaped irregularly, and larger than her fist, positioned as it was—

nestled between the woman's breasts—Mary couldn't help but compare it to a heart. She let her fingers rest upon this "heart stone" as she looked over the woman's peaceful, resting face. Her kissable, plump lips had been discoloured to a pale purple; a large, cute as a button nose; surprisingly, her eyes were wide open, though milky and colourless—Mary couldn't tell if that was how they'd always been, indicating this woman had been blind, or if that was a sign of her deterioration in death; and there wasn't a wrinkle in sight, the woman's age was impossible to tell just from looking at her like this. To cap off her appearance was a glorious crown of lustrous, brown curls in a large, neat afro that would've been half a foot high at least.

'That's my type of woman. God, what I wouldn't give to have met you while you were still breathing.' Mary chuckled and leaned down, staring at those irresistible lips as she wet her own. She pressed her pursed, thin mouth against the deceased woman's, kissing her softly. She held the kiss for a long time before pulling away. Her gaze drifted lower, drawn back to the heart stone as it seemed to shimmer. It must've been because of her torch. She fingered the stone carefully, lifting it away from the woman's chest and looking along the pearls wrapped around her thin neck. Her gaze followed the pearls and eventually looked the woman in her cold, dead eyes again. 'Sorry, love. But such a gem is wasted on the dead, even for a perfect bitch like you.' She slipped the necklace over that large crown of hair and drew it away. 'Fuck!' she exclaimed, her eyes widening with fright as she stumbled back and almost dropped the necklace, catching it by the pearls. Lifting the stone away from the woman's chest had revealed a nasty, festering wound right beneath it. Mary clutched the stone close against her own chest and shuddered. She thought the woman must've been stabbed with a knife carrying the plague or some other—just as hideous and deadly—disease. But it was so odd that the rest of her body appeared so perfect, as if she might've just been sleeping.

She turned the stone over in her hand, checking for any foul residue or signs of decay clinging to the back of it, though it was perfectly clean. Just as Mary was slipping the necklace over her head, another boom startled her. This time she *knew* it wasn't just her imagination. Her head whipped round to the door again, her torch acting as a crosshair as she pulled her stun gun from its holster and readied it, wishing it was the real thing. She crept out of the meat locker and edged her way down the hall; the noise had come from the morgue's entrance.

She was more curious than frightened, her heart steady as she slunk through the dark, her feet moving quietly and deliberately. There was no trepidation in her stride or mind; she'd been trained for shit like this. She didn't fear what she might find, it would finally answer a question for her: just why is security needed at a morgue anyway? She neared the corner into the lobby and saw two streams of light waving around in the shadows. She shut off her own torch and pressed against the wall, peering around the corner. The lights were coming from outside the glass doors of the entrance, two men pressed against the glass, desperately trying to see inside.

Mary laughed, then stepped into the open. Her question still only had one answer—security was needed to stop thieves like her. 'What the fuck are you clowns doing? Why are you making that racket? You should've just called me,' Mary said, walking over to the door and unlocking it.

'We did! Ya phone's off, ya moron,' the shorter of the two men said. His name was Sully—at least that's what Mary knew him by—and he was a real prick. He was ex-military, allegedly. The only thing confirming that story was his stupid buzz cut. When asked why *he* wasn't the one who took the jobs as security in their little act, he said it was because he'd never get hired with a criminal record. What crime he'd been charged with, he wouldn't say. Sully was much shorter than Mary, only up to her chest (maybe another reason why he wouldn't get work as a security guard), and within five minutes of meeting him, she knew he was insecure about it. Mary thought his real name would've been closer to Napoleon than Sully. He had a face like a bulldog's, only perpetually angry, and twice as ugly. Even now, when it was the middle of the night, he still wore a pair of aviator shades, and no matter how ridiculous they made him look, he could never be convinced of it.

'Yeah, yeah, whatever.' Mary held the door open for the two men, glaring down at Sully as he walked in, though she gave a respectful nod to the man who came after him.

Aaron was almost the same height as Mary, though he was shockingly slim, almost all skin and bones. Mary felt a lot more confident that Aaron was his real name too. Overall he was a much more open and trustworthy guy. Sure, he was a crook, and as dirty as they came, but his motivator was clear, he was doing it all for the money, Mary knew she could rely on people like that—they were the easiest to understand. Despite his meek looks, Aaron was cunning and ruthless, not afraid to break your hand just to squeeze a fiver from your grasp. His bald head and sharp eyes gave him a sort of reptilian look, and gold glittered around his neck from a locket that he *always* wore.

Sully carried a bag over his shoulder, it rattled with every step, full of the tools they'd need for the job. While Aaron had a large freezer tub with him, this one rattled too but with the distinct sound of ice sloshing about. Both men were older than Mary, though Sully's angry face held more wrinkles than both his partners combined.

'Quiet night?' Aaron said with a smirk.

Mary laughed and slammed the door shut behind him. 'Nah, they've been chatting my ear off, haven't had a second of peace 'til you showed up.'

Aaron chuckled, Sully wasn't amused. He stood in the middle of the entranceway, looking around impatiently. 'We haven't got all night.'

Mary rolled her eyes. 'Alright, jeez. There's no rush. It's not like they're gonna get up and walk away.' She laughed more and led them back to the meat locker.

'Here you are, your majes...ty...' Mary pushed open the door of the meat locker and froze. Jane Doe was no longer on her table.

'What's the matter with ya? Move out of the fuckin' way if ya just gonna stand there starin' at nothin'. Ya been smokin' again? How many times do I have to tell ya not to do that shit when ya on the job?' Sully growled and shoved past Mary, approaching the nearest carcass.

'Th-There was...' Mary was still staring in disbelief, pointing a finger at the empty table where Jane Doe should've been.

Aaron pushed past her, placing a hand on her shoulder and looking at her with concern. 'Are you alright, Mary? Maybe you need to go get a drink and some fresh air. We'll handle this first one.' He flashed a soft smile before moving along and setting out the ice box on a side table near the corpse. Sully slammed the toolbag onto the same tray and opened it up.

Mary shook her head rapidly. 'N-No there was ... there was a body right there. There should be a body right there! What the fuck is happening?!'

'What? Stop talkin' bullshit and get it together, woman. The grass makin' ya hallucinate?' Sully glared at Mary.

Aaron looked at the empty table and then at Mary again. 'You *really* need to stop smoking.'

'I'm not fucking hallucinating!' Mary slammed her fist against the wall, glaring at the men. Her heart raced. She stared at the disturbed and worried looks of each man, and then she laughed. 'Ohhh... hahaha. Right. I get it now. Very funny. You've brought on another partner without telling me, and while you distracted me at the door, you had them sneak in through the back and hide the body somewhere.' She laughed more though the men exchanged glances. 'Okay, very, very funny. But you can come out now. You got me good, but it's time to stop pretending.'

'Ya seriously gone off the deep end, Mary. If this is what ya gonna act like, maybe it's best if ya off the team.' Sully turned his attention back to the corpse. He and Aaron put on gloves. 'Let's get this tarp under him. Help me lift him.'

Aaron didn't say anything, looking at Mary with concern before he turned to the body. With Sully, he lifted the lifeless body. Once it was in the air, Sully had an easier time holding it in his arms while Aaron quickly laid a tarp across the table before they set the body back down.

An icy bead of sweat ran down Mary's temple. 'Y-You guys... I'm being serious. There really was a body right there.' Her voice grew more frantic, rising in pitch. 'If you didn't move it, who did?!'

'Enough!' Sully barked, slamming his fist down on the table. He pointed a knife at her and removed his shades, his large, bloodshot eyes almost fully white. 'If ya not gonna help, just go and grab all the expensive shit from the property boxes.'

Mary stared at the empty table as she backed out of the room before staggering down the hall. She tried calming her heart and breathing with no luck. She stumbled into another small room full of filing cabinets and a table with a registry book laid upon it.

Maybe she *had* hallucinated Jane Doe. She was lonely, and it had been a while since she'd gotten some action. Maybe her restless, love-and-sex-deprived brain had just conjured up the image of the perfect woman.

Her fingers graced the necklace around her neck. She tugged the chain out of her shirt and grabbed the stone dangling from it. It throbbed and glowed in her hand. She definitely hadn't made that Jane Doe up.

'What the fuck?...' She laughed hysterically and shook her head. She was losing it. How could that body have disappeared? Where did it go? If there was no body, where did this amulet come from? She stuffed the glowing, multi-coloured rock back into her shirt. She didn't have any answers, and rather than dwell on those questions and fall deeper into insanity, she decided to occupy her mind by sorting through the many possessions that all of these deceased people had been brought in with.

Each cabinet pertained to a different individual, and the book on the table had a detailed inventory of each item that had come with each body. Sorting through those lists and finding everything valuable wasn't tiresome or hard, it was brain-numbing, which was *exactly* what Mary needed.

It was only when she was done and had a good pile of jewellery, cash, wallets, and anything else they could make a quick buck with, that she realised she hadn't brought a bag to stash all this loot into. 'Fuck.' She headed back to the meat locker, slowing down the closer she got as her mind was brought back to the missing body. Panic and fear once again gripped her heart. Her chest squeezed tighter the faster her heart pounded against her ribcage, desperate to break free.

She peered inside, Aaron and Sully were just about finished with the first corpse, dumping the harvested organs into the icebox. Mary swallowed the lump in her throat then said: 'Hey. I need the keys for the ute, is it open? I need a bag for the goods.'

'Ya stopped freakin' out then?' Sully looked over, even with his shades back on, Mary could tell he was glaring at her.

Her eyes darted to the empty table again. She didn't answer him.

Aaron sighed. 'Look, maybe you can just sit out in the car tonight. Keep watch or something.' He picked up the ice box with Sully's help.

'Whatever,' Sully said. 'As long as she isn't in the way. We're goin' to the truck anyway so ya can get ya bag then. Now move.'

Mary darted aside as the two carried the box past and down the hall. Her gaze travelled to the hollowed-out body they'd left behind. The man's chest and stomach had been sliced open and ripped apart, leaving a massive crater behind from which they'd pulled out everything that had made him human.

Mary looked at the scavenged carcass coldly. It was strange to think this sight made her feel next to nothing, whilst the mere thought of a missing body almost paralysed her with fright. She hardly even noticed the horrid stench of putrid decay, shit, and death that came with this job anymore.

At least this one hasn't moved. She shuddered at the thought of this one getting up. She almost didn't want to leave the room and give it the chance to disappear while they weren't looking, but soon Sully's angry voice beckoned her.

'Mary! Stop spacin' out and come get the fuckin' door!'

She hurried to the front of the building, where Sully and Aaron were waiting by the door. Sully was still muttering about her being a "useless bloody woman". At least her rising anger from being ordered about like a dog didn't give her any time to worry about the missing body.

'Get the fucking door yourself,' she mumbled before opening it.

The men shuffled over to the modified flatbed of the ute, a domed roof now installed over it, and set the box down.

Sully fumbled in his pocket for the keys before swinging the door open. Together, all three of them lifted the box and half buried it into the bed of ice that blanketed the back of the ute. Mary went to the backseat to get an empty duffle bag, while the men grabbed another box, empty except for its own ice, for the next set of organs.

As they were closing the car back up, they heard a crash inside the morgue. Mary jumped, banging her head on the inside of the ute, and dropping her bag. 'What the fuck was that?!' She clutched her heart, though the stone was in the way of her hand.

Sully and Aaron both frowned at each other, then looked back at the morgue. The door was open. 'Maybe a cat got in? Or a possum?' Aaron said with a shrug.

'Maybe it was somethin' gettin' into the bins behind the buildin',' Sully added.

'Okay. You two. I'm serious right now. You really didn't bring a new member? If you're lying to me and trying to pull a prank on me, I will kill you both with my bare hands. I'm *not* fucking playing around.'

'Don't get ya fuckin' knickers in a twist. Ya on ya fuckin' period or somethin'?' Sully shook his head.

'Mary. On my baby boy's life. We are *not* trying to trick you. We didn't bring in a newbie.' Aaron moved over, putting his hands on her shoulders and looking into her eyes. 'It was probably just some animal getting into the bins, like boss man said.'

Mary breathed deeply, trying to calm down. 'B-But the body...'

'Let's go check it out, we'll look all through this building, and when we find nothing will you relax a bit?'

'O-Okay...' Mary nodded, it seemed reasonable. Her heart rate slowed.

'Is that alright, boss?' Aaron looked back at Sully.

Sully groaned. They could tell when his eyes rolled behind those shades. 'Fuckin' whatever. If it stops her from freakin' out, fine.' He turned away muttering the next part, 'This is why I hate workin' with women.'

They all turned back to the morgue, entering and leaving the new ice box, as well as the empty duffle bag on a desk by the entrance. The noise sounded as if it had come from the back of—or behind, as Sully suggested—the building. They ventured deeper inside, coming across an open door that led to the autopsy room.

A single, cold, metal table sat in the middle of the sterile room, and next to it, there was a tray table that had fallen over and spilt its utensils across the white, tiled floor.

'Somethin' fell over, that's what ya so fuckin' scared about? It's nothin',' Sully said.

Aaron examined the fallen tray and tools more closely, righting the table and setting everything back on top of it before shrugging. Mary looked around the room, but nothing else was out of place, no other drawer or cupboard was open.

'But...' Her voice still carried fear and worry. 'Wh-What knocked it over?' Her eyes continued to dart around the room.

'It was just the wind. We left the door open, and this door was open too.' Sully waved it off dismissively.

'Or it could've been a wild animal that got inside. We'll just keep an eye out.' Aaron said.

Mary slowly nodded, not truly accepting their explanations, but they had to move past it. They weren't going to accept her fears or even respect them, so there was no use dwelling on it. The faster they finished this job, the quicker they'd get out of there. And after all, maybe it *was just* the wind (even if it wasn't that windy outside), or a wild animal as unlikely as that seemed. Was a dead body getting up, vanishing, and then knocking over this tray honestly more plausible?

Returning to the entrance, they grabbed the ice box again, and Mary grabbed her bag before they ventured down the hall, the men returned to the meat locker, while Mary went back to the storage room. Mary was scooping the pile of valuables into her bag when she heard Sully scream out: 'Mary!'

She dropped the bag again, instantly imagining the worst as she rushed to the sound of Sully's voice, skidding to a halt in the doorway of the meat locker. She gasped, another chill shooting up her spine.

The hollow corpse was still on the tarp-covered table but now, every door along the freezer wall where the bodies were stored was open, the trays pulled out and empty.

'What the fuck...' Mary braced herself against the doorframe.

'What the fuck is right!' Sully exploded with anger. Mary realised that his shout hadn't been one of fright, but one of rage. 'What the fuck are ya tryin' to pull here? This is a fuckin' *dud*!'

'Wh-What?!' Mary took a step back. How was he trying to blame her? How was he so blind? Couldn't he see how fucked this was? 'I-I didn't do *anything*. What are you talking about?'

'There aren't any fuckin' bodies, why didn't ya tell us there was only one bloody corpse in this fuckin' shitbox!?' Sully kicked over the empty table where Jane Doe once laid. Mary flinched.

'Whoa, relax, Sully... d-don't you see how weird this is?' Even Aaron's eyes were wide with panic as he tried defusing Sully. Aaron couldn't draw his focus away from all the open doors and empty trays. 'Those were closed when we left this room, and the wind sure as hell didn't do all that.'

Sully looked back, huffing loudly with each ragged breath, the air fogging up in front of his face. '*She's* the one fuckin' with *us*. We brought a new member? Fuck off! Ya know we only work as a three-man group. Ya the one who brought somebody extra along and are tryin' to yank our balls. What are ya even tryin' to pull? Tryin' to keep it all for yaself?'

Aaron stood between Mary and Sully. 'What?!' Mary's fright was turning to outrage at Sully's accusations. 'You're *fucked* if you seriously think that. I'm telling you, something fucking weird is going on here.'

'And I'm *tellin*' *ya* that I don't buy it.' Sully turned away, shaking his head. 'Fuck this. Just grab what we've got and let's get out of here.'

Mary certainly wasn't going to argue about leaving.

'Aaron, grab the tarp while I lift this cunt off it.' Sully moved closer to the table with the corpse.

'No way. I'm with Mary on this. There's something wrong here. We need to go, like right now, fuck the tarp, fuck the bag, let's just go.'

'*Fuck*! Don't tell me ya fallin' for her bullshit?' Sully snarled. Aaron stood his ground. 'Fuckin' hell. I'll do it myself then, ya fuckin' pussy.'

Sully grabbed the corpse, going to lift the now much lighter weight off the tarp. However, when he grabbed the body, its arm shot up and grabbed onto his. Before Sully could react, the corpse lurched forward with a hellish growl and sunk its teeth into his arm.

Sully screamed bloody murder as the ... *thing* tore into his flesh. It bit down so hard it reached bone and even started to snap and crunch through that. Sully lashed out, bashing and punching the thing with his free hand as it ate him.

Mary screamed louder and more shrilly than she had even when she was a little girl. She didn't move, she was frozen in place by this vile, terrifying event. Even Aaron was stuck where he stood, like his feet had sunk into the floor. His mouth agape as he watched in silent horror.

Sully kept screaming as he futilely thrashed against the thing. 'D-Don't just stand there! Heeeelp! *Help meee!*' He cried out in agony as one of the bones in his forearm broke apart, and another large chunk of him was ripped away.

Both Aaron and Mary jumped into action, shaking off their fear. They sprung to Sully's rescue. Yes, he was an asshole, but he was still their partner and someone they'd been working with for over a year. They couldn't stand by and watch him get eaten by whatever the fuck that thing was.

They pulled the thing off Sully's arm, tendons and muscle stuck between its teeth as it was yanked away. It snapped at their arms as they held it down, before they quickly released it, stepping back.

Mary whipped out her heavy-duty flashlight, the thick object weighed a good couple of kilos but she flipped it around with ease. She lunged forward as the monster hissed and screeched at them, and brought the flashlight down atop its skull, smashing its head in. Brain matter shot out of its nose and mouth as its skull caved in, leaving a large dent behind. Then the thing tumbled off the table and splattered on the floor where it lay unmoving once more.

Sully was still crying and wailing, clutching his bleeding, ruined forearm, which looked more like a raw, half-eaten chicken wing at this point. 'What the fuck... what the fuck was that? My arrrmmmm!' Sully dropped to his ass, shaking his head wildly.

Aaron rushed to Sully's side, hands reaching for the injured arm though he had no idea what he should do. They had nothing to stop the bleeding or even bandage such a grievous wound. 'Oh fuck, oh shit, oh my god, what the fuck do I do!?' A thick stream of blood squirted out onto Aaron's shirt and he jumped away.

Mary ignored the screaming coming from the other side of the room, her attention firmly fixated on the corpse whose head she'd just bashed in, fragments of skull and brain clung to her flashlight. Looking closely, Mary saw under the shine of her bright light, that the skin was even further discoloured; the veins were more prominent, now a strange, sickly yellowy-green kind of colour, like puke; and there was a bite mark on its neck, which hadn't been there before, the flesh around it a rotten black colour.

'That's ... that's a fucking zombie. That's a zombie!'

'What?' Aaron's head snapped around to look at Mary. 'Now isn't the time for fantasy, movie bullshit, Mary. Sully needs help! We gotta get him to a doctor, *now*.'

Mary shook her head, backing away from the bitten and presumably infected man. 'He's bit, man. H-He's gonna turn into one of those things. I'm telling you. W-We need to get out of h—'

'*Yes* and get him to a doctor! Now fucking help me or go get the car started!' Aaron started to help Sully back to his feet, the injured man leaning on him heavily with his bitten arm tucked close to his chest, his good arm draped around Aaron's shoulders.

Mary stumbled out of the room and backed into a wall, still staring at Sully like he'd turn and start eating Aaron's face any second. Aaron and Sully shuffled through the door then stopped, staring down the hallway at another figure by the end of it.

Mary slowly turned her head towards the crooked, shadowy figure. With a shaky hand, she shone her light over the figure, revealing pale, grey skin, with those same, prominent puke-coloured veins. It had a gaping wound on its head which would've already put a normal human out of commission, and of course, the rotten bite on its neck.

'Oh fuck...'

The zombie screeched loudly and started sprinting towards them. Mary scrambled backwards, fumbling with her flashlight as she turned it around in her grip, ready to use it as a weapon.

The dark shape quickly closed in on them as Sully staggered away from Aaron, slipping his good arm away from the taller man and reaching behind himself.

'Bite this, cunt!' A blinding light filled the hallway and an explosion of thunder deafened the three thieves for a moment. Aaron flinched and covered his ears, though that did nothing to stop the ringing filling his head. Mary almost dropped her flashlight as she too clutched her head.

Sully held a pistol in his outstretched, wavering arm, smoke spilling from the barrel. The zombie staggered, blood gushing from its shoulder where the bullet had pierced straight through. Then it charged again.

Shots thundered through the hall, echoing off the narrow walls, and after the fifth bullet had been expelled, the zombie fell flat on its face, skidding to a stop just in front of Sully. A hole had been blown through the back of its skull. Hideous, gunky, off-coloured blood spilt from its wounds.

Sully staggered forward, stepping over the fallen corpse. 'I don't know what the fuck is goin' on, but I'm gettin' the fuck out of here.'

Mary stared down at the dead zombie and kept tight against the wall, shuffling after Sully. Aaron ran after Sully. 'Where the fuck did you get that? Have you always had a gun?!' he asked.

'Of course! Ya never know when ya might fuckin' need it.' Sully grimaced with every word, but he refused Aaron's help this time.

'The head … you have to shoot them in the head,' Mary muttered. If Aaron or Sully heard her, they didn't acknowledge it.

'Give me the gun I'll—'

As Aaron reached out for it, another zombie rounded the corner into the hall, only to be head-shotted by Sully. 'No. I'll hold onto it.' Sully stepped over this corpse and continued.

The trio reached the end of the hall and turned into the lobby, where a group of zombies crowded the front door. A few were bashing against the glass, trying to smash it open, but most were already facing the humans. In the midst of the horde, was Jane Doe, staring at Mary in particular.

'Oh fuck, oh shit. Th-There! That's the fucking body that disappeared when you guys got here!' Mary pointed her out with a shaky finger, her other hand clutching the stone hanging under her clothes.

'That one?' Sully raised his gun and fired, however, another zombie lurched in front of the bullet and shielded Jane Doe. 'Ya motherfuckers. I'm not dyin' here!' Sully kept shooting, one of the bullets sprayed wide and smashed through the glass windows.

Jane Doe raised an arm, pointing at the three, and screamed. The horde swarmed forward. Two more zombies fell, but Sully was soon out of bullets and there were still at least a dozen zombies charging at them.

'Run!' Mary bolted, and Aaron followed. Sully threw his pistol at the oncoming horde, but it did nothing to slow them. He tried to run, but was quickly overwhelmed and tackled to the ground. His death throes only caused Mary to run faster as she left him behind. Aaron refused to look back and tightly held onto the locket that bounced against his chest as he ran.

When Sully's agonising screams finally ended, it was a mercy to all involved. He had at least provided a good distraction while the zombies paused to tear into his flesh and gorge on his innards.

Jane Doe screeched again, her voice piercing through the entire building. A few zombies at the edge of the feeding frenzy snapped out of their hunger-fuelled bloodlust and rushed past her, dashing out of the shattered door. Most of the others rose and resumed the chase against the remaining prey.

Mary burst through a closed door, turning back and holding it open just long enough for Aaron to squeeze through before she slammed it shut. The two were now in the staff break room, a simple place with a barebones kitchen, fridge, dining table, and sofa lounge set up in front of a TV. Together, they pushed the lounge in front of the door, just before a zombie thumped against it loudly.

Hungry groans and growls persisted along with the thumping and thudding as the zombies tried to break the down door. Mary backed away, panting hard, her eyes darted around the room. She dashed towards the single window.

'Come on!' She threw it open and hurriedly climbed out, Aaron following right behind her as the window led out to the alley behind the morgue. A large, wire fence with a crown of barbed wire hemmed them in tight against the building, this fence ran along all sides of the building expect the front. 'Shit!'

Mary started down the alley towards one corner of the building, just as a zombie scrambled and skidded around the corner. She shrieked and turned right into Aaron, who quickly turned around as well, only to find another zombie coming around the opposite corner as well.

'Back inside!' He ordered, throwing himself back through the window and helping Mary in. They slammed it shut and started to push the fridge in front of the window as the zombies converged, smashing against the glass furiously. More zombies piled up against the glass, biting at it, and smushing their faces against the window in their endless hunger for the meat held within. The banging against the door was unceasing. They were surrounded with nowhere to go.

Mary shook her head, reaching into her pocket for her phone. She fumbled with it as she turned it back on. Aaron grabbed her arm and said: 'Who the hell are you calling?'

'I-I don't know, the police? The fucking army! Who does it matter? We need help right fucking now!'

'You can't call the cops. What the hell are you gonna tell them? That we're being attacked by walking corpses? Yeah, I'm sure they'll believe that. And even if they *do* show up, then what? We get arrested for harvesting organs? Hell no.' His hand moved back to his locket. 'I can't go to prison.'

Mary gulped. 'O-Okay well... I'll call someone else. A friend. I'll...I'll ask someone else for help. No cops.'

'What the hell are they gonna do?'

'I don't know! But it's better than nothing!'

Aaron bit his tongue but nodded, looking away as he got his phone out as well and looked through his contact list.

Mary's phone rang for a few dials before the call was answered. 'Vicky?! Oh my god, Vicky, please! I need your help. I'm at the morgue on Long Street and there's fucking zombies! There's even this fucking zombie queen bitch and she's after us and we're surrounded and they're gonna eat our faces off! They've already killed Sully and we're seriously in deep shit here! I need you! ... Just, no cops okay?'

A very tired voice on the other end of the phone answered Mary. 'Whoa... zombies? Damn... that's a crazy nightmare... mmm... you need me to come to your house?'

'What? No! No, this isn't a nightmare. I'm being serious! Don't come to my house. To the morgue! The morgue on Long Street.'

Vicky yawned loudly. 'That's a really... messed up dream... dude... I'm... sor...ry...'

'Vicky! *Vicky!*'

Only snores answered Mary now.

'Fuck!' She looked at Aaron. 'Any luck?!'

He held up a hand to silence her, his phone pressed to his ear. 'Pick up, pick up. Yes! Finally, Alexa—'

'Do you have *any* idea how late it is, Aaron? I have work in... two hours! This better be good,' a grumpy voice answered.

'I know. I'm so sorry, but you gotta come help me. I'm in the morgue at fifty-four Long Street, and I'm trapped. Th- There's a bunch of... zombies in the building, and I'm cornered. I need you to help me out.'

There was a long silence before Alexa spoke again, but she simply said: 'Goodnight, Aaron.' Then hung up.

'A-Alexa!?' Aaron stared at his phone, dumbfounded. He tried the number again. No answer. 'F-Fuck! Fucking, shitty cunt-on-a-stick! You goddamned bitch! I hope you rot in hell and get raped by Lucifer himself for all eternity, Alexa!'

Mary stared at Aaron. She'd never heard him swear before.

'She turned her phone off...' Aaron explained. 'I...I don't have anyone else who could help us.'

Mary bit her tongue and kept trying more numbers, but no matter who she called, they either didn't pick up, or if they did, they never believed her no matter how calmly and seriously she explained the situation.

She slumped down, tossing her phone away and putting her head in her hands. 'That's it... it's useless. We're fucked.'

Aaron moved over and sat down by her side. 'I guess... we just have to wait it out, and hope they leave. I-I mean. They're outside right? They can go wherever they want and find tons of other people to eat. O-Or. We wait, and when morning comes, someone else will come and find us, and we'll be saved.'

Mary looked over at him. She didn't think it very likely that the zombies would just up and leave. They don't get bored, they don't get tired. They'd bash on the window and door until either they or the building fell apart. Plus, there was likely another reason that they wouldn't leave them alone. Her hand clutched around the stone again.

Aaron looked at her, his hand went to his own chest, this time he pulled his locket free and opened it up. He used his phone's torch to light up the picture contained inside the locket. A smile came across his face.

'You haven't met my kid, have you? Or my wife. Sorry, ex-wife... I keep work and my personal life separate. I'm sure you understand.' He angled the locket towards Mary more, and she leaned over, looking down at the illuminated picture. It was of a beautiful woman, a head full of luscious, wavy black hair, thick lips curled up into a smile so warm and bright it could still be felt through the picture, with straight, shiny teeth, a small gap between the upper front teeth. Cradled in her arms was a chubby, giggling baby, with the same dark brown eyes as his papa, and the same, flat nose as his mama.

'They're beautiful,' Mary said, smiling. Aaron had to make it out of here.

'Thanks. Though, our boy, he's a bit older now. Heh, already in kindergarten, starting primary school next year... they grow up way too fast.' Tears welled in Aaron's eyes as they stared at the loving, serene picture for a while longer.

They stayed that way for a long time, curled up on the floor, Mary hugging her knees as she tried to ignore the groans and thuds. Aaron kept stroking the edge of his locket, never taking his eyes off the picture, and occasionally he'd mutter the odd prayer while they waited.

More than an hour passed, nothing changed. Sunrise was still far away, the morgue opening even further away, and the zombies were still tirelessly pounding away. The door had started to give way. With each thud, it rattled harder, and the wood splintered inward more; it wouldn't be long until they broke through completely.

Mary stood, stretching her cramped legs. 'We can't wait around any longer. There's no point. Help isn't going to come before they break in. We have to do something.'

Aaron slowly picked himself up as well. 'You're right... but... what can we do?'

Mary looked around. She flipped over the small, wooden table and grabbed onto one of its legs, yanking hard until the thing popped off. She snapped the end of the leg across her knee, making a sharp, jagged point, and then tossed it to Aaron. 'We can fight.'

Aaron caught it and looked at her like she was crazy.

Mary shrugged. 'Or you can stab yourself through the brain and never see your kid or wife—sorry, *ex*—ever again. Your choice.' She looked through the drawers, finding the biggest knife that she could. She held it in one hand, her flashlight in the other, then nodded to the lightly barricaded window. 'We go out the back, there's less of them there.'

Aaron was still unsure. A hand smashed through the door, part of it fully caving inward. A zombie pressed their face up against the gap, a sickly arm reaching in and groping at the air.

Mary started pushing the fridge out of the way of the window, grunting with the effort. 'Look. I'm fucking leaving, you can stay here or you can come with me.'

Aaron moved over and helped her shove the fridge aside. Five zombies stood clawing and pressing on the glass. 'Okay,' Mary said, 'we open the window a bit, deal with the fuckers as they try to climb through, then we hop out and make a run for it.' She paused a moment. 'You go right, I'll go left. If we split up so will they, and we'll have a bigger chance of making it.' She didn't tell Aaron that she fully expected the zombies to prioritise her and the stone; she hoped Aaron would get away even if it cost her her life. It's not like she had anyone waiting for her.

'O-Okay.' Aaron gripped his makeshift spear tightly.

Mary grabbed the window's latch, and after a slow countdown—during which they both took repeated deep breaths—she threw the window open.

Aaron stabbed the first zombie that clambered through, jamming the pointy end of the broken leg straight through its already missing eye. Mary took out the next, stabbing a woman through the top of her skull. Mary then started to climb out the window herself, slashing and bashing away hands, kicking one zombie in the face and stomping on it as she jumped outside.

'Come on!' She called for Aaron to follow as she shoved past another undead and started down the left side of the alley. Two of the remaining three zombies started following her. Aaron scrambled out of the window, the last zombie—that was still on the ground—latched onto his leg. He yanked himself free before it could sink its teeth into him, and stabbed it through the mouth. His "spear" got stuck in the ground, but he quickly abandoned it and made a dash towards the right.

Neither Aaron nor Mary looked back to see how the other was doing, and as Mary neared her corner, she started shouting to draw even more attention to herself. 'Hey! You undead zombie fuckers! I'm over here! Come and get me you rotten shitbags!' She felt a hand grab her from behind, whirled around, and took the offending zombie's jaw clean off with a strike from her flashlight. She then shoved it into the other zombie that was lagging behind it, both of them toppling over to the floor for a moment.

She sprinted around the corner, rushing through the narrow side alley to the front of the building, thankfully no zombies were in her way, though that was also concerning regarding her self-sacrifice plan. She only hoped Aaron was faring as well as her.

She rounded the corner and burst out into the open at the front of the building, she saw Aaron sprinting towards the ute. 'Aaron! Shit, look out!' Zombies were flooding out of the front entrance, and as Aaron reached the ute, one slammed into his side.

He kept his feet, trying to fend the monster off, though as he shoved its face away, it chomped onto his hand, biting off a couple of his fingers. He screamed and kicked it off, throwing open the car door. He crawled inside and started it up.

'Fuck!' Mary watched as more zombies were streaming towards the car. 'H-Hey!' She clanged her knife and flashlight together loudly, trying to draw their attention, and she did succeed in distracting a few, but more continued their charge towards the car as the engine sputtered to life.

Aaron reached out to close the door. The zombie who took his fingers, this time took a chunk out of his arm, latching onto him and crawling into the car as well.

As Mary fended off and evaded another zombie, she was helpless and could only watch in terror as the car jolted forward, Aaron's pained voice crying from within as the machine raced out of the lot and crashed straight into a telephone pole, the horn blaring loudly and continuously.

The zombies swarmed the crashed vehicle, obstructing any path off the front of the property.

Another zombie came from behind Mary. She shrugged it off, shaking and slashing its hand away before she scrambled towards the entrance of the building. She could loop around and head out the back door and then jump the fence, barbed wire be damned—a few cuts would be better than being made into a meal.

She rushed inside, hurrying through the corridors, sliding around corners and stopping herself against walls. However, when she got to the back door, she froze—the zombie queen stood in her path.

The staff room. Mary turned and headed for the staff room next, though her path was cut off by a regular zombie this time.

She shrieked as it lunged at her, and she just barely shoved it off before its teeth could latch onto her flesh. She fell over, scrambling and crawling backwards rapidly, her flashlight clattering to the floor. She turned over and scrambled to her feet, almost slipping over again as she ran harder, darting into the first room she came across, which just so happened to be the meat locker.

'Shit!' She didn't have time to turn back, the zombie was right behind her. She tried to slam the door shut, but the zombie stuck its hand through the doorframe, using its decrepit body to prevent it from closing fully. 'Fuck! No, no, no!' With each "no" Mary slammed the door against the zombie as hard as she could. Eventually, it stuck its head through the gap during one of her backswings, and when she smashed it forward, the zombie's skull messily splattered from the impact.

Its truly dead body fell forward, and the rest of the horde burst through the door after it. '*Ahh!*' Mary stumbled backwards, still clutching her knife. Again, she plunged it through the top of one zombie's head, but as the body fell away, it twisted the knife from her grasp, the blade still lodged deep inside its brain.

She staggered back, now defenceless as the last of the horde filled the room ... but, they held back and didn't instantly swarm around her and start tearing her into pieces. Mary backed away, almost tripping when she bumped against a table. Then her back was against the wall, and she had nowhere else to run as she stared at all the bloody, pale, lifeless faces staring her down.

There was no hunger in their eyes, there was no expression at all on their faces, they didn't even move as they stood there. Not even the slightest twitch. The only difference between these zombies and a bunch of statues at that moment was the thick, dark saliva that spilt from their mouths.

What were they waiting for, what did they want?! 'C-Come on and eat me then!' She roared at the horde. Her heart felt like it would explode it was beating that hard and fast; the waiting felt worse than what she was sure would come next. She'd already resigned herself to her fate, she just wanted them to get it over with now.

Instead of moving forward, the depleted zombie horde parted, and Jane Doe stepped into the open. Mary gawked, locking eyes with the dark queen. Hers were the only eyes that still held life, and while there was still some drool running down her chin, her lips were curled into a smile, instead of hanging open listlessly. Mary gulped. Her heart was still pounding, but, maybe there was still a chance of survival. 'Th-The stone? Is that it? Is that what you want?'

Jane Doe said nothing; it was likely she couldn't speak. Her smile faded, and she tilted her head, watching Mary closely.

Shakily, Mary reached into her shirt and started to retrieve the stone. When Jane Doe saw it, her eyes flashed the same eerie colour of the stone's glow. Mary's breathing hitched and she quickly pulled the necklace off over her head and then thrust it out towards Jane Doe. Mary's hand shook uncontrollably as she held out the necklace in a tight fist, her knuckles whitened as she panted hard, staring into the vibrant eyes of the ebony zombie before her. 'Please... I'm sorry just... just take it.'

Jane Doe looked at the glowing rock that hung from Mary's fist. She reached out, her cold fingers pressing against the warm stone, lightly caressing it.

Mary smiled softly, unable to take her eyes off the zombie as she caressed the stone. This could work! Maybe she'd be freed from this nightmare, never to defile the dead ever again.

It was as if the zombie could sense the hope building up within Mary's heart and instinctively sought to crush it. Literally. Faster than Mary could blink, a coldness burst through her chest. She turned her eyes downward and saw the zombie's entire left hand buried deep into her body. The zombie drew her fingers away from the stone, focusing solely on a more interesting gem. She pulled her hand from Mary's chest, her fist still wrapped around that beating, bloody heart. A metallic taste filled Mary's mouth just before she puked up blood, the viscous liquid flowing down her chin and spilling to the floor like a waterfall. She could see her own beating heart before her eyes, the zombie holding it up for her to see clearly in her final moments, letting her watch as she took a bite from that pulsating organ.

Let Me Taste You

Alex sat in his dark apartment, illuminated only by the images on TV. He couldn't draw his eyes away from the news as the major headline that night was about yet another young boy's mutilated body being found. Alex was so enraptured by the details of the story, that he didn't even notice an envelope slip under his door. The only marking envelope had was a red love heart that looked like it'd been finger-painted. When Alex finally shut off the horrific story and crawled into his bed, he didn't sleep a wink.

> "My love, I can't say thank you enough! You are the light of my
>
> world, the sun of my day, and the moon of my night. Ohh how
>
> utterly dull it had all been until you came along. So lifeless,
>
> colourless, and void! My life had been totally empty and hollow.
>
> But you. ohhh, you. You have brought the spark back into my

> soul and the joy back into my heart. No other beauty can compare to you, your fair skin is too pure for this earth, ..."

'Christ, this creep is just going on and on ... what's this bit? Did you scribble it out?.' Izzy brought the note closer to her face, squinting at the ink, trying to discern what words had been covered up by such heavy and repetitive scratches that the paper was almost torn.

'No, it came like that. My secret admirer must not've liked it after reading it again. Though, I made out one of the words: skin,' Alex said, pointing the word out. 'Maybe they'd forgotten they'd already said that part.'

The two were standing behind the counter of the little cafe where they worked. Alex had brought the letter after he found it that morning, thinking Izzy would get some entertainment out of the bizarre contents.

'You don't seem all that freaked out by it,' Izzy said.

Alex shrugged. 'Oh, when you're as beautiful as I, you can't help but get the odd letter from such a smitten admirer every so often.'

Izzy rolled her eyes and Alex laughed before apologising half-heartedly.

'You really shouldn't sound so happy to receive such a creepy letter! Ugh...' She huffed and looked away, resting her cheek on her hand.

Her eyes scanned Alex. They were both wearing the same uniform: a form-fitting, collared and buttoned, green shirt, as well as tight, sleek, black slacks, and a black apron over the top of it all.

Alex wears it better, she thought. *It's not fair.*

Her brown hair was tied in a messy bun, whilst Alex's blond locks were neatly trimmed and brushed, perfectly framing his soft, freckled face, the tips of his hair dyed pink, making his unique, pink eyes pop even more.

People always notice his eyes, always compliment them. Her eyes—as brown as mud—were rarely noticed, and when they were, it was usually just for how tired they looked.

It's not fair.

She looked so frumpy in her uniform, but Alex looked like he moonlighted as a model and didn't deserve to be in a place like this, even if the uniform hugged his curves and wide hips so nicely.

It's not fair this fa— Izzy was knocked from her train of thought when Alex bumped her hip with his. He nodded towards the tired-looking man on the other side of the counter.

'You've got a customer, hon,' Alex said.

Izzy shook the nasty thoughts out of her head and turned to the customer.

Why am I even getting jealous over some creeper's weird love letter? Ugh, get a grip, girl.

Izzy rang the man up and got to work making his coffee. When she handed it over to him, he didn't even thank her before he turned away and left the shop.

'I don't think that was the admirer... he didn't even look my way,' Alex said.

'Huh?' Izzy looked at Alex, confused.

'My admirer.' He waved the letter about. 'Don't you wanna know who it is? They'd have to come see me at work, right? I bet they come here every day. Ahh... I hope they leave big tips~'

Again Izzy rolled her eyes. 'You're not taking this seriously enough! This isn't some cute little schoolyard crush! This is a stalker. They could be dangerous! What if they hurt you?'

'H-Huh?! Wh-Why would they hurt me? They're in love with me.' Alex stood up straight, his face paler than usual.

'Well, they're crazy, right? Only crazy people stalk someone, and... they're probably ugly or something, weirdos are always ugly. And then if they confess to you, and you reject them, they could get mad and try to hurt you!'

Alex trembled, staring off at nothing. He almost jumped out of his skin when the next customer entered and the bell chimed.

'Fuck, Alex I didn't mean to spook you,' Izzy said. 'Just, don't worry about it, I'm sure nothing bad will happen. Go take a breather in the back, I'll be fine up front for a little while. You relax and calm down.'

Izzy rubbed his back and guided him towards the break room before she returned to deal with the customer. Alex was still shaking a bit as he clutched the letter tightly against his chest. He looked it over again, his eyes focused on a word that came up repeatedly throughout.

Taste.

I imagine the taste of your lips to be sweeter than any cherry. I can't wait to finally taste your nectar. I need to taste you on my tongue each morning and night and every waking moment!

Alex shuddered all over and closed his eyes, gripping the love letter tighter against his pounding heart, the paper crumpling in his hands.

He was in the back for nearly ten minutes before he returned to Izzy's side. She looked at him apologetically. She felt responsible for the mini panic attack. 'You okay?' she asked.

'I-I'm fine now, thanks ... you're such a great friend.' Alex smiled up at her. Izzy smiled back, though she couldn't tell if he was just putting on a brave face. She looked away as the lunch rush was getting underway, thankful for the distraction from her guilt about her jealousy.

As the day continued, Alex seemed much more alert and focused when it came to dealing with the customers. Each time either he or Izzy finished dealing with a customer, he'd lean over and ask her if she thought they could've been his stalker.

It was hard to tell. None had shown any obvious signs, at least not what Izzy was looking for. She expected some shady individual to show up, all fidgety and stuff, thinking it'd be obvious to see them fawning all over Alex and being all handsy with him, or someone who asked specifically for him. But nothing like that happened, so she started to look for subtler signs. Alex was constantly watching them all like a hawk. He even drew a complaint when he creeped out an overly jittery woman with his constant staring, and Izzy had to apologise on his behalf.

When they were both taking their lunch break, she brought it up with him. 'Look. I'm glad you're trying to figure this out, Alex, but you can't freak out the customers. Maybe you shouldn't worry about it so much, I mean, they might not even be an actual customer, maybe just someone who sits in the park across the street and watches you through the window,' Izzy said.

Alex gasped and stiffened again. 'You think they're some peeping tom? Oh my gosh! What if they've got like, binoculars or something and are watching from really far away?' He started to shake again, hugged himself tightly, and whined.

Izzy bit her lip. 'Trust me... I'm sure it's nothing like that okay? Just, don't worry about it, I'm sure this isn't really that big of a deal right? I mean, didn't you say you're used to getting letters like that?' She suppressed another pang of jealousy. 'Nothing bad has come from those before, right? So I'm sure it'll be fine this time too.'

'Y-You really think so?' He looked like a frightened little animal, desperate for comfort as he pouted up at her.

She couldn't help but smile at him. 'I know so.'

He threw himself at her and hugged her tightly. He sobbed against her chest. 'Thank you! Ohh, thank you, Izzy! I don't know what I'd do without you. You're my best friend!'

Izzy gasped. Her fingers trembled as she wrapped her arms around Alex and squeezed him close. She held him for a while. He was so soft.

Even in his distressed state, Alex noticed the pounding of Izzy's heart. Eventually, he tried to pull away.

'Uh... heh, th-thanks Izzy... you-you can let me go now.'

Her arms dropped away from him. 'Oh! Sorry. Hah. You okay now?'

He nodded again, still smiling softly.

'Okay, good.' Izzy nodded as well. 'Oh! And um, you shouldn't bother the female customers.'

Alex tilted his head. 'You don't think it could be a girl? The letter didn't say if it was a man or woman.'

'It didn't, but like, when do you ever hear of a woman stalker right? This kind of thing is always some creepy guy, and uh... especially for someone like you, it just makes sense that it'd be a guy.' She held back from mentioning her belief that it couldn't be a woman because they'd be more likely to be jealous of his looks—just like her—rather than attracted to them.

Alex's brow furrowed as he thought it over. 'Hmm... alright, that makes sense.' Looking back on his past relationships, he always attracted more male attention. Even though he was bisexual, he couldn't remember his last romance with a woman.

'Alright, you ready to get back out there?' Izzy said.

'Yeah! Sorry, I'll try not to bother any more customers I just... really gotta figure this thing out.'

Izzy patted him on the shoulder. 'I'm sure you'll figure it out sooner or later.'

The day continued like normal, and the two closed shop later that night. As they were cleaning before locking up, Alex went over some potential suspects he'd narrowed it down to. 'So! There are some regulars I've got my eye on.'

'You have? Do tell,' Izzy said.

'First! That writer guy. He's like always here. Every day. For so. damn. long.'

'The one with the scarf?' Izzy's eyes drifted away from Alex as she pictured the man he was talking about.

He'd always sit in the corner booth. He was skinny, probably cause she couldn't remember him once ordering any food, despite getting a coffee every hour that he was there. He was pale, almost as much as Alex, tall and really long too. The tapping of his keyboard was such a regular occurrence that it completely faded into the background and joined the drone of all the other noise she'd subconsciously tuned out after working at this joint for so long.

'Yeah! That's the one. He must have a long neck under that scarf. Blegh.' Alex's tongue stuck out as he shook his head. 'But, he always looks at me every so often. And whenever I give him his coffee he always makes sure to brush his fingers over my hand.'

Izzy nods. 'Okay, so that's suspect number one. Who's next?'

'The jogger!'

Izzy groaned at the mention of him and knew exactly who Alex was talking about. Another guy that'd visit the shop every day. Though he wouldn't stay as long as The Writer, he'd show up twice a day, every day, always at the same times, like clockwork. And he'd stink up the place with his damn sweat!

First, he'd show up at 2:35 pm, in a lycra tank top and these tiny shorts, he'd get a coffee—always standing too close to the counter and rubbing his sweaty body against it—then he'd stand around while he drinks it before heading back out and continuing his run. While he was quite fit and admittedly handsome, he always stank and seemed super inconsiderate too, and cocky. The next time he'd show up would be 45 minutes later, and this time he'd get a muffin, find a table, soak a seat in his sweat, eat his muffin, and then walk out of the store and down the street.

'Why him?' Izzy asked.

'He's always flirting with me, and giving me eyes like he's trying to see through my clothes. I swear he like, flexes at me and stuff whenever he needs to grab his drink or muffin, or hand over cash.'

'Okay okay. So, Mr Jogger is suspect number two. Anyone else?'

'Last one. They're not quite as regular, but you see them every so often and they showed up today! They're a lot more shy, and even if they ain't the stalker, they've definitely got a crush on me! They're all quiet and nervous whenever they speak with me. Uhh, kinda short and heavy. They get a tall black and a chocolate chip cookie each time, and they always have a novel with them.'

'Oh! Oh!' Izzy exclaimed. 'Kinda greasy, black hair? Always wearing a hoodie?'

'Yep! That's him.'

'Huh... yeah, he does prefer being served by you...'

'Right?'

'Mm, he fits the profile more than the others, I reckon.'

'Maybe I should confront him next time he comes in...'

Izzy's face paled and she grabbed Alex's arm. 'Whoa, no way! That's stupid, don't do that. They could freak out and you might just make it worse. The best thing to do is keep an eye out when you're walking home and to work and stuff. And get some pepper spray or something.'

'Oh...' realisation washed over Alex's face, he hadn't thought about how his stalker would react after he confronted them. 'Okay, I'll get some of that. But... uhh, speaking of walking home... do you think you could walk me home tonight? Or uh, maybe I should get an Uber?'

'I can walk you home!' Izzy stood up, smiling wide. 'That's not a problem, and it's like, what? Two blocks to your apartment? That's nothing, no need for an Uber.'

Alex held onto Izzy's hand, the tension leaving his body. 'You're right. Thanks, Izz. I don't know what I'd do without you~'

Izzy squeezed his hand gently. The pair smiled at each other, then finished closing up shop before heading off into the night and starting down the streets towards Alex's home.

As they walked along—the sounds of their steps echoing off the buildings—Alex couldn't help but think the streets were overly quiet and empty. It wasn't that late, but even beside Izzy, he felt so isolated. He couldn't shake the eerie feeling of predatory eyes upon him, the type of nerve-racking sensation that made the hairs on the back of his neck stand on end. He squeezed Izzy's hand, and kept his head down, focusing on their feet and the ground ahead of them. What he didn't know was, that his stalker was closer than he would've liked, and that he was being watched by them every step of his way home.

The stalker was so focused on Alex, they'd blocked out everything else around them. Not like there was much to block out that night, it was almost as if everything was frozen in place around them. The air had that kind of crisp chill to it. There wasn't even the usual scent of the city in the air that night: garbage, rubber, piss and shit. Nor did Alex's scent reach his stalker's nostrils, and that saddened them. Alex usually had such a nice scent, flowery and sweet, like honey-coated rose petals. But it was as if the day and night had robbed him of his sweet scent... they wondered if his taste had been robbed as well, or if he would still taste as sweet, rich, and juicy as he looked.

The stalker wetted their lips with their tongue, creeping along, matching Alex's every step, making sure to never let him out of their sight. But they were cautious, even with such a quiet night, they couldn't make their move yet. They had to wait. Until Alex was completely out of sight from the rest of the world, truly alone and trapped. Then they could pounce. It was decided, after watching this boy for longer than any other, they would finally make their move. Tonight, they couldn't wait any longer.

It wasn't long until Alex and Izzy arrived at his apartment building. Still, he didn't let her go.

'Izz...? Um, c-can you walk me up to my room, too?' he pleaded, looking up at her with big eyes as his bottom lip quivered.

'Geez, this has really shaken you, huh? What's next, gonna ask me to tuck you in as well?' She giggled.

Alex pouted and pulled his hand away. 'It's not funny! If you're gonna be like that, I take it back, you can go home now.' He crossed his arms over his chest.

'Aww, come on, I was just joking. I'm happy to walk you up to your room.' She tugged on his arm, trying to uncross it.

He gave her a side eye before his pout faded away. 'Fine, fine, okay.' He smiled a bit before he entered the code to unlock the door, then held it open for Izzy. She slipped inside and hooked her arm with Alex's heading up the stairs with him.

When the door swung shut, Alex didn't know the stalker had slipped in, and he was now trapped inside with them.

Alex and Izzy took each step one at a time, staying quiet as they kept close to one another. Once they stopped in front of Alex's door, he slipped away from her grasp, and started to unlock his door. When it clicked open, he stared down at the handle for some time before speaking up.

'Would you... care to come in, Izzy?' He pushed the door open, entered the lightless apartment. He didn't look back.

The door closed again before she responded, but he'd heard her step inside. 'I'd love to. Thank you for having me, Alex.'

'Oh, no, I should be thanking you for walking me home... who knows if that crazy stalker would've attacked me if I was alone tonight. Would you like anything to eat or drink?' He walked further into the darkness.

Izzy frowned and flicked on the light, seeing Alex disappear around the corner into his kitchen. 'Oh no. I'm fine, thanks,' she said. As she followed him, she slipped something from her purse and hid it in her hand and along the inside of her forearm. Her nose turned up as she walked further into Alex's home, this was only the second time she'd been inside it, but she didn't remember it having this metallic stench last time. 'You know... I've been waiting for this for some time now...' She stepped closer to Alex. He had his back to her. She stopped when he turned.

'Oh. I know. Trust me, I've been waiting for just the same thing... I was beginning to wonder if you'd ever make your move. I've had my eye on you for such a long time as well~' Alex's voice was different. His sweetness was dripping off every word, but there was a sultryness underneath that honey.

Izzy hesitated. Her brow furrowed and her eyes darted around. Something was wrong here. Alex was different. That stench was stronger. *Is it coming from the fridge?*

'Ahh... your heart is racing~ That's perfect,' Alex purred. His tongue swiped across his ruby lips. He took a step towards Izzy. She retreated.

'St-Stay back!' Her heart continued to pound as she brandished her knife, all sense of threat and menace was gone from her actions, and instead, she was the one under duress. She still wasn't entirely sure why, but she was no longer in control. How long had she been the one ensnared in a trap?

A fanged smile warped Alex's face. His soft eyes morphed to a harsh, sharp red, though they hardly took notice of the blade in Izzy's hand, instead focusing on her delicate, bronze neck. 'Mmmm... don't disappoint me, Izzy, I know you'll taste exquisite!' He lunged at her. Izzy's knife clattered to the floor.

Even though Izzy's scream penetrated the entire building, not a soul thought to investigate the noise that came out from Alex's apartment. The next day, no one even thought it suspicious when Alex told them the reason Izzy hadn't made it to work was because she had gotten sick. Life continued as normal, and Alex already had a shortlist of candidates for his next meal. Though he wondered if any would come close to tasting as delectable as the woman who played at being a monster.

M.P. Seipolt

The Tapping in the Wall

Tap tap tap.
Dexter woke from a state of half-sleep. Had that sharp rapping noise come from the wall? The door? Or his dreams? 'Hello?' he said into the darkness.
Silence answered.
He lay there, staring into the dark. The rise and fall of his chest was the only movement in the room.
Tap tap tap.
He sat up, breath hitching. He flicked his bedside lamp on and winced at the explosion of light. He shielded his eyes as he stared at the off-coloured, floral wallpaper that covered the wall on the far side of his room. It was an interior wall, so he knew it couldn't be a branch or a bird tapping against it from the outside. But... what was it?
Tap tap tap.
He threw off his doona and slinked out of his room. He was silent as he peered around the corner and down the hall that was on the other side of the wall. His eyes adjusted to the dark, picking up shadowy shapes and outlines of furniture, but he couldn't see anyone. It wasn't either of his younger

siblings pulling a prank, nor his parents, nor even their Cocker Spaniel, Brucie.

Maybe they were hiding, or he was too tired and didn't spot them in the dark. 'Who is it? I'm trying to sleep, so knock it off.' He saw no movement, and no one's voice answered him.

Tap tap tap.

Again! This time the sound came from inside his room, but still in the same spot on the wall. His heart rate quickened, and he hurried down the hall, almost knocking over a vase as he followed the wall to where the tapping had originated.

He pressed his hand against the smooth surface, rubbing over a small area. He wasn't even sure what he was searching for, but he found nothing, it was just a regular wall. Was there a rat inside somehow? It didn't sound like something scurrying around inside the walls, it was a distinct tapping, like a *person* tapping their bony knuckle against the wall.

Dexter swallowed; his mouth and throat were dry. He leaned closer to the wall. 'H-Hello?'

Thud!

He jumped back, eyes widening. Someone was inside the house. *Inside the wall.*

He scrambled out of the hall and to his parents' bedroom, bumping into chairs and drawers as he navigated the dark house in a panic. He burst into the room without even knocking. 'Mum! Dad! There's someone in the house. They're in the walls.'

'What?!' Dad, although groggy from sleep, stumbled out of bed and grabbed a cricket bat that was resting against a nearby wall.

'What are you saying?' Mum sat up, more reluctant to leave her comfy bed.

'Th-There's someone. I can hear them, i-in the walls. They keep tapping on the wall in my bedroom.'

Dad lowered the cricket bat, his darkened, angry expression turning to that of confusion. 'What? Someone in the walls?'

'What's he saying about the walls?' Mum asked.

'He said—'

'—There's someone in the walls,' Dexter and his dad both said.

'Don't be ridiculous... it's just a nightmare Dexie... go back to sleep,' Mum said. She laid her head back down and turned over.

Dad sighed and set the bat down, shaking his head. 'Don't be stupid, Dexter. Of course, there isn't anyone in the bloody walls, you idiot. Waking me up for this nonsense.' He sat back in bed, still grumbling.

'B-But, there really is someone in there,' Dexter desperately pleaded his case, but they were as effective as a match in a blizzard.

'I don't want to hear it. It's just the wind, or mice, or the house settling, or you're just making shit up to yank my leg. Now, *go back to sleep.*'

Dexter flinched then backed away, closing the door as quietly as he could. He sulked back towards his room, stopped in the hall, and peered through the darkness.

Tap tap tap.

He thought about running back to his parents, dragging them out of bed and physically showing them what was going on. He thought better of it. He doubted they would've followed him, and it's not like he could drag his dad anywhere. He chewed on his lip. If he showed his siblings, his parents would have to believe them all.

He sped through the shadows of the home, much more used to the dark now, not running into anything. He even managed to hurdle over Brucie—who was snoring in his bed within the open plan kitchen—as he hurried to the opposite end of the house where his siblings' rooms were. He started with his little brother, Axle.

He eased the door open and poked his head inside the darkened, still room. 'Axle?' he whispered. There was no response, so he called again, louder. He took a step into the room, hearing Axle stir. He approached the single bed where he knew Axle lay under his soccer ball-covered doona. He reached out and gently shook the small mound. 'Axle, wake up.'

'What time is it?...'

'Don't worry about that. It's still night, just wake up, I have to show you something.' He didn't give Axle much of a choice, pulling the doona off him.

Axle sat up, struggling to keep his eyes open as he yawned loudly. 'What's going on?' he said.

'I told you, I have to show you something, but you have to be quiet for now ... it's a secret. There's something in the walls.'

Axle's bright eyes shot open, sleep evaporating from them as he looked up at his older brother, full of curious wonder. 'Really? What is it?'

'I don't know. We're gonna check.' Dexter had no idea, and right now, he didn't quite care about figuring out what exactly was in there—that problem could be solved later—right now, he just needed someone else to hear it too, so he knew he wasn't going crazy.

He helped a now eager Axle out of bed and took his hand. He led him from the room, though tugged the boy back when he started down the hall, and pulled him towards their little sister's room first. 'We have to get Luna too.'

'Aww, but I wanna see it now.'

Dexter shushed him, and then pushed open Luna's door. She was a few years younger than Axle, and her room was so bright, that it wasn't even dark in the dead of night. The pinks of the painted walls, the colourful cushions, stuffed teddies, and posters all about the room, even shrouded in shadow, were jumping out at Dexter.

'Luna?' He had to keep a tight hold of Axle's hand so he didn't run off trying to find the tapping on his own. They didn't have to step far into Luna's room—she was awoken much more easily. The second time Dexter called for her, she raised her head up, a black shape rising from that dark, pinkish bed.

'Who's there? Mummy?'

'No, Luna. It's me, Dexter.'

'Wh-Why are you here?'

'I've gotta show you something, but you gotta be quiet okay? Just come here with me.'

'Dex says there's something in the walls.' Axle said excitedly.

Dexter shushed him again.

'Wh-What?! What's in the walls?' Fear was already evident in Luna's voice.

'We don't know, but it's okay, it's just something tapping in the walls. You need to come hear it too.'

'Yeah, don't be a scaredy-cat,' Axle teased.

'I'm not!' Luna tried to hide under her pink, pony-covered doona.

'You're not helping, Axle.' Dexter strode over, once again throwing aside his sibling's doona. He put a finger to Luna's lips. 'Mum and Dad are gonna get mad if they find out you're awake when you shouldn't be.'

'*You* woke me up.'

'Mum and Dad won't care. You'll still be in trouble.'

She pouted and her lips trembled but she didn't utter a single peep or squeak. Dexter took her hand and helped her from her bed.

'How'd a person get in our walls anyway?' Axle said. 'Do you think they fell down the chimney?'

'That's not how chimneys or houses work. And I never said it was a person. I don't know what it is.'

'Someone's in the wall?' Luna squeaked.

'No! I...I don't know.' Dexter gritted his teeth. Maybe this was a dumb idea after all. 'Wait here,' he said firmly and then hurried to the kitchen, taking one of the larger knives from the fancy wooden block Mum kept on the counter. He tucked it into the back of his waistband, slipped the back of his shirt down over it, and then returned to his younger siblings as Axle was pestering Luna with a bunch of questions about what might be in the wall, and Luna was doing her best to ignore him so as not to be frightened any more than she already was. Dexter took them both by the hand and then—keeping a firm hold—marched them through the house to the entryway hall. He stopped right where he had heard the tapping.

Luna clung tightly to his hand, pressing against his side as she rubbed sleep from her eyes. Axle stared at the wall, excited but impatient. 'Now what?' He looked up at Dexter.

'Just, give it a moment, it was driving me crazy before, I couldn't sleep.' He let the kids go and stepped closer to the wall, reaching out and feeling it before he slowly pressed an ear against the plaster, listening for any sound or movement.

Nothing.

Axle moved closer and mimicked his brother, closing his eyes as he did so.

Luna stayed back, shifting on her feet as she watched her brothers. 'I-Is someone there?'

'Shh.' Dexter held up a hand, still listening.

Axle moved his head back. 'No one's there.'

'Hold on, sometimes it waits a bit. Just... I swear it was right here.' Dexter waited a moment longer. 'Hello?' he said to the wall. Axle's impatience was growing, but he stuck his ear against the wall once more.

Silence.

Luna's fear and trepidation were slowly turning to annoyance after being dragged out of her blissful sleep and cosy bed for seemingly no reason. Dexter grumbled and then stepped back. 'Let me try something.' His siblings watched him raise a fist and quietly knock on the wall.

He waited.

Nothing.

He waited more. A full minute, during which he'd tap and knock in various places around the wall, but still there was *nothing*.

Axle groaned and moved away. 'Great... good one Dex, you really got me.' He yawned and shook his head. 'Here I was all excited and it's just a prank.'

'No, it's not a prank I prom— ow!' He hissed and lifted a leg, clutching at his shin where Luna had kicked him.

'You...You big, meanie head! You got me scared for nothing. I-I should tell Mummy on you.' Her lip was trembling as she turned and stormed off.

'Hey, wait. I-I wasn't trying to trick you, there really was something tapping in the walls before.'

'Yeah, yeah.' Axle walked away as well. Then, just after he had disappeared into the shadow of the hall leading back to his room, a knock came from within the wall. Dexter's eyes widened and his head whipped towards the sound. He had heard it clear as day.

'There it was, did you hear that? It just knocked!' He struggled to keep his voice low.

'I'm not falling for that twice, idiot.' Axle kept walking away.

Dexter's shoulders slumped, defeated. The tapping sounded a couple more times in quick succession, as if it was taunting him. He glared at the wall and thumped on it—it thumped right back. 'Are you happy now? And they said I was tricking them. I hope you're satisfied after making me look like an idiot. I know I'm not crazy. I know you're in there. I know you're real, and...and if I have to, I'll smash open a hole with a hammer and drag you out. You won't like tapping so much then, will you?'

Tap tap tap.

He gritted his teeth, growling in frustration. He kicked the wall. An identical thud echoed his. 'I'll call the police? How about that? Then, I'll...I'll get them to come in and tear down the wall and then they'll drag you out and off to jail. How about that?'

There was silence. Silence except for Dexter's panting breaths. He waited longer, but no more tapping came. Satisfied, he turned to leave. More taps came in a playful, mocking rhythm. He clenched his fists but didn't retaliate. He stormed out of the hall and back to his room. Maybe he was just going crazy, he had just argued with a wall after all.

He sat on his bed, staring at the wall. It was quiet for now. *'How could a person be in there? How would they have gotten in?'* He couldn't think of any holes they had in their home, inside or outside. It's not like they were stuck inside the chimney. But... if it wasn't a person, then what? Could it really be a mouse or a bird or any other kind of little critter stuck in there, scurrying around and bumping into the wall over and over? It just didn't make any sense.

He clutched at his head, another few knocks came from the wall again, but they might as well have been coming from right inside his skull they jarred him that much. He shuddered and turned his back to the wall. He laid down on his side and curled up into a ball. He'd ignore it.

It had to be in his head, there was no other explanation. He was just, that tired, or sensory depravated, or some other reasoning for these auditory hallucinations. There was *no way* a person or animal could be *in* his wall. He just needed some sleep. It'd be gone in the morning.

But what if whatever was in there crept out in the middle of the night? Dexter could see it now, a long, gangly arm, stretching from a yawning, black hole in his wall. Dead skin peeling from the limb, bones protruding from the rotting, sickly flesh. Talon-like fingers stretching out, looming over him. They were right above his head, then they closed in around his eyes and mouth. He tried to scream, but no sound came out, and then he'd be whisked from his bed and dragged into that hole, never to be seen again.

He shot up, panting hard. He didn't want to look, he didn't want to see that arm reaching out for him. Maybe if he never saw it coming, it wouldn't be so bad. He had no idea if the kitchen knife could do anything to whatever was coming out of the wall, but he gripped it tight in his shaking hands; he had to look.

He took a deep breath and slowly turned his head, eyes trying to turn away, refusing to look. Eventually, his gaze fell upon the wall, and there was nothing. It was the same wall he'd always had, ever since he moved into this room years ago.

It's just in your head. All in your head. He was still breathing heavily as he settled back down, staring at the wall as he tried to convince himself that nothing was truly in there and that he was only imagining things. *If anything, just a mouse, or a loose piece of dry wood scratching the wall as the house settles.*

He closed his eyes, trying his best to block out the tapping and knocking and thudding ... it was no use. No matter how hard he tried, there was no escaping it. He squashed a pillow against the sides of his head, he burrowed under his doona and sheets, but he could still hear it. It was never constant enough to become white noise and easily drowned out like from a stereo or TV. At the same time, it was frequent enough that right in those long gaps, just before he was about to drift off, another tap would rattle through the wall and jolt him awake. It was torture.

He barely slept, if he got any sleep at all. The knife was constantly by his side, but that didn't help ease his anxieties. The morning rays of sunshine peeked into the room around the edges of his curtains, and he lifted from his bed like a zombie—looking even worse than one—his eyes almost crusted closed. At least the tapping had stopped, and he might've gotten an hour's sleep at most, but then it was his alarm's time to shake him awake.

He *really* wasn't up for school that day, but it's not like he had a choice—his Mum could always sus out when he was "faking" his sick days. There was nothing he could do.

He sat on the edge of his bed, staring at the wall. It was silent this morning. He stared for a good long while. Five minutes passed. Nothing. Ten. Still nothing. His mother's voice called out, yelling for him to wake up. He started to get changed and organised for the day ahead, occasionally glancing over at the wall as he did so. Not a single tap or knock disturbed him.

See? It really was just in your head. A faint smile touched his lips. He picked up his bag and went to the door, his growling stomach reminding him of his need for breakfast. He pulled open the door.

Tap, tap, tap.

His smile dropped.

He ate in silence, barely touching his food. He didn't even react as Brucie nosed and pawed his leg, barking for attention and the usual morning dosage of pats, love, and affection he was accustomed to. Brucie was the only one who seemed to notice his strange behaviour, the kids just glared at him, still angered by their rude awakening last night, and he might as well have been invisible to his parents as they fussed about getting ready for work and the school run respectively.

He set his half-eaten bowl of cereal on the sink, and then he was out the door to catch the bus, muttering his goodbyes to his family before he left. The kids' school was in the other direction, so Mum would be dropping them off before she went to work. Dad was lucky and could just head straight for work today.

At least school would get him away from that incessant tapping. He prayed it'd be a good day, one where he'd be left alone.

Of course, he could never be so lucky.

It was on his way to the second class of the day that he ran into Brock and his loyal dogs. Or more accurately, that Brock and the others ran into him.

Brock and his friends—who followed at his heels like obedient puppies—had been on his ass since the first week of school. Dexter had no idea why they had picked him of all people, he guessed that it was because he was at the bottom of the pack when it came to PE so they knew he was weak, but they never gave him a reason or an answer as to why.

Maybe they didn't need a reason. Dexter was an easy target, and maybe that's all the excuse they needed to exert their "power and dominance" over him. He had no friends, no allies, no one to protect him, no one to stop them from using him as an outlet to make themselves feel better about their own miserable lives. It certainly made Dexter feel a lot worse.

It showed him just how isolated he was at school. No one ever came to his defence, not even the teachers. Brock and his dogs would just get a slap on the wrist, or a week-long "suspension" (more like a vacation) at worst. "Boys will be boys" they'd say, or, "you just need to stand up to them and then they'll stop." Yeah, the last time he did that he almost ended up in a hospital.

It didn't help that Dexter was as skinny as they come, and one of the shorter boys in their year. With pasty skin that was prone to acne and freckles, they loved to remind him of how ugly and pathetic they thought he was.

Brock was nearly the complete opposite looks-wise. He had shaggy, blond hair; a good physique that he seemed obsessed with; he was nearly the tallest in the school; and he had a flawless, tanned complexion.

Brock shoved Dexter aside causing him to stumble into the wall. Dexter was surrounded. His shoulders slumped and he shrank back. 'Ugh, fuck... what do you guys want?'

Brock answered with a punch to Dexter's gut. The others held him up to stop him from crumpling to the floor. 'Hmm, now that I think about it,' Brock said, 'I could really go for a Coke. Run along and get me one, bitch.'

'I have class!'

Apparently, that tone was too assertive. Dexter received another gut punch to make him rethink using that kind of voice around Brock. This time the dogs shoved him to the floor. Dexter looked at a boy walking past, their eyes met— the boy lowered his head and walked faster.

That hurt worse than anything Brock did to him.

Dexter's attention was drawn back to Brock as he crouched down. 'I don't care,' Brock said. 'Get it during break, you dumb cunt. And don't even think about disobeying me, or you'll be sorry.' Brock stood and kicked Dexter's head against the floor. 'Don't forget!' After the dogs had given Dexter similar kicks, they all walked away, sneering down at him as they left him to pick himself up.

'Assholes...' Dexter muttered under his breath then groaned as he stood. He dusted himself off.

Tap, tap, tap.

He gasped and spun around to face the wall behind him. That's not where the sound had come from, it had come from all around ... from within.

Tap, tap tap.

He clutched his head. *I really am going crazy. It's all in my head.* He laughed. He laughed even as a tear trickled out. He shook his head. He took a deep breath, wiped his eye, and he made his way to his next class, acting as if nothing had happened, though his heart still pounded. When the teacher asked why he was late, he came up with a half-assed excuse about needing to use the bathroom—he saw no point in telling them about Brock, or the tapping.

The tapping persisted throughout the day, infrequently, but always popping back up just when he might've forgotten about it. He didn't leave during the break. He was fed up, and he wasn't going to kowtow to Brock and his dogs any longer. They could find a new punching bag to boss around. He knew he'd get a beating for going against them, but he didn't give a shit.

When school was let out, he walked home, keeping his head down as he wondered what to do about the tapping in his skull. *I can't go see a psychiatrist*—tap—*they'll think*—tap—*I'm crazy*—tap. He clenched his fists and ground his teeth, the tapping was hardly letting him think. He couldn't tell anyone about this, they'd lock him up in a mental facility. Then his reputation would plummet even further.

"You see him?" they'd say, "That's Dexter Mooney, he's a schizo freak!"

He shook his head. It was just tapping. He'd be fine. It'd go away if he ignored it.

What if whatever was in your walls, got in your head while you were sleeping? He had to stop for a moment. *Now that is crazy.* Then he thought about it some more. He saw a shadowy, ghostly demon seeping out from some imperceivable crack in his wall, stretching across his room to his sleeping form, circling him as the room darkened and he lay completely unaware. It plunged into his ear and squeezed its way into his brain.

His hand reflexively covered his ear. 'It's all in your head,' he reminded himself.

Exactly! It's all *in your head ... now.*

He hurried home.

That night, he brought Brucie into his room. The dog was always happy to join one of the kids in bed. Mum and Dad, not so much. They'd scold the kids if Brucie was caught snuggling under the covers with any of them.

Dexter stared at the wall, one arm wrapped around Brucie as he waited, and waited.

Tap ... tap ... tap.

He tensed up, but Brucie didn't even flinch. 'So, it really is just me who can hear it, huh, Brucie?'

Brucie looked up at Dexter, tilting his head.

Dexter thought about sending Brucie out, so that whatever was tormenting him wouldn't affect the innocent little pooch, but decided against it, insisting Brucie would be the perfect defence and nothing could come crawling out from the wall or his own ear as long as Brucie was there.

Even with Brucie by his side, Dexter still didn't get much sleep.

This continued for a week.

Over that time, Dexter had received a thorough beating from Brock and his dogs, Still, no one helped him. He just hoped they'd get bored with him and move on to a different victim sooner rather than later.

Dexter also hadn't figured out what to do about the tapping. He was still too scared of being laughed off and seen as insane to tell anyone else about it, but it wasn't like he could ignore it when it followed him wherever he went and nothing could block it out from his own mind. He had no idea what to do. He knew one thing, though—he couldn't go on living like this.

He didn't know what caused the tapping, or why it hadn't done anything else; why it was still waiting to make its move. Maybe it was waiting for him to go truly insane, and then it'd leap out and slurp up his brain once it had turned to mush. He wasn't going to wait around and find out, however. If it wasn't going to act, then *he was*. Ten nights after the tapping first started tormenting him, he leapt out of bed, and went to the wall. He traced his hand along the old, flowery wallpaper—it had been there before they even moved in almost ten years ago.

He pressed his ear to the wall and closed his eyes. All was silent, except for a dull, rhythmic tha-thump, tha-thump. He couldn't tell if that was his heartbeat or the walls. He stepped back and looked to the floor. He saw the wallpaper was somewhat peeling at the bottom, part of it already ripping away from the wall like it was trying to fly off. He reached down, his hand shaking as he pinched the beginning of the peel and started to pull it back further. He revealed old, partially rotted, wooden panels, and a long, narrow crack stretching from the floor up to eye height. There was a slightly wider portion at about the height of his chest, so he leaned down and pressed an eye to the hole. Total darkness looked back at him.

Tap, tap.

He jumped back. Even when the tapping sounded, he had seen no movement; it was too dark to see what had made that noise. He put an eye to the hole again. His hands braced unsteadily against the wall. Tentatively, he said: 'H-Hello?'

Tap-Tap.

'What do you want from me?'

There was a moment of silent contemplation before another tap answered him.

He frowned and leaned back, looking at the crack with a furrowed brow. His heart beat loudly. He couldn't stop now. He slowly slid a finger into the hole. He tensed and expected something to bite it off, but nothing happened. He gripped the panel and started to pull, prying it looser until it snapped off the wall.

He set the broken chunk aside and looked into the wider hole. He couldn't see anything until he flashed the light of his phone in there, but he saw nothing other than a dusty, cobweb-filled, narrow passageway, one just like any other that he expected to find inside every wall.

His forehead wrinkled as he scanned the immediate area behind where the tapping had occurred. There was nothing, no monster, not even a tiny little mouse. Then he heard the tapping come from further within the hole, far away to his right, at the edge of his room.

He couldn't see that far through the still too-narrow hole, so he quickly got back to work prying more of the wall apart, widening the gap until he could squeeze his head through.

He peeked inside, but it was too dark. With another chunk torn off, he could fit his arm through. He flashed the light down the right side of the narrow passage, and saw a corner, rather than the dead end that should've been there.

He pulled his head back and imagined the other side of the wall. The hall was straight, parallel to his room it was impossible for there to be a corner inside the wall.

He stuck his head back inside and double-checked. The corner was still there, bending to the left.

Tap, tap, tap.

The noises came from around the bend this time. Dexter bumped his head as he flung himself out of the hole. His heart thumped like a machine gun. 'This can't be real.' With shaking hands, he tried to smooth the wallpaper back into place. It was no use, whenever he took his hands away, it rolled back up and revealed the gaping hole in the wall.

'Perfect... now you've done it. Now you've opened it, and now whatever the fuck is in there is gonna come crawling out. You freed it, you bloody idiot.'

He paced around the room, trying not to focus on the image of some hideous, multi-armed monster of impossible girth squeezing out of the hole, hundreds of tiny claws clack-clacking and tap-tapping along the walls and floor as it scuttled along, leaving a slimy, disgusting trail in its wake. Then it'd rear up, revealing a gruesome maw on its belly, an unending void of teeth that would swallow him up and grind him into sludge.

He shuddered. There was only one thing to do. He had to go in there and find the monster first. Before he knew it, he was pulling apart the wall until the hole was large enough for his entire body to fit through. He pulled himself through the gap and into the rank, narrow passage.

Only when he was on the other side of the wall, did he realise what he had done. It was as if he had done it instinctually, without thinking, he hadn't even brought his phone or a knife. He turned to go back, and slammed face-first into the wall.

He groaned and massaged his nose, it wasn't broken at least but what the hell was that? He groped the wall in front of him, feeling solid wood where the hole should've been.

His blood went cold. His heart palpitated. He groped the wall more, moving side to side, thinking he must've gone past the hole, but there wasn't even any light that should've been coming through from his room. 'H-Hey!' He began pounding on the walls, but it didn't even sound like he was making much noise. It sounded like he was hitting a pillow.

He panted heavily, each breath sucking in dust and the foul, musty odour of this place. Again the tapping sounded from deeper within.

He whirled toward the noise. Now slightly adjusted to the blackness, he could see the curve of the corner. He bit his cheeks and crept towards it—if he couldn't go back, he had to go forward.

He rounded the corner and saw the end of another long, narrow passageway before it took another corner. Again, it seemed impossible, it just shouldn't exist, there were no walls like this anywhere within the house let alone his room. Tapping came from the end of this hall and disappeared around the corner. He took a deep breath and inched his way through the narrow, winding passages.

He felt as if he had been walking for an hour. It was only when he noticed a tight passageway that required him to crawl that he realised the walls and ceiling had been closing in tighter and tighter all around him; he was hunched over, arms tight to his sides.

He stared at the crawl space for a long while before he shook his head. He waddled in place to turn around, only to be met with a blank wall that was directly behind him. His eyes widened as he pushed against it—it was real and completely solid. 'Oh shit.' His eyes darted to the crawl space again. His loud breathing filled the space. He tried to calm down before he sucked all the air out of the suffocating passage.

Tap, tap, tap.

The tapping came from within the crawl space.

'Please let this be the end of it,' he prayed. He dove into the crawl space, hurriedly dragging himself through it as quickly as he could so that it'd be over faster.

This tunnel began to close in as well, getting increasingly narrower the deeper he delved. He tried to shuffle back at one point, but his feet pressed against a flat wall. The way back was blocked off, of course it was. He closed his eyes tightly. *It's all a bad dream. You're stuck in a nightmare. Wake up.* 'Wake up!' He banged his head against the ceiling, but all that did was make him dizzy for a moment.

This was no dream, or at least not one he would so easily wake from.

Tap, tap, tap.

It came from the tunnel floor ahead of him—it was urging him forward. He closed his eyes and powered onward.

Eventually, the crawl space became so tight, that Dexter couldn't even crawl along on all fours, and instead had to wriggle himself through like a worm. Then, just when he thought it was going to become so tight he could no longer move at all and he'd be entrapped in this unreachable place forever, like a cave explorer who hit a dead end, his head popped free into a much wider room.

He gasped, the air feeling fresher as it filled his lungs. His eyes locked onto a black door before him, it was riddled with scratch marks and missing a handle. A faint, orange light shone down upon the door, a flickering lantern hanging above it.

He pulled himself free from the crawl space and stood in the spacious room. It felt like he was standing in an empty, Olympic-sized pool after being stuck in that tunnel for so long. He couldn't take his eyes off the door. He didn't even dust himself off as he slowly approached it.

Tap tap tap

Three gentle knocks came from the other side of the door. It sounded dense and heavy. He walked close enough to press his hand against the door, fingers tracing over the grooves of the scratch marks.

'Hello?'

An angelic voice, as sweet and smooth as honey, answered him. 'Will you stay with me? It's very lonely here.'

'Who are you?'

'Your friend. ... I can be if you open the door. You'll be happy here. I promise. I won't ignore you or hurt you, not like they do.' He could feel a hand on the other side of the door, right against his own. '...Or you can turn back, and return to the life you left behind, and we can both be lonely.'

Dexter stayed quiet. He looked back. The room was much smaller now, the crawl space was gone, but the hole in the wall had returned. He could see his bedroom. It would be as easy as stepping through the hole and falling into bed and then he could forget all about this. He looked at the door again.

'Who are you?' he asked once more.

'A friend. Nobody. Just like you. I've been watching you. You...You're just like me. So very lonely, with no one to care for you. Everyone else is always so busy with someone or something much more important. They have no time for us. I have time for you. In here, there's nothing but time. Together, we won't be lonely.'

Dexter's brow knitted together. Could he really leave his life behind, and abandon his family? He didn't have friends at school, that was true. No one helped him when he was being harassed by Brock and the others. But... his family still loved him, didn't they?

Do they? He looked down, his head resting against the door. His parents were always so busy with work, or looking after Axle and Luna, or worrying about each other.

"You're big enough to take care of yourself now," that's what they said. Big enough that he didn't need them, and they no longer needed him.

Axle and Luna as well. When was the last time either of them looked up at him with amazement after he had done something for them? Did they even look up to him anymore? He felt like he was only a nuisance to them now, like they wanted to get away from him as quickly as possible and go back to their own fun lives without him.

Sniffles and muffled sobbing came from beyond the door. 'Do you really wish to walk back into such sadness? Am I that undesirable that not even *you* would wish to spend time with me?'

'How can you—'

'Because we are the same. I feel as you do, Dexter... please, my heart could not bear it if you were to walk away.'

He felt a heartbeat through the door. It was slow, steady, sad. He closed his eyes.

'I promise. If you stay with me, you will never know another day of sadness or heartache. Just open the door, please,' the voice said.

He opened his eyes and looked down to where the handle should've been. He saw a metallic, silver knob materialise from thin air. He inhaled slowly, shakily, and then he turned back to the hole. He looked at his bedroom, his old life. *What about Brucie?* He looked at the doorknob again.

Still shaking, he reached towards it. He clasped the warm metal. It clicked heavily, deeply, like a great lock had been opened as he twisted it. The door swung out from him, slowly and smoothly, revealing a wall of darkness.

A thin, jet-black arm reached forward from the abyss, a hand with three blade-like fingers stretched towards him. He stood frozen in place, he shut his eyes and flinched away from what he was sure were the claws that were about to rip out his throat, only, that didn't happen. Instead, his face was caressed, as gently as a mother's kiss.

He was dragged into the blackness by an unseen force, the hand still on his cheek. He couldn't see what the arm was connected to. There was a knock to his left, and a series of candles lit up all along the walls of the cosy cabin. A black figure was illuminated in front of him. She was tall, having to stoop to fit in the room. Her elongated neck bent down, and a long, angular face stared at him. It housed no mouth, no nose, no features other than a dozen eyes all in two straight rows of six side by side, running vertically down her face. Each dark eye was like a galaxy of stars, and they all twinkled and smiled at him. Dexter was utterly captivated.

'I'm so happy to finally meet you! I've been waiting so long for another friend.' Even though the figure had no mouth, her voice rang like bells through the air.

Dexter relaxed, and smiled up at her before stepping into her embrace. A second arm wrapped around him, and then a third and fourth—they all held him tight against her.

He didn't hear the door swing shut behind him, nor did he hear the lock clicking back into place.

M.P. Seipolt

Help Wanted

Kira already knew her interview was a disaster; from the moment she had sat down she wished to fling herself out the window. *I told you, Mum. I told you,* she thought. The suit she wore was stifling. It was trying to strangle her, worse than that, she was *so* out of place because of it. Her eyes darted around the room as she rocked back and forth in her seat. She had told her mother there was no need for her to dress so formally for a job interview at a fast-food place, but had her mother listened? Of course not. Now here Kira was, looking like a child wearing their parent's clothes—which she was—in the middle of the busiest *Burger Bucket* she'd ever seen, surrounded by customers that were wearing flip-flops and singlets. As Kira wiped the sweat from her brow, she envied and cursed those people. It was the peak of summer, and she was wearing a damn suit.

Can this place have worse air conditioning? Is it even on? And where the hell is that manager lady?! It feels like I've been sitting here for ten minutes. Kira couldn't hear the hum of any AC unit above the din of people, music, and beeping machinery. She was about to completely lose it and run out of the store, already standing from her seat when the manager returned. Kira stumbled back into her chair and sighed.

The manager smiled—a smile that was just a little too wide for Kira's liking—and took her seat opposite the young woman. 'I apologise for the wait. I had trouble finding the questionnaire. Silly me.' As the manager laid a piece of paper on the table, she kept smiling. It was the kind of smile that never reached her beady eyes—eyes that were far too small for her face.

'Oh, no th-that's okay. It really didn't feel that long.' Kira chuckled nervously, watching the manager's long, bony fingers smooth out the paper, trying to read the upside-down words.

A sharp, black nail came to rest under the first line of words, which the manager used as a pointer to read along. 'Firstly—Kira, was it? How old are you?'

'I-I'm twenty years of age.' Kira shifted uncomfortably in her seat. She knew she was nearly five years late getting this whole, part-time job at a fast-food place, she only hoped her embarrassment didn't reach her face.

'And you have no prior experience?' The manager asked. Kira couldn't tell if her tone was mocking or genuinely surprised.

'N-No... I... well, I'm still at uni, I'm going for a bachelor's in engineering but... well... th-that's not really working out jobwise just yet.'

'I see.' The manager was still smiling as she turned her attention back to the paper. 'What times are you available?'

Kira perked up. 'I can work whenever! I've already talked it over with my school and they can move me over to night classes if that's what's necessary.' She bit her tongue and slumped back down a bit, worrying that she'd come across as over-eager.

'Oh! That's just wonderful!' Now the manager's eyes sparkled with delight.

Kira breathed a sigh of relief. Maybe this wouldn't be so bad. Surely a place like this couldn't reject her, right? No one got rejected for a job at a fast-food place, right?

The interview continued, with the store operating as normal in the background. Kira was quizzed about how she'd handle difficult customers, her knowledge of mathematics was tested—though it was just simple addition and subtraction—and she was asked about whether she'd prefer to work in the back or upfront with customers, to which she answered that she was happy to do both. It was a short interview in the end—at least from what Kira expected—and when it was over, the manager grinned, revealing a mouth full of yellowed teeth. 'When can you start?' she asked.

Kira was surprised, she didn't think it would be *that* easy or quick. 'I-I... t-tomorrow! I can start tomorrow! Ah... but, um, don't I need a uniform?'

The manager laughed. 'My! So eager, how wonderful. Yes, yes, you do need a uniform.' Those dark eyes looked Kira up and down quickly. 'Mmm, I think we may have a spare uniform in the back in your size. Hold still. I will be right back.'

The manager slid out of the booth and disappeared into the back of the restaurant.

Kira shook with joy. She pulled out her phone and excitedly wrote a text.

"Ash! Guess what! I totally got the fucking job!"

She didn't have to wait long for a response that read: "Woo! I knew you could do it babe <3"

Kira giggled. "<3 Sorry, I've kept you waiting out there. Won't be much longer now, just waiting for them to get me a uniform then I'll be right out."

The manager returned quickly, and offered a uniform that looked to be Kira's size, as well as a small business card. 'Here you are. Please try this on when you get home and let me know if it fits. This card has my number, so give me a call if you need a different size, I can tell you where to buy a uniform from, and we'll compensate you for it, of course.'

'Thank you so much, ma'am!' Kira stood, bundling the clothes into one arm and slipping the card into her pocket. 'You won't regret hiring me, I promise.' She reached out and shook the manager's hand, it was shockingly cold, sending a shiver through Kira's hot body.

The manager flashed her yellow grin again and enthusiastically shook Kira's small hand. 'Oh, I'm sure I won't. After all, we can never have enough fresh meat here.'

Kira laughed nervously as she stared into the manager's eyes; the handshake lasted a tad too long. The manager held on for a second more as Kira tried to pull away. 'R-Right. Of course. W-Well... I'll see you tomorrow then!'

Kira slipped free from the manager's grasp and hurried out of the restaurant. The manager followed her to the door, waving goodbye. Kira threw herself into Ashley's car and was dragged into a tight hug.

'I'm so proud of you babe!' Ashley kissed Kira. Kira kissed back. The two held hands as they left, unaware that the manager was still watching from the doorway.

Kira showed up for her first shift, bright and early. The uniform was a little baggy on her, thankfully, the belt tight around her waist kept her pants up. *Maybe I should ask about getting a new one in my actual size.*

She entered the restaurant, it was strange to see one so quiet and empty. She approached the counter, she couldn't see anyone in the back, but the door had been unlocked, she couldn't have been too early. 'Hello?' she called. No response. She was about to call again when a man poked his head around the corner.

He looked her over with squinting eyes and stepped out. His face was much too small for his chubby, round head, like it had been smushed together. Deep wrinkles cut into his fat jowls, making his tiny mouth look like that of a puppet. His thin nose was constantly upturned, though thankfully, with how short he was—his shoulders only just visible over the counter—Kira couldn't see up his nostrils. His name tag read "Colin", and denoted him as the assistant manager. 'Yes?' he said, his nasally voice conveying his irritation.

'Ah, it's um, my first day and I uh, I don't know the code?' Kira gestured to the door that led to behind the counter, or more specifically, the electric num-pad above the handle.

Colin rolled his eyes, as if getting the door for Kira was the greatest burden ever placed upon anyone. He held it open for her, and she thanked him quietly. He stopped her, before she went through, one of his greasy mitts holding her wrist. 'Pay attention now,' he said, 'I'll only show you this once, and I won't help you again, new girl.' He let her go and then his pudgy fingers punched in the code to unlock the door.

Kira watched closely, though his fingers moved quickly, and she wasn't sure if she'd seen correctly. She didn't dare ask him to repeat it, and only hoped that she would remember it. She thanked him again.

'Mm, it's not my job to be babysitting you. Go through the back and find Sarah, she'll tell you what you need to be doing.' Colin waddled away.

Kira chewed on the inside of her cheek, hoping that not everyone would be as much of a prick as Colin. She passed through the back of the kitchen, spotting another boy—a bit younger than her maybe—moving trays of uncooked produce out of a freezer, but kept moving, not bothering him by asking for where to go.

She wandered into an empty hall, still gnawing the inside of her cheek. Her footsteps echoed through the empty, narrow corridor and her eyes darted to each closed door that she passed. Nothing was labelled, and her nerves wouldn't let her try any of the doors, it felt like it wasn't her place to be opening random doors. She got to the end of the hall and saw a long staircase leading down to another lone door, a faint light coming from underneath the frame, but otherwise, the door was shrouded in darkness. It was certainly odd, and she hadn't expected a place like this to have a basement. She wondered what could be down there, what reason would there be to have a place like that, though just as she was about to head down the first step, a hand touched her shoulder.

Kira shrieked, and almost fell down the stairs before she regained her balance, one hand braced against the wall as she whirled around and saw a female worker standing there.

'Oop! Sorry, didn't mean to spook, you. You alright?' they said with a smile. It was Sarah. At least that's what the nametag said.

Kira held a hand over her thumping heart and caught her breath. She let out a nervous laugh and shook her head. 'N-No, you're fine. Phew, s-sorry I was, I was a little lost actually.'

'Hah, I reckoned you were. The name's Sarah, though, I'm sure you saw that already.' The young woman gestured to the nametag. 'You must be the new girl. Don't worry, I'll look after you.'

Sarah moved her hand away from Kira's shoulder, but the sense of comfort it had given didn't go away. Kira steadied her breathing, taking in the sight of this polite, smiling woman. Sarah was maybe just a year or two older than Kira, but it was hard to tell. Her bright smile was so soothing and reassuring to look at, the kind of smile that told you everything was going to be alright. Kira was amazed by how bright and calming Sarah's large blue eyes were—Kira couldn't help but stare. Sarah was the same height as Kira, with her blonde hair pulled back into a ponytail, which stuck out from the back of her cap. And Sarah's uniform fit much more nicely and looked a whole lot better on her than it did on Kira.

Yeah, I really need a proper uniform.

'So, ready for ya orientation?' Sarah asked.

'Oh, yeah, definitely um… but uh, what's that door down there?'

'That would be my office.' The manager's voice startled Kira. She whirled around to find the smiling woman standing halfway up the stairs. Kira's heart raced again; she hadn't even heard the door open or close, nor the sound of the manager's footsteps.

'I'm so glad you could make it, Kira~' The manager said. 'I hope you're excited for your first day. Here. I have this for you.' She held out her hand, and Kira saw a nametag in her palm.

'Oh, thank you, I guess I can't really work without one, huh?' However, when Kira reached to take it, the manager moved her hand back.

'Allow me, please.' The manager kept her yellow smile as she gripped the name tag between her fingers, going to poke the sharp pin through Kira's shirt.

Kira held perfectly still, watching the pin slide through the fabric. 'Ow!' She flinched away, wincing as the pin had pricked her skin. When the manager pulled the tag back, a drop of blood covered the tip of the pin.

'Oh no, I'm so sorry dear, please, hold still, it won't happen again,' The manager said, her smile hadn't changed at all.

Kira remained unmoving, though her breathing was heavier as with wide, trembling eyes, she watched the pin approach again. This time, the manager gripped Kira's shirt and pulled the fabric further away from her body, slipping the pin through without any issue and locking it safely into place.

She patted down Kira's chest and her smile widened. 'There.'

'Th-Thank you...' Kira was still shaking, still trying to get her heart under control.

'Enjoy your first day, dear.' The manager slipped past both girls, and disappeared down the hall.

'Ah, sorry about that, the boss is a bit... strange. But, she's sweet and chill enough,' Sarah said. 'You okay?'

Kira nodded meekly.

'Alright, let me show you around and tell you what you'll be doing today.'

Kira stuck close behind Sarah, there wasn't much room in the back corridors, if they tried to walk side by side they'd be squished up against one another with their shoulders touching. Sarah showed her around, pointing out which door led to what room. On the left was the back door out to the bins, on the right was the toilet, and just past that was the break room. Then there was another door on the left for storage of cups and lids and boxes and paper bags and all that junk.

When Kira prompted, Sarah also said that she was 22, and had been working there for almost half a year.

'I've worked in other fast food joints before this though, but man, this place is hectic. It's like, the most popular place in town, even compared to other Burger Buckets. I hear we're the most popular in the country, and we do the most sales by like... a lot. But uh, I guess because we're so busy, we have a lot of turnover when it comes to workers too, like even just while I've been here, you're like, the fiftieth new employee, and people are always quitting,' Sarah explained.

Kira's face must've been looking extra pale, cause Sarah laughed and smacked her shoulder. 'Don't worry though, you'll get the hang of it, it sounds a lot worse than it actually is, trust me.' She smiled. 'And I'll be right there to help you out.

Sarah also ran Kira through the operating system with the computers up front and how to take someone's order.

while more workers filed in to fill up the kitchen as opening hour rapidly approached.

'For your first shift, I think you'll be upfront mostly, but I'll be here too, so if you've got any questions or you need help, I'll be right by your side.' Sarah scratched her chin, her eyes wandered to the ceiling and she lost herself in thought for a moment. 'Nope, I'm pretty sure that's all I need to tell you. Any questions?' She looked at Kira expectantly.

'Uhh... when's my lunch break?' Kira shrugged.

'Hm, when do you get off?'

'I think I'm supposed to finish at three.'

'Alright, I'd say taking your break at eleven would be good, then. There's a board in the back where you can pick your time, just so everyone knows and we don't *all* go on break at once. Go ahead and put yourself down for eleven 'til twelve.'

Kira nodded and then hurried over to the door leading to the back halls, finding a whiteboard right behind it that had a table for all the different break hours everyone could take. Kira signed the slot she wanted.

When she came back to the counter, the bell above the door chimed, and the first customers of the day walked in. 'Looks like you're up, Kira,' Sarah smiled, giving her a thumbs up.

Kira stood behind her computer screen and took a deep breath, looking over the two men who came up to her. 'Hi sirs, um, may I take your order?'

The day flew by like a tornado, and Kira was swept up into it without much say in the matter. Sarah tried to help her out as much as she could, but being busy was an understatement when it came to this place, and Sarah had her hands full with her own customers most of the time.

Kira tried to keep a level head, and serve her customers as quickly as she could, though she struggled to not get completely thrown around by the storm of impatient, demanding customers. There were always so many voices, shouting over one another, and the beeping and whirring of the kitchen equipment and other machinery in the store, plus some music over the top of it all, it was a recipe for the migraine of a lifetime. Kira wondered if she'd ever get used to it.

It didn't help that if she made any fuck up, no matter how small, Colin would hound her for it. Take too long to serve a customer? Colin would give her an earful. Fumble someone's change? That's another excuse for Colin to scream at her. Forget to note that this order didn't want pickles on their burger? You'd think she'd have shot their dog with the way both Colin and the customer berated her. It was like Colin's *only* job was to yell at her—she hadn't seen him do anything else throughout the day.

Kira was thankful when it was finally time for her break and she could get away from that chaos.

She flopped face-first onto the couch and relaxed, only realising just how tense she had been now that she finally let go of everything and emptied her mind. Though even back in the staff room she could still hear the beeping and the occasional shout from a customer or staff member.

She sat up and looked around the room. She was the only person in the small space, and she hadn't turned on the light, but it was still bright enough with the sun streaming in from the singular window. A table was in the middle of the room, and on the wall opposite the couch was a long counter, with a sink, and a small fridge and freezer at one end. Staring at the fridge, Kira remembered that she hadn't brought any actual lunch with her. *That's great... now what?* She decided that maybe she'd just go without today, it was her own fault after all. But after sitting there for fifteen minutes, her grumbling stomach wouldn't let go of the fact that it was still empty.

She got off the couch, and crept back to the kitchen, poking her head through the doorway. *Surely I can just, have some of the food here, right?* Though she was hesitant to ask, and she definitely didn't want to run the idea by Colin, no way he'd allow that. She wanted to ask Sarah if it was alright, but could see that she was still swamped with customers, another boy out there manning the counter alongside her now.

'Is everything alright, Kira?' Again, the manager's voice startled Kira. She turned her head. The tall woman smiled down at her, that smile always sent shivers down Kira's spine no matter how many times she saw it.

'Oh um, well... I didn't bring any lunch today and so—'

'No need,' the manager interrupted. 'We have all the lunch you could possibly need. Please, have your own meal. The kitchen won't mind.'

Kira wanted to ask if the manager was sure, but before she could, the manager was whisking her away towards one of the grills, a large hand spread across Kira's back.

'Excuse me, I need one of the station's clear, thank you.' The manager spoke extremely calmly. Without any backchat, everyone in the kitchen obeyed and cleared a path for her as she brought Kira over to one of the grills and fryers. 'Now, in the future, feel free to ask anyone back here, or even make something for yourself when you go on your lunch break, dear Kira. But today, what would you like me to make you?'

Kira gulped, staring down into the bubbling oil of the fryer, then she gazed up at the eerie smile staring back at her. 'Uhh... j-just, maybe like, nuggets, an-and some chips?'

'Of course~ they won't be a moment. Go and get yourself a drink from the fridge too.'

Kira nodded, slipped away from the hand on her back, and quickly grabbed a bottle of soft drink from the fridge. When she returned to the manager's side, she stood there awkwardly and watched the nuggets cook. As Kira watched them in that vat of oil, she couldn't help but wonder if these really were the best in the country. Throughout the day, she'd seen the customers dig into their various meals like ravenous beasts! *Surely they can't be that good, right?* She'd had food from Burger Bucket—albeit from different locations—plenty of times before, and no matter how hungry she'd been, she never devoured it like *every* customer she'd seen today had. You'd think they hadn't eaten in weeks the way they tore into their food.

'Done.' The manager offered Kira a small box, full of chips and a dozen nuggets, all coloured a perfect golden brown.

'Oh, th-thank you.' Kira took the box, though before she left, the manager spoke again.

'Wait. Try one of the nuggets. I'd love to see what you think of them.'

Kira felt her mouth dry up. She stared into the manager's eyes and felt that she couldn't refuse, like she would be fired on the spot if she did so.

She picked out a nugget from within the food pile and brought it to her lips, withering under the intense, unwavering gaze of the manager. She took a nervous bite into the richest, juiciest, most perfect nugget she'd ever tasted. The meat was surprisingly sweet, and so very tender. The battered skin had just the right crunch to it, and enough salt to balance the savoury sweetness of the meat. Before she even knew it, she'd already stuffed the rest of the nugget into her mouth and had munched it down completely.

The manager's grin widened, and she reached forward, swiping a bit of drool from Kira's chin.

'Holy shit!' Kira exclaimed, so lost in flavour heaven that she wasn't even perturbed by what the manager just did to her. 'Those are the best fucking nuggets I've ever tasted. I've never even had nuggets like that from any other Burger Bucket, how'd you do that?'

'Shhhh.' The manager brought her drool-glazed finger to her thin lips, which quickly curled up into another grin. 'That, my girl, is a secret~ Now, run along, you won't get to enjoy your break at this rate.'

Kira didn't need much urging to head towards the back again, already stuffing her face with another nugget as she went. She never looked back to see the manager lick the slimy drool from her finger.

Kira's break went by in a flash, spurred by her thorough enjoyment of each nugget, though when she'd finished them all, she still hungered for more. She hadn't touched a single chip before all the nuggets were gone, and as much as she'd enjoyed the nuggets, she was equally disappointed by how mediocre the chips were, they tasted just like any other and did nothing to sate the hunger that the incredible nuggets had left her with.

Her day continued at the front counter, dealing with more customers, yet now she understood why they were in such a rush to get their food, and why they chowed down so vigorously.

The manager would flitter by on occasion, checking in on how things were going, or when the lunch rush hit, she'd man another computer to ring up more orders as well, and for those orders that were dining in, she'd personally deliver their food to them. She'd also make sure to go around and ask people how they were enjoying their food, her smile only growing with each positive remark she got.

Colin continued watching Kira like a hawk, and he constantly reminded her of her mistakes no matter how small. So, when Kira looked up to serve her next customer near the end of her shift, and instead saw her Ashley, she wasn't exactly happy.

'Babe?' Kira blinked and looked around. Five other customers waited behind Ashley.

'Hey, baby! How's your first day going?~' Ashley leaned against the counter, a smile wrinkling her face.

'Uhh, y-yeah I mean, it's pretty crazy but um, I'm doing okay I think. A-Are you here to order?' Kira leaned forward, her eyes still darting to the other customers.

'Huh? No, silly, I just came to say hello and check in on you. I've missed you~ When are you getting off? Heh, I wanna get you off~'

Kira blushed and stood up straight, clearing her throat. 'N-Now's not a great time, babe. It's really busy. I get off in a little over an hour, I'll see you then okay?'

'Ugh!' Ashley pouted, laying her chest and head against the counter. 'But I'm *so* bored... why do you have to work so long? Can't you take a break and hang out with me?~'

Kira's eyes widened more and scanned the faces of the waiting customers more frantically, she could see those hungry beasts growing angrier, some of them stepped closer.

'What's the hold-up?' one of them said.

Kira swallowed the growing lump in her throat and said: 'Babe, I can't. I already took my break, please, you're holding—'

'Pleeeease!' Ashley latched onto one of Kira's hands. 'Just a quick smoke outside.'

'Is there a problem here?' Sarah moved over from her station and yanked Kira away from what she perceived to be a crazy customer.

'No it's jus—'

'Who the fuck is this?' Ashley said, glaring at Sarah. 'No there isn't a problem, I'm just talking with *my* girlfriend, so get the hell away from her and leave us alone, no one invited you.'

'I'm sorry but you can't touch a worker, I'm gonna have to ask you to leave,' Sarah said.

Kira couldn't get a word out.

'Excuse me? You can't tell me what I can and can't do with *my* girlfriend.' Ashley continued to grow angrier and her voice got louder.

'Why isn't anyone taking my order!?' Another customer raged.

Kira's breath came in panicked gasps.

'Kira! Why are you holding everything up!? What are you doing?' Colin's voice joined the shouting, swirling noise.

Kira retreated more, she didn't know where to look, so many voices screamed through her skull and bounced around it. She gnawed on the inside of her mouth.

'*Kira!*' The manager's voice cut through it all and Kira's world went silent as her eyes focused on the tall, slender woman standing in the doorway to the hall. 'Staff room, now.' She turned and disappeared through the door.

Kira breathed a sigh of relief. Even if she dreaded what may come, at least it pulled her from the chaos. She hurried to the staff room.

Sarah glared at Ashley. 'I'm not gonna ask you again. If you don't walk out that door right now, I'm calling the cops.'

'Hmph! Fine!' Ashley stormed out.

Kira found the manager in the break room, already sitting at the table. The manager gestured for her to take a seat as well and Kira did so. Now that she was away from the raging storm up front, a new fear crept in. *Am I about to be fired?*

'What was that about?' The manager asked.

'I'm really sorry, ma'am. My girlfriend, she... I told her that I was working and that I still had an hour left on my shift, but she wanted to talk with me and she, she's an artist you know? So she doesn't have a job right now, and I didn't either before all this so we've always been together and I guess it was just a bit much me being away from her for so long but I tried to get her to leave and then it was just, I couldn't see any other customers and, and—'

The manager raised a hand to cut Kira's rambling short. Kira took a breath, shaking all over.

'I see. I will warn you this once. Please, don't let that happen again. I will not tolerate outside drama within my business. Learn to keep your personal life and your work life separate, or you will not have a work life in the future. Understood?'

Kira nodded rapidly.

'Good. Now get back to work, you've got to clean up the mess you just made.' The manager stood and exited the room with just two strides.

Kira stayed seated at the table for a moment longer after the door closed behind the manager. She took a few more deep breaths, trying to steady herself before she exited as well.

When she stepped back up to her spot on the front counter, Ashley was gone, but she could feel her phone buzzing over and over in her pocket. She quickly checked it to see multiple messages from Ashley, with more coming in and even a missed call or two. Kira turned her phone to "Do Not Disturb" and put it away again.

When her shift was finally over Kira was overjoyed. She stepped away from the counter, and thanked Sarah for all her help that day, even apologising for the trouble that Ashley caused.

Sarah smiled and put a hand on Kira's shoulder. 'Hey, don't worry about it. If she ever bothers you like that again, or does some crazy shit, just give me a call.' She quickly slipped Kira a piece of paper with her phone number on it and got back to work, Sarah's shift wasn't done just yet.

Kira went and apologised to Colin, though regretted doing so as he told her "If she continued to fuck up like she had today, he wouldn't hesitate to fire her", which was *very* reassuring.

And of course, she also thanked the manager for being so patient with her and apologised to her as well. As a token of good faith, and to show that she held no ill will towards Kira, the manager sent her home with another box of nuggets, which Kira gratefully accepted. Even despite her throbbing headache, the soreness she felt all over, and being incredibly drained after her first shift, Kira's ravenous hunger was awakened once more by the smell of those fresh nuggets. It took all her willpower not to disgustingly devour them all on the spot. At least she made it out the door before popping them into her mouth like candy.

She went straight home, getting the bus rather than calling Ashley to pick her up, in fact, she didn't even respond to any of Ashley's messages for the rest of the night and flopped right into bed the moment she got home. She was exhausted and just needed a break from everything. After all, she'd need all the rest she could get, tomorrow would promise more of the same, but she hoped she'd have a better handle on things, seeing as it would be her second day.

She went to sleep with a strange feeling as she reminisced about the day's events—the job was stressful, but the money was good. With it, she'd finally be able to get that holiday she and Ashley had always talked about. And Sarah was really nice, oh and the food! Of course, she couldn't forget about the food as one of the great perks ... but, there were still plenty of downsides. Colin was probably the biggest one, he was such a tool, and Kira didn't think it was any wonder why the store went through so many workers if he was driving them all off. Plus the customers were also an issue. She expected to have some horrible experiences sure, but it was so extreme! It was like trying to deal with starving children. And finally, the manager was nice, in her own way ... but... there was also something off about her, and that damn smile. Kira just hoped she wouldn't have nightmares about that smile.

Can I really do this? ... Do I even have a choice?

Three months had passed since Kira began working at Burger Bucket, and instead of growing used to the verbal abuse thrown at her from both sides of the counter, it had only piled on top of her until it reached the sky and buried her within the dirt. Working in the kitchen as a chef wasn't any better, that just had different people barking orders at you, and if you were a little bit slow, or heavens forbid you under or overcooked something, there was hell to pay. Oh and cleaning? *That* was the *worst*. Kira had seen unspeakable things within those bathrooms. *Un-speakable*.

There was nothing to look forward to each work day, only her lunch break now. Throughout the months, she'd tried each item on the menu to find what would be the best meal for her, but nothing could top the combo of a cheeseburger and a handful of nuggets. The quarterpounders were too much to handle, the fish sandwiches were too mushy for her liking, and the chicken drumsticks and wings were too finicky with their bones getting in the way.

But she couldn't quit. She was so close to getting that holiday, she'd almost had enough saved up, then she'd get the break she so desperately craved and needed. Just a few more paydays, she reminded herself.

One thing she *had* gotten used to, however, was the amount of noise that penetrated her eardrums daily. The cacophony of noise from customers, the many machines and appliances in the back, and music had become nothing more than white noise to Kira. However, when she would get off work, she'd always find the outside world and other people to be a little hard to hear, sometimes needing things to be repeated multiple times, and there were instances when Ashley would complain about the radio being turned up way too loud.

Another bad thing was that Sarah had stopped showing up to work recently. Apparently, she was another one of those employees who couldn't take it in the end and quit. Kira envied her resolve, maybe she'd end up following Sarah one day, though, she hadn't heard from her since she didn't clock in a week ago.

That reminded Kira, she was going to be training a newbie tomorrow. She thought it'd be interesting to see what that was like from the opposite perspective. *Am I even ready to be doing that? Did Sarah feel like this when she was showing me around? She seemed as calm as anything back then.*

Maybe she wouldn't have to worry about tomorrow, not now that she'd seen Ashley walk in.

Despite being warned to *never* let an incident like what occurred on her first day there, happen *ever* again, Ashley still showed up plenty of times after that. While it never got to be as much of a big deal and disturbance as the first time—mostly because Kira took her break whenever Ashley came around, and talked to her outside instead—Ashley still caused a scene, but Kira had yet to be fired for it. Maybe today was the day she would finally receive her just punishment.

Kira's eyes darted to the clock hanging from the wall and ticking slowly. Her shift was almost up, but she'd already been forced to take her break. Looks like there wasn't any avoiding it this time, maybe she could talk her down.

'What is it, Ash?' Kira said.

'Wow, I can really feel the love. Is that any way to greet your girlfriend, baby?' She spat the last word with such venom, using her most frequent pet name for Kira as a weapon to stab her heart.

'I'm at work, Ashley. We've gone over this. Please, I'm off in like, fifty minutes. Can't this wait?'

'I *always* have to wait for *you*. You never have time for me anymore.'

Kira ground her cheek between her teeth. 'I've asked if you want to get a job here as well, you *always* walk by that help wanted sign, it's in the window right by the door, *every* time you come in.'

'And I've told you that I wouldn't have any time for my art if I did that. Do you even care about my dreams? What I want?'

'It's *always* about what *you* want. You, you, you're just so selfish!'

Ashley's eyes flared wide. '*I'm selfish?!*'

'Kira!?' Colin roared. He stomped over to the counter.

Kira could taste blood in her mouth. She started to relax and breathe deeply. 'Please leave, or I'll call the police... you're gonna get me fired.' She pointed to the door.

Ashley slammed a fistful of money down onto the counter. 'No way, I'm a paying customer now, you *have* to serve me. Now get me some nuggets ... bitch.'

Kira shoved the money back at her, some change spilling onto the floor. 'No, leave this store. Now.'

'Kira!' This time it was the chilling voice of the manager. Kira slowly turned her head, the manager stood in the doorway to the back. She'd never seen the manager with such an angry look on her face, she didn't even know those beady eyes could hold such powerful hatred within them.

Kira sighed, fully turned away from her smirking girlfriend and stomped through to the staff room to speak with the manager, while Colin took over the front and rung up Ashley.

Help Wanted

The manager's arm outstretched towards the vacant sofa, gesturing for Kira to take a seat in the stuffy room. She did so, and then the door shut loudly, Kira flinched at the impact and sound of the slam, glancing up at the manager. There was an icy chill hanging about the woman, even though the heat from the recent summer had yet to dissipate. Kira squirmed in her seat, hands picking and scratching at her lap.

'Having relationship troubles, Kira?' the manager asked.

Kira gulped before responding. 'I-I'm sorry. I've told her not to—'

'Please, save your excuses. You are on *very* thin ice.'

Kira crushed her cheeks between her teeth again, sitting there in silence now as the manager glared down at her, not having taken a seat herself.

'I do like you, perhaps too much. I've let you get away with these shenanigans, disrupting *my* restaurant for far too long... you should be very thankful that I will allow you *one* more chance.' The manager's bony finger trembled in front of Kira's face as the woman leaned down before her. 'But trust me, my sweet Kira. If you continue this kind of behaviour, you won't last long. The machine will be more than happy to grind you up and spit you back out!' There was such a strange, chilling emphasis on the way the manager said this, that Kira couldn't help but shudder. 'That is what happens to cogs who disrupt the machine.' The manager turned away. 'You can go home early today, Kira. I do hope you've learned your lesson, I'd hate to lose you.'

The door closed again and Kira inhaled deeply. She slumped forward and hugged her knees. Her holiday couldn't come soon enough. Just a few more paydays, she reminded herself. She hoped the cruise could solve her issues, both with work, and Ashley.

Kira grabbed her things, and hurried outside, keeping her head down as she passed Colin, avoiding his hateful, condescending gaze. Thankfully, he didn't say anything as she passed him. Something worse was waiting for her outside, however. As Kira stepped out, a car veered in front of her and blocked her path, beeping its horn. The window rolled down. It was a familiar car, of course, it was. Kira didn't even have to look through the now-open window to know it was Ashley in the driver's seat.

'Get in,' Ashley demanded, and Kira knew better than to draw this out and try to argue about it; if she refused and tried to walk away, Ashley would just follow along, screaming at her and honking that damn horn until Kira relented.

With a sigh, Kira opened the door and sat down on the old, stained, leather seats. The instant after the door shut, Ashley locked them all. They drove in silence for a short time, though it didn't take Kira long to notice that Ashley was just circling aimlessly.

Kira turned to face Ashley. 'What do you want? I don't have time to play this silly silent game of yours.'

Ashley glared sideways at Kira, though she finally turned around and actually started heading to her apartment. 'Do you love me?' Ashley broke her silence.

Kira groaned and rolled her eyes, turning away again. 'For fuck's sake, don't start this again... of course I love you. I tell you that every day.'

'It's not enough to just say it! I could say I'm the fucking prime minister but that doesn't make it true does it?!' Ashley started to speed up.

Kira gripped the handle above her window tightly. 'What do you want me to do? You're the one who doesn't want to fuck anymore.'

'Oh is that all I am to you, huh? Just someone you can crawl back to and fuck whenever you want? Is that the only way you can express "love" now?'

'Keep your eyes on the road! And slow down, Jesus fucking Christ.' Kira tensed, feeling herself slide around in her seat as they rounded a corner rapidly.

'You never have time for me anymore, when's the last time we went out on a date? Or that you even did anything romantic?!' Ashley only continued to accelerate.

'What? Well, I... yeah but when was the last time *you* did anything for me? This is a two-way thing. The least you could do is have a nice meal cooked for me when I get back home from work.'

'There it is. Work, work, work, work, work! *Work*! You're always fucking working!'

A car horn blared at them as they sped through a red light.

Kira's knuckles turned white she was holding onto that handle so hard. 'A-Ashley! Slow down, please! Fuck, why do you think I'm always working so much? I'm doing it for you!'

'*Bullshit!*' Ashley slammed on the brakes and the car skidded to a halt. Two stretches of black tyre marks burned into the asphalt behind them. Kira was almost thrown from her seat, and she would've been if not for the seatbelt slingshotting her back. She panted hard, looking at Ashley with widened eyes.

'Get out,' Ashley growled.

'Wh-What?'

'You heard me! I said get out!'

'B-Babe wait I—'

'Don't you dare call me babe! Get out!'

Kira reached for her phone. Surprise be damned, if she could just show Ash the cruise tickets, then she'd understand. Before she could even get the phone from her pocket, the bottom of a fist connected with her cheek. Then another on her temple, and shoulder, then nails started scratching and clawing at her as she leaned against the car door, curling up and covering her head.

'Get out, get out! *Get out!*' Ashley screeched, continuing her feral attack.

Kira fumbled with her seatbelt and the door. Once she got it open, she tumbled out onto the edge of the road. Without even waiting for the door to be closed, Ashley sped away, tyres squealing again, leaving smoke in their wake. Kira coughed heavily, shivering as she rubbed at the side of her face and her upper arm. Her hands came away with small amounts of blood on them, claw marks stung her cheek.

She crawled to the curb, and sobbed. She couldn't hold back the tears. Her life was over. It had just sped away from her and left her in the dust. She'd lost Ashley, and she didn't know what else she had anymore.

She dragged herself back to her mum's house instead of her shared dorm with Ashley. She didn't explain why she was there, or what her injuries were from. She barely said anything, no matter how much her mum pestered her, she just crawled back into her childhood bed and buried herself under the covers. She never wanted to emerge again, she just wanted to go to sleep forever.

Unfortunately, she woke up the next morning.

She didn't know why, but she still went to work that day as well. It was like her body was moving on its own, working off of repetition. She was also supposed to be looking after a newbie and showing them around, so she went in even earlier than usual. When she saw that newbie's face, it reminded Kira that it hadn't been that long since *she* was the one being shown the ropes. If she could go back in time to that day, she'd have made sure to run as far away from this place as possible, maybe then things would still be alright.

Or at least, if Sarah was still here, maybe things wouldn't be so bad. *Where are you, Sarah? Why didn't you take me with you? Wherever you ran off to...*

'Um, are you alright, ma'am?' Kira was snapped from her thoughts by the voice of the boy in front of her. This new hire sure was young. He was a fresh-faced, pimply young boy. A nervous sweat was already running down from under his ill-fitting cap, and he kept fidgeting in place, his big, innocent eyes never able to stay in one place for long. He was short, but had some meat on him, maybe he and Colin could bond over their similar stature, though this kid was still taller than that tiny cunt. Kira wasn't even sure if this kid was old enough to be working, but that wasn't her problem to deal with.

'Don't call me ma'am.' That title made Kira feel way too old.

'S-Sorry um...' He looked at her name tag. 'M-Miss Kira.'

'That's ... better. I might as well ask what your name is.' Her mind wasn't focused on this conversation or orientation at all. *Maybe it isn't too late to go back home.*

'Um, I'm Jacob.' He stood there, looking up at her expectantly as her vacant gaze was aimed elsewhere. 'M-Miss Kira? A-Aren't you supposed to be showing me around?'

'Yeah yeah, don't get your knickers in a twist,' Kira grumbled.

She began very unenthusiastically showing Jacob around and showing him how everything worked around the store. Eventually, their tour brought them before the stairs leading to the basement door.

'And down there is the manager's office, but I mean I've never—'

'Oh! G-Great, I actually had something I need to show the manager. I don't think she has my bank details yet so...' Jacob hurried down the steps to the basement, uncrumpling a piece of paper from his back pocket.

'H-Hey wait!' Kira's heart started to race for reasons she didn't understand. Why did she feel so uneasy about him going towards that door? It was just an office right?... But... Kira had never seen anyone go in there, and she'd never once been behind that door herself even after months of working here.

She hurried down the steps after Jacob, but she couldn't reach him before he knocked loudly on the metal door.

'Miss manager?' he called. He got no answer. He knocked again.

'I don't think she's in, we should just...' As Kira reached for the back of his collar, Jacob tried the handle. The door wasn't locked.

Silently, the door swung inward. Kira held her breath. The room beyond the door was dark, and perhaps a little cramped, but it looked like a standard office. No one was sitting at the lone desk in the middle of it. Only one thing was odd about it, and that was the open door on the right side of the room. Maybe it was just a personal bathroom was Kira's first thought, but then what was that strange red glow coming from it?

Kira's heart pounded harder. She couldn't stop Jacob from stepping further into the office. He moved towards the red door and called out again, 'M-Miss manager?'

'I-I don't think she's in, maybe we should just go back and wa—'

Kira jumped as a horrible grinding sound came from beyond the door. It was like an entire drawer of silverware was put into a blender on max power.

Jacob stopped in the open doorway. Kira stepped behind him. Both of them stared down yet another stairway leading even further down. The dark, stone steps were illuminated by the red glow, and they seemed wet, like they'd just been drenched with some kind of liquid. At the end of the stairs, there was another open doorway where the red light was coming from.

'Miss... manager?' Jacob called once more. Only the grinding answered him. Both Jacob and Kira flinched at the loud, grating noise. Jacob stepped forward and started down the first step.

'Wait.' Kira reached out to stop him, but he shrugged her off, never looking away from the red doorway. Kira's chest tightened as Jacob carefully descended. She followed behind him. As she crept down the stairs, a strange but almost familiar smell hit her nostrils. There was the damp, mouldy stench of the stone walls and steps, but, under that, there was a meaty smell not dissimilar to that she found whenever she went into the freezer upstairs.

Jacob reached the bottom of the stairs and went through the doorway. He was met with a sharp corner, and upon turning it, he stopped dead in his tracks. 'Oh... god... what is that?' All the blood and colour rushed out of his face.

Kira rushed down the final steps and hurried over to him, almost running into him as she stopped just past the corner as well. She couldn't help but let out a horrified shriek before covering her mouth.

Past the corner, was a round room filled with red light. In the centre of the room, was the source of the horrible grinding noise. It was some weird machine, with a big, three-headed drill...claw thing above a wide metal bowl. The bowl was filled with chunky, pinkish goop, and rested over the base of the machine with a tube leading out into a wide tray. There was a lever connected to the side of the base, as well as a few buttons.

Next to this horrible, strange machine, was a much more frightening and shocking sight. A disgusting creature stood there with its back to them. It was hunched over greatly, if it stood straight its head would surely touch the ceiling. Its spine and ribs were protruding from its spotty, black skin. It had four, extremely long, bowed legs, spread far out under it, and the bottom half of its hunched torso bulged out fatly, like a beach ball that was one pump away from bursting. Its arms were almost as long as its legs, and it also had four of them, each with elbows as sharp as knives, and massive hands, all of its fingers were like thin, long blades.

The creature turned its head one-eighty degrees to look back at Kira's shriek. The creature had the face of the manager except with eight beady black eyes. ... The creature *was* The Manager.

'O-Oh fuck. *Run!*' Jacob cried.

He turned and bolted, getting caught up on Kira who was slower to turn and flee. As the two went to round the corner again, The Manager let out a horrid screech and shat out a sticky white fluid from the rear of its gross, fat bulge. The tough webs caught around the fleeing pair's legs, tripping them up and sending them crashing to the floor.

'*Heeellllp!!*' Jacob screamed. The Manager approached. Jacob frantically clawed at the webbing around his legs, desperate to tear it off though struggling to do so. Each time his hands touched the webs, it took a great effort just to yank them free let alone rip any of the webbing away from his ankles.

Kira cowered and curled up, closing her eyes as she felt The Manager approach. She was biting down so hard on her cheeks, that she thought she'd ripped them off. She awaited whatever grisly death this monster had planned for them, but... The Manager simply passed them by, stepping over them and squeezing itself through the narrow passage as it crawled up the stairway to the thick, heavy door leading back to its office, shutting it and locking it. Jacob was still trying to free himself, and even Kira struggled with the webs while The Manager's back was turned, though she stopped and curled back into a ball when the great spider passed them again. Kira watched as the monster returned to the machine. Then Kira took a longer look around the eerie red room.

On the far wall was a large bench, with a bloody tarp covering a lumpy mass. Kira didn't want to know what was under that tarp, though she had a good guess. Around the left side wall, was another bench, this one with numerous bloody utensils like butcher's knives, tongs, and mallets, as well as a great big sink full of ice and... oh god, that was a hand sticking out of it. The right side of the room elicited another scream from Kira. There were 3 glass tubes, filled with a strange, greenish, transparent liquid, and floating within these test tubes were butchered and mutilated human corpses. One tube was empty, but in one, Kira swore she saw a young man who had been caught trying to dine and dash just last week and, worst of all, in the tube just next to that, Sarah's head was floating around, the rest of her body almost entirely gone, only a few chunks and a foot left in there as well.

The Manager reached into the sink and picked out the severed arm from the ice. It then moved over to the grinder, and dumped the arm into the pink gloop in the bowl. It pressed a button, and the drills whirred to life, spinning rapidly. It grabbed onto the lever and pulled it back, lowering the drills into the gloop, pressing it down as that horrible grating sound shook the whole room, and that pink gloop splattered around the room. It held the drill down for ten seconds, then stopped, hitting another button and pushing it back up. It pressed another few buttons and then moved to the large tray and its dispenser tube. It leaned down, watching as the tube gurgled out a small excess of gloop before producing a perfectly formed, juicy, raw patty, just like the ones used in the burgers.

Kira watched the whole process in stunned silence. Blood filled her mouth from how hard she gnawed on her cheeks, and as she gulped it down, she realised that the meat here had always had a similar metallic, soothing aftertaste.

She laughed. Jacob thought she had lost her mind but couldn't blame her. He got himself free and then ripped apart the webs holding Kira down, freeing her as well. He sprung up, and grabbed the nearest knife that he could. 'C-Come on!' He urged Kira to get up. 'There's two of us and just, just that one ... thing! W-We can kill it before it kills us.'

Kira picked herself up, still staring at that perfect, thick, succulent patty. Her hand blindly fumbled around on the benchtop before she latched onto a mallet, some brain matter still caught between its many grooves.

The Manager tilted its head, its many eyes blinking as it stared down its two prey. Kira stared back, she was perfectly still, while Jacob's whole body was vibrating rapidly.

Kira looked at the grinder, and then around the room again. Her eyes fell upon the tubes again. No wonder this place went through so many employees. But... the food here was to die for. She looked at Sarah's lifeless face and imagined Colin's stupid, fat mug there instead. She looked across to the empty tube and imagined Ashley submerged in that sickly green liquid. She wondered if someone as beautiful as Ashley would taste just as beautiful, or if her toxic personality would taint the flavour.

'Kira! We have to do this now! P-Please... together, we can do it together,' Jacob wailed. He was still shaking, tears running down his face now, and piss running down his legs.

Kira slowly nodded. The Manager hadn't moved, still just watching them.

Jacob stepped forward, raising his knife. Kira raised her weapon as well. Jacob let out a warcry and rushed forward, but his final shout was cut short when Kira's mallet crashed through the back of his skull and killed him in one blow.

His lifeless body crumpled to the floor in front of The Manager, and Kira tossed aside her mallet. Both spider and human stared down at the fresh corpse on the floor, neither monster said anything for a while before Kira finally spoke.

'Help me get him in the grinder?' she said.

The Manager stared at Kira now, unmoving, unspeaking.

Kira gulped and extended a friendly hand to the massive creature, smiling up at it. 'Please, ma'am. I'd love to continue working here. I can see now, why this is the most popular chain in the country, and I'd love to help you grow this place and expand it.'

The Manager laughed, a shrill, high-pitched laughter as it flashed its sharp, yellow grin. One of its long, bent arms reached out and took Kira's—comparatively tiny—hand in its own. 'You want to be partners? Mmm... I wonder just how efficient this place could get now that I've got an assistant manager who is on board with the program and shares the secret to my special recipes. Welcome aboard, dear Kira~'

Kira smiled, relieved as she happily shook The Manager's massive hand. 'Thank you ma'am, I won't let you down...' She looked at the empty tube again. 'And I know just who would be perfect for our next batch of meat.'

The Manager chuckled again, still grinning. 'Yes~ I don't think we'll need *two* assistant managers. Ahh, but looks like we'll need to keep that "Help Wanted" sign up for a little longer yet.'

As Kira and The Manager fed Jacob into the grinder, Kira realised, she still had so much to live for—it was her duty to share this unforgettable, irresistible food with the rest of the world.

Fool's Gold

John listened to the slow, shrill beeping of the gold detector. His eyes never left the device's wide, flat head as Levi deliberately waved the detector back and forth mere inches above the golden sand. The two men hoped the beach was as golden underground as it was on the surface.

'Thanks again for bringing me along, mate,' John said.

Levi paused and raised the device, the steady beeping faded. 'No worries mate. I saw how interested you were when I showed off those little nuggets the other day, and hey, the more hands out here the merrier ... as long as you're gonna share your treasure with me.' He nudged John and they laughed together.

'Of course, of course. But, I'm not worried about that. I mean, if it was easy to find a boatload of gold, everybody would be doing it, wouldn't they?'

'Yeah, true. It's just a good excuse to get out of the house, get moving and enjoy some natural beauty.' Levi's gaze focused on the iridescent shine the mid-afternoon sun gave the sea's rolling waves. 'The gold's a bonus at that point.'

John looked over the glittering ocean, then his eyes wandered around the shore. It was a picturesque day—not too cloudy but not too blue and hot either; the beach wasn't crowded nor were they alone; and there was just the right amount of wind to carry a cool breeze across the sea, along with that rich, ocean smell. John closed his eyes and soaked in the moment. 'Yeah. What a beauty of a day.'

While it was a wonderful day and great for them to take a moment to stop and take it all in, they had come out here so Levi could show John the ropes of prospecting in case he wanted to make the investment and get his own gold detector. So they didn't pause long before moving onward again. However, before Levi lowered the detector back to the sand and continued their slow crawl along the beach, he turned to John. 'How about you take a go at it now, mate? It's a pretty simple thing all said and done, and maybe your luck will be better than mine.' They'd been searching for only fifteen minutes, but with Levi at the helm, they hadn't gotten close to gold.

'Really? Sure, I'll give it a whack. I'll be real careful not to drop it though.' Levi handed over the device, and John handed over the spade and bucket he'd been carrying. Once they'd swapped over, John strapped the detector to his arm and aimed it at the sand. A wide grin spread across his face. 'Thanks again, mate.'

'Hahaha, you can thank me by finding us some gold.' Levi nudged him once more, and as they laughed, they set off.

John combed over every strip of sand ahead of him in a wide, slow arc. He went from the wet sand of the tide, all the way to the steep sandy cliffs that separated the beach from the road. While he covered a lot of ground, he wasn't moving forward quickly. However, it was ten minutes later when he found his first hit.

'Hold it right there, mate,' Levi said. He dropped to his knees and started shovelling sand aside in great heaps with the spade. He dug until he revealed a glittering speck. 'Ohh that's a good sign!'

John's heart rate rocketed skyward as his friend groped the shining object and then dug some more around it. It didn't take long for him to unearth it. John was a little disappointed with the size, but Levi was astonished. 'Holy shit, mate. Look at that nugget!' Levi held it up, turning the oddly shaped, golden rock in his hands as it continued to sparkle in the light.

John crouched down, looking at it, gobsmacked. 'That's...That's gold,' he stammered, 'Real gold?'

'As real as you and I, mate. It's a bloody big chunk to boot, that might be worth a grand right there.'

'What?! You're joking.'

Levi shook his head. 'I'm bloody serious. They don't need to get that big to be worth a lot of moolah. Go on and hold it for yourself. It's heavier than it looks.'

John took it in his shaking palm. His hand sagged. A thousand bucks, sitting in the palm of his hand. He laughed, staring at it.

Levi whacked him on the back. 'You hold on to that one. Fuck me, my first bit of gold was just this tiny, little fleck, and you've got a damn big rock like that. You lucky bastard. I should've brought you out here ages ago.'

'I can't believe it. I'm holding it and it still doesn't feel real.'

'Hahaha, yeah I've been there. Come on, let's get a picture of the big moment.'

They stood, the ocean behind them. John held the nugget up to his face, his massive grin incomparable to the beautiful glamour the gold held. Levi's smile was much more reserved. Both men put an arm around the other's shoulders. John was the skinnier of the two, with a roundish face that was too small for his head. In the picture, his dark, beady eyes were glued to the nugget, a reflection of it could be seen within them. Levi was bulkier—he *used* his gym membership—and had a stubbly beard with dark, shaggy hair. He was rugged, but in the way that made him popular with the ladies.

After the photo, John's eyes dropped back to the sand. 'Let's keep looking, there could be more right under our feet.'

'Yeah, alright, you keep searching, I need to fill that hole back in, always gotta remember to fill your holes in.'

John nodded, but Levi wasn't sure if he'd heard what was said, the detector already beeping again.

They scanned around the hole where they'd found the nugget, but nothing else was hidden there. That didn't quell John's excitement, however, and he continued his search, Levi—happy to placate his friend and not wanting to rain on his parade—followed him along the rest of the beach. It was a great day after all, and he was happy to enjoy the walk and the beautiful vista, and if they found any more gold, so be it. Unfortunately, they didn't have any further luck. They got their fair share of hits after finding the nugget, but only dug up junk buried for who knows how long. The only thing that was somewhat exciting was an old pair of car keys—they doubted whatever rust bucket the keys operated was nearby.

Eventually, there wasn't any more beach to search. A cliff face barred their way forward. The sun crept closer to the horizon. John was frustrated they hadn't found more. He felt in his pocket where he'd kept the nugget, then looked over to a pathway that led off the beach and up the cliff. 'What's up there?' he asked.

'Up there? A park, some nature reserve I think. You're not tired yet?'

'Not tired at all. Can we search up there?'

Levi laughed. 'Jesus, I think you've got a bit of gold fever, mate. Yeah, I guess we can give it a look, no harm in that. Might as well get this fever out of your system before we head back.'

'Thanks a bunch.' John grinned, eyes gleaming as he hurried up the path. Levi tagged along behind him. When they got to the top, Levi directed John down a hiking trail, and after a ten-minute walk, they reached a woodland area Levi knew was good for prospecting.

'Just keep going until we reach a shack, that's when we've reached the area close enough,' Levi said. 'There were gold mines here back in the day, sometimes you can still find the odd bit here and there, something they thought was too small and threw out.'

They followed the winding path, delving further away from the beach and city. The longer they went, the more trees sprouted up around them, until they were surrounded by the woodlands with nothing else in sight. A little later, they found the clearing and a small, rundown shack. Beyond the shack, the forest darkened and became much thicker, with gnarled and near-dead trees. John spotted a narrow path through the dying trees, but wooden boards blocked off the entrance and a danger sign was erected nearby. Despite all this, John found himself drawn towards the path, even as Levi was moving across to another, wider and more welcoming-looking area of the forest, trying to explain that was where he usually went.

John could almost touch those wooden boards, his fingers stretching towards the wood when a gravelly, old voice cut through the air. 'Hold it!'

John stopped and spun around, shocked to find a strange, small, old man, who looked like a homeless Einstein, only twenty kilos lighter. The old man stood in front of the shack, glaring at John. He pointed a shaking, bony finger at John. 'Ye step away from there, sonny. Don't ye even *think* about steppin' foot in ol' Widow's Wood or I tell ye it'll be the last thing ye ever do.'

'Excuse me?' John bristled, the last part sounding like a threat.

Levi hurried to John's side, putting a hand on his shoulder. 'Whoa, it's alright. We weren't going in Widow's Wood, Mr McNeely. Sorry, it's his first time out here. I'm showing him the old mines.'

'If he's a friend of yers ye better make sure he knows not to go out into Widow's Wood! Not unless he wants to get eat'n by the Widow herself! Don't say I didn't warn him!' McNeely wagged his finger at them.

Levi laughed awkwardly, pulling John away from the barren, black trees and towards the lush, green area of the woods opposite. 'Oh don't worry, we wouldn't dream of it.'

McNeely's bloodshot eyes were almost bugging out of his skull as he watched them until they disappeared down the "correct" path.

When the shack and the old man were out of sight, John turned to Levi. 'What the hell was that?'

'Oh, that? Right, I should've warned you. Sorry about him, but that's Old Man McNeely.'

John raised a brow.

'He's uhh, well he's the local around here, that's his shack. I think he was one of the miners from when this place was operational. Now he's just the crazy old coot who lives in the woods.'

'And what was that about Widow's Wood?'

'That old ghost story? It's a bunch of bullshit. The old man must've seen ... *something*, probably nothing, but, well, you know how people can get when their mind starts to go. Don't worry about it. His advice on where to look for gold and old stuff out of the mine is pretty good, and he's actually an alright fella when he's not ranting and raving about the ghost story. So...' Levi shrugged. 'Just go along with it. Better to not have him yelling at you, plus, I think this might be his property anyway. If he lets us explore out this way that's fine by me, and if he doesn't want us going through Widow's Wood, then that's fair enough.'

John looked back the way they came, sympathy replacing his bewilderment. 'Poor guy, going crazy all alone out here. I wonder what happened to his family?'

'Bugger if I know. Probably took the riches he dug up from the mines and then ran off after they shut down, left him behind when he wouldn't leave this place.'

John looked back. 'Do you think ... you think *he's* the widow? And his wife is buried in those woods or something?'

Levi stopped, looking back as well. He shuddered. 'Bloody well might be. But let's not think about morbid shit like that, 'specially not out here. Come on, don't you want to find some more gold?'

'Right.'

The two continued deeper into the woods. Levi showed John where the old mine shafts and their run-offs were. Of course, John needed to have a look, even though Levi kept telling him that countless people had gone over those hillocks. John insisted on giving them a once-over himself. Levi relented, because with stuff like this, you never knew, something could've been glossed over amongst all that dirt and rubble. Sometimes it felt like you could check the same spot two days in a row, and on the second day, you'd find something, as if the gold was waiting for the right moment.

As luck would have it, the first hillock they searched, John found something. They got to shovelling, having a harder time with the tougher, more compact earth and rock compared to the loose sand on the beach. Eventually, they dug deep enough to find what had sent the detector into a frenzy.

They came away with another couple of nuggets, albeit these were much smaller, still, Levi couldn't believe it.

'Bloody hell, you really are one lucky bastard, you know that?'

John held one of the pebbles up in the light of the fading sun, grinning as he looked it over. 'Yeah... guess I've got a knack for this thing, huh?'

'One hell of a successful debut. Just try and leave some gold for the rest of us!' Levi laughed. John laughed with him, passing over one of the pebbles.

'You can hold on to this one, as thanks for showing me all this, and letting me use your kit.'

'Gee, thanks, mate. You sure you don't want me to have the first nugget?' He nudged John.

They both chuckled. Then, John put the head of the detector back to the ground and started scanning away, moving from the hillock.

'Hold on, mate,' Levi said, tugging his arm. 'We better call it a night for now. It's getting late, and you've already found plenty. Besides, not like the gold can get up and walk away.'

John wanted to continue, he almost voiced his desire to do so, but he remembered it wasn't his equipment. It wasn't up to him if they kept going. He frowned, but surrendered. 'You're right. Sorry, guess I was getting carried away. Hah, might take a bit longer for that fever of mine to die down, what do you reckon?'

'Hey, if I had your luck I'm sure I would've been out here every day. Come on, I'll take you home. Geez, with what you've found already, you'll be able to buy some top-of-the-line gear yourself. I can tell you about the place I got mine from, they were real helpful, explaining all the differences between the machines and all that.'

'Sounds great. Thanks, mate.'

As the two retraced their footsteps, they passed by Old Man McNeely's shack again. McNeely wasn't anywhere to be seen, but John's eyes were again drawn to that dark patch of land known as Widow's Wood. A golden glint caught his eye. 'Oi, Levi, wait.' He moved closer to the dense wall of trees. He gripped one of the branches as he peered through the gangly, pointy bracket, but he couldn't find that glint again. Levi looked over expectantly. 'Hmm... never mind. I thought I saw something in there, some gold.'

'You've got gold on the brain, haven't you? I doubt there's any gold left in there.'

'You're probably right.' John kept looking, squinting his eyes. If it was lighter maybe he could've seen better, maybe that glint would've shown again. He saw something move deep within the dark recesses of the wood and he stepped back, though he jerked around as his hand stuck to the branch he had grabbed. He tore himself away, stumbling back. He looked at the branch, seeing it was covered in a thin layer of webbing. 'Ugh, fuck me.' John shook his hand, wiping it off on the leg of his shorts. Of course, something had moved back there; it was a bloody forest. There were probably tons of things in there he couldn't see.

'You alright?' Levi asked.

'Yeah, yeah I'm fine. Sorry. Let's get out of here.'

* * *

The next day, John went to the store Levi had told him about and bought a top-of-the-line gold detector, it even came with the ability to detect the different forms of metal in the ground, and make specific beeping tones and patterns for different kinds, meaning you could tell if what you'd found was junk or gold without needing to dig. He even traded in the pebbles and flecks he found to help pay for the device, as he found out just how pricey they could be. He was sure he'd make the money back in no time with his luck. He could've sold the nugget as well but decided to hold onto it as a good luck charm, and a reminder of why he's doing this.

With his own detector, John was free to head out prospecting as much as he wanted—which was quite a lot. It started with just the weekends. He'd return to the beach and the little woodland area past Old Man McNeely's cabin, scanning every bit of the ground he could reach, and overturning every rock he laid his eyes on. Soon it progressed to an extra trip during the week, then two, then three, then finally (hardly a month had passed since his first time with Levi), he was out there every day.

It was all he could think about, all he wanted to do, and thankfully, his luck continued to flourish those first couple of weeks. He found many more flecks, pebbles, and nuggets—

though none as big as his first. It was like he was sitting on a horde of gold buried just beneath the earth.

He'd had such a great amount of success, that he stopped showing up to work so he could be out there more, after all, if his luck kept up, he wouldn't need to work ever again. But, gradually, the days became less fruitful. This only heightened John's gold lust. Each time his haul was less than that of the previous day, his desperation grew. It was no longer just a fun hobby or a good pass time to earn some extra cash, it was his life. Old Man McNeely could see that, even if John himself couldn't.

The old geezer confronted John one day after he'd made his usual climb up the hill. 'Turn back!' McNeely said. 'There's nothin' left for ye to find here 'cept old bones, disappointment, and things best left undisturbed.'

'What?!' John was taken aback, though his surprise was soon replaced with fury. 'What would you know, you old coot!? Have you been taking the gold when I leave, is that it? You're keeping it for yourself, aren't you? You greedy old bastard!'

'I ain't dug up nothin' since before ye were born, boy! When ye dig too deep, ye find things ye wish ye never unearthed.'

John's eyes narrowed. He didn't believe McNeely. The crazy wildman just wanted to run him off, he thought. Now that he'd been finding all the gold, McNeely wanted it for himself. He'd probably thought the forest was dry, but now that it'd been proven to still be full of riches he wasn't going to let anyone else have it. He wouldn't let anyone else in again, he'd keep it for himself. John's gaze drifted past Old Man McNeely towards Widow's Wood and his eyes gleamed gold for an instant. *Keep it all to himself. Don't let anyone else in.*

'Don't ye dare set foot in that cursed place, boy, or it'll be the last thing ye do.' McNeely straightened his crooked back, standing taller to come back into John's vision.

John glared down at the old man. 'Are you threatening me?'

'Do not play with nature boy!' Old Man McNeely rose even taller, briefly regaining some of his youth. 'I do not threaten ye, it is the woods itself that would put yer life in peril! Heed my warnin', no man who goes into those dark, cursed woods,

ever comes out.' There was a crazed, fervourous look in McNeely's eyes, a look of great fear and belief; a look so convincing that a tiny bit of fear seeped into John.

'Bah!' John turned away, storming off down the other path, disappearing into the greener forest.

Old Man McNeely staggered back, panting softly as he hunched over again. He looked at Widow's Wood. He could feel the woods staring back at him. He was no longer a visage of his younger self, he was back to a frail old man, shaking in the wind.

* * *

A few days later, John hadn't found even a fleck within the usual spots. That marked a week without gold. It was then that Levi came to the beach, meeting John there. Levi was shocked by what he saw as the two met up. 'J-John? My god, what happened to you? Have you been sick?'

John manically said: 'what no what are you talking about I'm perfectly fine'

Levi's concern only deepened. 'H-Have you seen yourself?'

John tilted his head. 'i feel better than ever'

'Uhh, n-never mind.' Levi looked John over again. John looked years older than he had just a month ago. His hair was frayed, and even his clothes were unkempt as if he hadn't washed in weeks. His skin was dark and weathered, wrinkling from excessive time in the sun, and he was much skinnier as if he hadn't been eating regularly since they last saw each other. His eyes were sunken but brighter.

'my only problem is i cant find any more gold i dont know where its all gone there was a sea of it here before'

'Well uh, I mean, it's not infinite, how much have you been coming out here?'

'every day'

Levi's eyes widened. 'Geez. I mean, you've probably found it all, man.'

'oh'

'Maybe it's time to try a different spot, you know, there's plenty of gold out there all over the place, you just gotta know where to look.'

John's eyes darkened, but he still spoke rapidly. 'Yes i see i must look in the right places where no one else has been yet' He nodded a few times, and then looked up the hill. He had the perfect place in mind.

'Right, but I think a break would do you more good. There's no point running yourself ragged over this. How about we go to the pub tonight and watch the game?'

'no no thank you thats fine i have something i gotta do'

'John ... I really think you should—'

John took a breath 'Levi.' He smiled reassuringly. 'I'm fine.'

A change washed over him in the blink of an eye. John looked better; more like his normal self. Levi was confounded. 'A-Alright, well, you just remember what I said. Be sure to take some days off from this.'

John waved goodbye to Levi. When Levi was out of sight, John turned and marched up the hill. Widow's Wood was the only thing on his mind. Widow's Wood had to be full of gold— Old Man McNeely's private stash. That's why he didn't want anyone snooping around in there, it was his nest egg, better than any bank account.

John stormed towards Old Man McNeely's cabin. He stared at the door. Old Man McNeely wouldn't dissuade him this time, he wouldn't let that greedy old wretch horde all the gold to himself. He started down the path towards Widow's Wood, but this time, McNeely didn't burst out to stop him. John looked back at the cabin, confused. Even old hermits had to leave their cabins sometimes. Fate must've been on John's side for John to have caught Old Man McNeely during one of his rare trips into town. It vindicated him, he knew he was justified in his actions, even fate, even the gold itself didn't want that old wretch to horde it selfishly, the gold *wanted* to be found.

Widow's Wood was a dark place, even without any leaves on the trees, they were packed together so closely they blocked out most of the sun. John wasn't deterred. He set to work quickly, making sure to journey far enough into the woods that the cabin disappeared from view before he began.

He was so set on his path that he didn't notice any of the large, intricate webs stretching between the trees.

It didn't take him long to find gold, and it was a spectacular find. The nugget he pulled from the earth was the largest chunk he'd ever found. It sparkled in the darkness. He whooped loudly, hopping around as he held it aloft. His slump was over, and he was right, Widow's Wood was rich with gold and ripe for the taking.

He pressed further into the woods, delving deeper into the dark, leaving the rest of the world behind. There was no noise within Widow's Wood, only the beeping of his machine, and the crunch of the previously untrodden dirt and sticks underfoot. It didn't even seem like anything lived in those woods, it was like he was off in his own world, where he was the only inhabitant. He was wrong. He was so transfixed on the beeping of the detector, that he never saw the signs of life—and death—all around him.

He crept further along the dark path. He didn't see the butterfly flutter overhead with deep blue wings, as pretty as any specimen ever recorded. He didn't see the butterfly flutter straight into an unbreakable web, never to rip itself free and flutter again. He didn't see it squirm.

There were a few times when he walked into frail strings of webbing that had been abandoned and never completed, but they were mere nuisances to brush away or wipe off his face, nothing large enough to hold a man. He didn't see the much larger webs just off to the side, so thick that they completely walled off branching pathways.

He never took his eyes off the detector, so he never saw the discarded bones lying unburied, covered only by a thin layer of dirt and foliage, picked clean of any meat that might've once clung to them. He never saw that the bones varied in size and shape, that they belonged to many different beasts, both large and small, nor did he see the human skull, old, discoloured, and cracked.

He was so focused on the beeping, that he didn't notice he'd walked in a circle. He didn't see the hole he'd failed to refill until stepped in it. His ankle twisted and he fell to the ground, the detector crunching under him. He gasped, and lifted off it, all thoughts of his ankle, and the pain it brought vanished. He shakily picked up the detector and checked if it was broken.

He was so concerned with it, that he never heard the the trees creak. He never noticed the great shadow looming over him. Nor did he notice the Widow's stinger, dripping with toxins, not until it was jammed deep into his back, and by then, he didn't have time to notice before he was paralysed completely.

A golden gleam was forever held within his greedy, eyes. His petrified expression was perfectly preserved for as long as it took the Widow to eat it right off his skull.

Visions of the Blind

Jasper's pale brown eyes squinted at the near-translucent image he held. He raised the large sheet to the fluorescent light of the doctor's exam room, but it would not grow shaper or more visible; the shapes were blurred and distorted. 'Gavin, what... tell me what it looks like?' Jasper held up the picture for his partner beside him.

Gavin wiped his watery eyes, focusing on Jasper's face. 'You really can't see it?'

'What do you see, Jasper? Explain it as best you can, please.' Dr Linwood said as she sat across from the couple.

Jasper turned the picture back to himself. 'O-Okay I...I can *see* it, but it's all...all blurry. I can't make out the details, it all looks the same. Just, one big shape.'

Dr Linwood's pen scratched across her notepad.

'Isn't there anything we can do?!' Gavin exclaimed.

'I can write your husband a prescription for lenses with a higher magnification but... with the way his vision is degrading, we can only look for temporary solutions.

'Oh...' Jasper's voice was hollow as if he hadn't fully understood the severity of this outcome.

'That's...That's all you can say?'

'I'm truly sorry, Mr and Mr Longly.'

'What about his art? How is he going to—'

Jasper reached out and caressed Gavin's cheek. 'Gavin, dear, it's okay.'

'I have heard of some blind artists who work more with texture and can still create beautiful masterpieces,' Dr Linwood said.

'Yes, thank you, Doctor. I'm sure I'll find a way to continue doing what I love. Even if my vision is lost, I'll never forget the beauty of the world.' Jasper looked at Gavin as he said this, and again Gavin had to wipe the tears from his own eyes.

Gavin and Jasper soon made their way out of the office. A follow-up appointment was set a month away. Gavin held Jasper's hand tightly as he led him to the car.

The ride home was silent and slow. When they arrived, Jasper instantly went through the small brick house to his art room. He looked at his easel, then glanced back to the doorway where he saw the shape of Gavin watching. 'Remember our honeymoon, how the sun would crest over the mountains every morning?' Jasper said.

'It was beautiful ... almost as beautiful as our wedding day.'

Jasper smiled. 'I never did paint those mountains, or that sunrise. Let's change that today.'

Gavin looked at the canvas worryingly. 'That sounds like a lovely idea. I'll get dinner started. Call out if you need me.'

'Thank you, dear.' Jasper picked up his brush and Gavin stepped away. He turned back once, worry still heavy over his heart. With a sigh, he left Jasper to his work.

Once dinner was ready, Gavin returned to inform Jasper, and to check how the painting progressed. He popped his head through the doorway. 'Food's ready.'

'I'll be right there.' Jasper finished his last stroke and then set the brush aside. He heard Gavin approach. He sat back holding his breath. 'How is it? Be honest now.'

They stared at the canvas. While the painting wasn't finished, it was most of the way there. It certainly wasn't pretty. The mountains were misshapen, the sun was wobbly, the trees were blotchy, and while the colours were mostly fine they all blended into one another. It was as if everything in the image was melting. A sniffling sob was all Jasper needed to hear to know the verdict.

'... What a waste of paint,' Jasper said.

'N-No it's not... it's good in its own way.'

'You don't have to sugarcoat it for me, Gavin. I always want to hear the truth. But it's okay. I'm just... getting used to this new... obstacle. I'll keep giving it my all.'

'That's wonderful, sweetheart.' Gavin sniffled again and wiped away a tear before he leaned in and kissed Jasper on the cheek. 'Now, let's have our dinner before it gets cold, you can keep practising another time.'

The night passed quietly and somberly. It was as if a heavy cloud was resting over the household. Gavin told himself it was just the shock and that it'd go away soon.

The next morning, Jasper was up bright and early. Gavin found him in the art room. However, he wasn't painting. He was staring at last night's unfinished painting. He turned his head as the floorboards creaked under Gavin's feet. 'Can we move this into the bedroom?'

'Oh, of course,' Gavin said.

Jasper took the current canvas off the easel and set it aside. Gavin grabbed the easel and brought it to the bedroom.

Their bedroom wasn't grand, at least Gavin didn't think so. Most of the space was occupied by their king-sized bed—always neatly made every morning—which lay in the centre of the room, and had more pillows on the right—Jasper's—side; the simple, wooden floorboards—which felt like ice in the winter—were blanketed by a large, cashmere rug they'd been gifted as a housewarming present by one of Jasper's art friends; a single shelf hung over the bedhead, stocked full of books within easy reach for any nighttime reading; a long, mahogany dresser was against the wall opposite the bed; a mirror covered the wall above the dresser to the ceiling; and on the far end, there was a tall wardrobe, that was right next to their ensuite bathroom.

Together they set up the easel between the bed and dresser, and while it was a little cramped, they were as well able to squeeze in Jasper's stool. They returned to the art room, however, when Gavin went to pick up the unfinished painting, Jasper stopped him. 'Leave that one,' Jasper said. He went over and picked up a new canvas instead.

'Are you sure you don't want to finish the mountains?'

'I will one day, but for now, I have a better idea.' He took the fresh canvas and brought it to the easel. 'Each day, I'll sit right here, and I'll look into that mirror, and I'll paint myself. Surely I can still paint myself.'

'I'm sure you'll do great.' Gavin kissed his head. 'Are you coming for breakfast or will you begin right away?'

Jasper picking up his paintbrush was answer enough.

'I'll bring you a coffee.'

When Gavin returned with a steaming mug and some buttered toast to go along with it, Jasper had some of the outlining done. It didn't look bad. Sure it was just basic shapes but they weren't wobbly or misshapen. Things were looking up. Maybe there was a way for Jasper to keep making art. 'Will you be alright today? I've got to go to work.'

'Yes, dear. Thank you for worrying but I'll be quite alright. I'm not an invalid just yet.'

'I didn't say you were, darling. Well, I'm sure Jess would be happy to come help you if need be. Give her a call if you need anything.'

Jasper chuckled and rolled his eyes. 'Yes, Dad.'

Gavin laughed with him.

When Gavin left, the two exchanged quick "love you"'s as part of their farewell, and Gavin went off with high spirits.

Jasper settled in for his work with a deep breath. His vision wasn't so bad he needed a carer. Honestly, he was a little insulted Gavin had suggested he give Jess—their neighbour—a call and hassle her if he needed something. Besides, it was only up close when things got fuzzy; he could still see the big picture ... so to speak.

He shook the thoughts from his head and picked up his paintbrush. 'No more delays. No more distractions. Just work.' He turned his gaze to his blurry reflection in the mirror, put brush to canvas, and began painting what he saw.

* * *

'I'm home!' Gavin announced. The house was dark, the curtains still drawn over every window. He left them as is, seeing no point in opening them during the twilight hours. The only noise he could hear was some soft classical music emanating from their bedroom at the back of the house. Gavin followed the noise. 'Jasper?'

'I'm in here,' Jasper answered from the bedroom, the faint glow of one of their lampshades poured out of the doorway.

Gavin found Jasper right where he had left him, however, where there was once a blank canvas, now was one filled with paint. From side on, Gavin couldn't get a clear look. 'Have you moved since I left?'

'I haven't soiled myself if that's what you're asking ... and I did have some food earlier. A ham and lettuce sandwich.'

Gavin smiled slightly. 'And what about the portrait? How'd it go?'

'You'll need to be the judge of that.' Jasper pushed his stool away from the canvas, and Gavin moved closer. Jasper looked up at his husband expectantly. Gavin leaned over, hands on Jasper's shoulders as he looked at the painting closely.

One didn't need to stand close to see that while the shape of a portrait was there, the details and features hadn't hit the mark. If Gavin didn't know what it was supposed to be, nor if he wasn't so familiar with the subject, he doubted if he would've recognised who the person in the portrait was. It was definitely human, but the finer details like eyes, nose, smile, even the hair, it was all ... off. The shapes weren't right, they weren't sharp and didn't stand out. It made the face distorted in a rather uncanny way. The border of the canvas was black, which faded lighter and lighter towards the centre before opening into an oval shape for the portrait ... something about it sent shivers up Gavin's spine.

'Well?' Jasper was still looking at Gavin, eyes dimly sparkling with hope.

Gavin squeezed his shoulders, then leaned down and hugged him. 'Oh, my darling ... I'm sorry it's just...' He sighed. He knew Jasper only ever wanted the truth, *especially* when it came to his work. 'It's not good.'

Jasper's heart sank. 'Is that so?...'

Gavin bit his tongue for a moment, but he couldn't stop there. He relayed exactly what was wrong with the painting from his point of view, how unsettling it seemed, and how queasy it made him.

Once he'd heard all the feedback, Jasper said, 'Thank you. I'll do better tomorrow, I have stuff to build off of now. But, how was work?'

'It was good. It's always good. There are plenty of talented young artists out there, and I'm always happy to help guide them down the right path. It's so wonderful nurturing their creativity and seeing it bloom before your very eyes...' Gavin looked at the portrait. 'Maybe...Maybe you could come in and show off some of your older pieces, give some advice to the kids.'

'Thank you, Gavin, but we've talked about this. You're the teacher, I'm the creative. I'm no good at giving advice it just... it's always come so naturally to me. It's like instinct. I'm no good at explaining it to others.'

'Okay, okay. How about I get some dinner on?'

'I'll help. I can still do that much.'

'Hahaha, oh I'm not one to pass up an opportunity where I can boss around a sexy assistant.'

'Mm, yes chef.'

The two laughed and shared a kiss.

* * *

The next day went through much of the same routine. Gavin left for work after making sure Jasper had a fresh canvas and enough paint on hand, then after the work day was finished, he'd come home, and find his love sitting in the same spot; the painting being completed was the only indicator Jasper had moved.

Again, the portrait was misshapen, the details fuzzy, oddly shaped and bent out of order. Whilst Jasper hadn't shown any improvement, he also hadn't gotten worse. Not right away. After a week of this same routine, the latest portrait hardly resembled a human at all. It had lost all shape, and gone beyond even the abstractness of Edvard Munch's "The Scream" to a messy swirl of various colours.

Gavin almost broke down when he saw it. Holding back his tears, he left the room and called Dr Linwood. He reached only the answering machine. He left a message, requesting they call him back as soon as possible to discuss pushing their follow-up appointment forward.

The following day, while at work, the doctor's office called him back. He stepped outside of the classroom and answered.

'Dr Linwood?'

'How can I be of assistance, Mr Longly?'

'I think it'd be for the best if you saw my husband earlier than we agreed. I've seen some worrying signs that his eyesight is getting worse.'

'Can you describe the signs?'

Gavin told her about the paintings and their degrading quality throughout the week.

'How is he around the house? And during his daily life outside of these paintings?'

'What? Uh, well, I've been working most days but... I haven't noticed any problems around the home. He can navigate fine, it's not like he's bumping into things, and typically when he helps me out with cooking he can still find the things I ask for.'

'Perhaps he's experimenting with a new style. Maybe he's leaning into his condition and making things more exaggerated, more abstract, on purpose. As long as his daily life is unaffected, there's no need for concern. We'll keep the original appointment for now, but thank you for bringing up these worries. If it makes you feel better, you should continue to keep an eye on him and if any problems do occur, I'm just a phone call away.'

'But ...' He wanted to tell her that Jasper's painting *was* a part of his daily life. Gavin swallowed his worries. 'Thank you, doctor. I'm probably overreacting.'

'You're just worried, it's a perfectly normal response in situations like this. There's nothing wrong with being concerned for those you love. Enjoy the rest of your afternoon, Mr Longly.'

'Ah, you too, Doctor.' Gavin hung up and after a deep sigh, re-entered his classroom.

Another week passed, and again, the "portraits"—if they could be considered such anymore—continued to deteriorate. The colours became more and more muted, there wasn't any attempt to even create a portrait it seemed, and they grew darker and darker. Then, they were fully black.

During all this, Jasper was still doing okay around the house. Gavin had noticed he was a bit slower, a bit more careful as he moved about and performed tasks, as if he was relying more on memory than sight. Sometimes Gavin found him feeling his way through the corridors but ... he was still functioning; still taking care of himself.

Gavin thought he was fine.

Gavin's worries and anxiety flared when he noticed a strange addition to Jasper's latest painting—which was a swirling, black void—he found two red dots by the top corner. The hairs on the back of his neck stood on end when he saw them, and he didn't know why. Gavin took the canvas from the easel and looked at it more closely, staring at those red dots. He recoiled and quickly set the canvas back in its place. They weren't dots, they were *eyes*. Dark red eyes, like a window straight into hell. Gavin could've sworn the area around them was slightly darker, as if there was a head shrouded in the darkness, the rest of the features unable to be seen in the blackness, but he dared not look again.

'What do you think?' Jasper said, his voice empty as he blankly looked at Gavin.

'Why...Why are you painting this?'

'Do you not like it?'

'I didn't say that. Why are you painting *this*, what happened to your portraits? This is—'

'If you don't like it, you can just say that, Gavin.' Jasper stood up and Gavin stepped back. 'I think I'll order Chinese for dinner tonight.'

Jasper walked out of the room. Gavin stood, speechless.

The following day, Gavin struggled internally. He didn't know if he should call Dr Linwood again and insist the appointment be pushed forward, or if he was overreacting again.

He couldn't focus at all during work and there were multiple instances where he thought about leaving early using some excuse that he wasn't feeling well—truthfully that wasn't a complete lie—but he stuck with it and saw the day to its conclusion.

The painting he found waiting for him tonight, subsided all his fears, however. As usual, Jasper was still on his stool, and another portrait was in front of him, the paint still fresh. It was better than any painting he'd done since they started this routine. The details were crisp, clear, almost lifelike; it was like his paintings of old, the ones Gavin had been enthralled by the moment he saw them. The way they seemed to capture life and hold the world to a standstill was stunning.

Tears formed in Gavin's eyes, there was a flicker of hope that somehow, Jasper was getting better, that his sight was returning. 'Oh, darling... it's beautiful!' He hugged Jasper close, pushing aside his worries about the previous paintings and the descent into blindness they could've represented. Jasper must've been experimenting with a new style, he must've grown bored of the lifelike portraits and was trying something new and strange, that's all. That's what Gavin told himself.

The coming days poked holes in that theory and extinguished the flickering flame of hope Gavin had regarding Jasper's recovery. Jasper's eyesight was getting worse, even as his paintings grew more detailed and picturesque. He'd constantly bump into things, and he couldn't read anything no matter how far away, or how close, he held it. In contrast, his portraits were expanding. He still kept his reflection crystal clear, but now he began to add a background instead of leaving it blank and having all the focus on himself. He started to add the bed, the lamp, and even the back of the canvas in the foreground, so it was as if you were truly looking at him through the mirror while he was painting.

Gavin was confused and his struggle continued. He had no idea how Jasper could be improving so greatly when it came to his art, yet around the house, he was doing worse than ever. No matter how he racked his brain, he couldn't understand it. But their appointment was less than a fortnight away; was there any need to push it forward?

As he chewed on this question, he was moving the latest portrait into the art room, where they'd been storing them until they figured out a more permanent solution—Jasper was adamant about keeping them.

Gavin examined the portrait. Jasper had painted it the day prior. By now the whole bedroom was on display and Jasper himself was just a small part of the foreground. Every detail was perfect, exactly how it was in real life, even down to the crinkles and folds of the bed that now remained unmade behind him for the whole process. Though it was all shrouded in a grey shadow—Jasper now kept the light off while he worked—it was spectacular. Gavin couldn't contain his smile.

As he absorbed every minute detail, Gavin suddenly dropped the painting. He backed away, ice spreading throughout his veins as his heart thumped desperately. He stared in horror at the painting as it lay on the floor, facing upwards.

The eyes were back. They appeared near the top right corner of the painting, as if they were peering in from the doorway ... and worse than that, the head around them was clearly defined. Those eyes belonged to a countenance that could only be described as horrific, monstrous ... *demonic*. Even as it was hiding in the deepest blacks of the painting, Gavin could see every last unnatural detail of that terrible thing.

Gavin shuddered and turned away. Then he stopped. With overwhelming dread, he turned to lay his eyes upon the stack of paintings. He slowly approached them—he didn't want to, but he *had* to. Each step was as if he was walking through rapidly solidifying concrete. He reached the pile and even though his eyes were frantically trying to run away from his head, he forced them to look upon the painting at the top of the pile.

He was immediately drawn to the dark, upper right corner. His heart tried to leap from his body. The eyes were there, that face, that *thing* was there, staring at him. He shoved the painting aside and looked at the one underneath. Again! The eyes were staring. Again, again, again. It was *always* there.

Gavin shrieked and shoved the rest of the pile to the floor before he sat back against the wall, head in his hands.

Jasper appeared in the doorway. 'What's wrong?'

Gavin stared up at him, his whole body shaking with every panicked breath. He pushed himself up and stormed past Jasper without responding. He went straight to their bedroom to see the current painting Jasper was working on. It was finished, but Gavin didn't care about anything else in the painting aside from the doorway.

He fell onto the bed when he saw it. The inhumane face was even clearer and larger than ever, and not only that, but now the shadowy thing had a shape, a more defined figure, a mass of black that Gavin feared was its vile, monstrous body standing in the doorway, taking up most of the space.

'Gavin?'

Gavin gasped loudly, his head spun to the doorway. But it was only Jasper standing there—*only* Jasper. A cold sweat trickled down Gavin's body.

'Are you alright?' Jasper asked.

Gavin gulped. 'Just fine,' he lied. 'What about you? How are you feeling?'

Jasper smiled. 'I'm perfectly fine. Well ... as fine as I can be, all things considered.'

'Then... w-would you like to explain your paintings?'

'What about them?'

'What the hell is that? In the corner.' Gavin pointed a shaky finger at the canvas.

'What are you talking about?'

'C-Can't you *see* it? You painted it! That thing! The thing in the top right corner.'

Jasper strode over to the painting and leaned down to inspect it more closely, he felt the top right corner, some of the black coming off on his fingers. He looked back at the doorway in the corner of the room, Gavin slowly turned his head in that direction as well, expecting to see the thing looming over them, but there was nothing, no matter how hard he peered through the shadows, they were just that—shadows.

'There's nothing there, dear, just shadows,' Jasper said.

'R-Right... just shadows.'

'Are you sure you're okay?'

'Yes I'm...I'm fine.' Gavin pushed himself up and started towards the doorway, hesitating as he neared those shadows. He didn't dare look away from them as he addressed Jasper again. 'I-I'll get started on dinner... you just relax. I'll take care of everything tonight.'

'Aww, how sweet. Thank you, dear.'

Gavin practically leapt through the doorway and hurried to the kitchen, pulling his phone out as he rapidly dialled Dr Linwood's number.

She answered after a few rings. 'Hel—'

'Dr Linwood! Please, it's Gavin Longly, my husband, he's gotten worse. I'm seriously worried about his condition. We *have* to reschedule for an earlier date, as soon as possible, please.'

'Okay, I hear you, please try to keep calm, Mr Longly. Can you describe what's been happening? I'll fit your appointment into my schedule as early as possible.'

'It's... well he's been getting worse throughout the house. He can't read anything or even differentiate labels. He's bumping into things. B-But it's more than just that... I can't explain it right now, but when I see you I can. Please, I'll even pay anything if you have to move other appointments around.'

'That won't be necessary, Mr Longly. It's going to be okay.' She sighed heavily. 'Honestly, examining the results of your husband's previous tests, it's inevitable that he'll lose over ninety percent of his sight. Unfortunately, there isn't anything we can do. I suggest learning brail, and I can point you towards the proper facilities to purchase walking sticks. I'll even fill out a form to request a guide dog if you'd like.'

'But—'

'I'm sorry, Mr Longly. My schedule is incredibly tight at the moment. I'll have to see what I can do about moving appointments around, but I'll need to get back to you when I've made those changes. Maybe take a few days off work and help him around the home for the time being. Goodnight.'

'Dr Linwo—' the line went dead as she hung up.

Gavin stared at the phone in disbelief, his jaw still hanging open, his words falling out soundlessly.

'Is something the matter?'

Gavin jumped at the sound of Jasper's voice. He turned and looked at him standing just outside of the kitchen. Jasper wasn't looking at anything in particular, just, staring.

'I keep telling you, I'm fine. Now, go and sit down.'

'I was just making sure. I didn't hear any sounds of cooking, so I was a little confused, that's all.' Jasper raised his hands submissively and backed away. He fumbled his way to the living room and felt around for the remote.

Gavin watched him for a moment before turning to the stove. He stared at it, but he had no idea what to cook; his mind could only focus on one thing. He hurried over to Jasper. 'You need to stop painting.'

'Pardon?' Jasper laughed and looked up at him with a bemused smile.

'You heard me. I think you should stop painting. Or at least give these portraits a rest.'

'Why?'

'Well... because... they're as good as they're going to get. You've clearly got your rhythm back, you don't need to do them anymore. Now you can go back and finish the view of the mountains from our honeymoon suite which is sitting there, collecting dust.'

'I could. But I like these portraits. I want to paint them. They're therapeutic. Are you *sure* you're alright?'

'Yes! Bloody hell I'm fine! You're the one who... ugh!' Gavin stormed off. 'I'm ordering Chinese!' he shouted.

* * *

Gavin took Dr Linwood's advice to stay home from work ... but he didn't tell Jasper. The morning went as usual, he set up a fresh canvas for Jasper, he made sure Jasper had plenty of paint on his palette, and then, after a kiss on the cheek, Gavin left the room to "head to work." Only, after he walked through the house and opened the front door, he closed it without leaving. He slipped off his shoes, then, silently, and very carefully, he tiptoed towards the bedroom. He stopped at the doorway and poked his head in, observing Jasper as he worked.

Jasper didn't react after Gavin looked in. He seemingly hadn't heard Gavin creep through the house, nor seen his head poking into the room in the mirror's reflection. He continued painting as if nothing had happened.

There was no noise except for the soft, wet strokes of the brush against the canvas. Jasper didn't listen to music today, nor could Gavin remember the last time he'd arrived home to hear music coming from their bedroom. Jasper didn't hum or say anything to himself, he hardly even breathed while he worked, his focus was on nothing but his art. Eerily, his gaze was locked on the mirror, and for as long as Gavin stood there, watching the whole process unfold, Jasper never turned his eyes away from his reflection. As Gavin watched, his breathing became so shallow and light, that one could've thought he was dead on his feet. He was a statue whilst he watched for hours upon hours as the next painting came to life under Jasper's masterful strokes.

Gavin's horror grew as he watched it unfold. Without watching what he was doing, Jasper perfectly recreated the environment surrounding him. Though Gavin was far away, he knew it was a flawless masterpiece. When the painting was seemingly done, Jasper started adding more shadows to everything. He cast the already dim room into an even blacker darkness. When that was finished, he brought light back into his creation as he added swirling, dark flames within the shadows. The innocent recreation of their bedroom turned into a hellish mockery as the painting was wreathed in flame and shadow.

Gavin couldn't stand it. He burst into the room. 'What is the meaning of this?!'

Jasper froze mid-stroke, then slowly pulled his brush back. He overcame his shock quickly. When he spoke, his voice was calm and level and showed no signs of anger or confusion regarding Gavin's trickery. He said: 'I didn't hear you arrive. Welcome home, dear.'

'Don't give me that. What are you painting this time why are you...' Gavin was startled when he inspected the painting more closely. 'Wh-What kind of sick joke is this...' Even though it was the most sickening painting yet, Gavin couldn't help but reach out and snatch the canvas from the easel. He couldn't believe his eyes; he had to confirm what he was seeing. He brought it close to his face, his breath quickening the drying process as he stared, unable to tear his eyes away from the terrible sight.

'Why? Why are you painting this? This...This sick *thing*. What is this even supposed to be? I don't quite like this joke or being made a fool of Jasper, so you best answer me at once and answer me clearly! What the fuck is this?!'

Jasper tilted his head, not understanding why Gavin was being so emotional, or why he was even confused. 'You ask me why and what I am painting? Well, that's a simple answer, my love—I'm painting what I can see.'

Gavin's words failed him. His mouth opened and closed soundlessly. His dread was realised, and it was worse than he could've imagined. His trembling hands couldn't loosen their grip on the painting. His face was devoid of colour and his heart felt as if it would burst at any moment. His irises and pupils shrunk to almost nothingness; his bloodshot eyes were wider than they'd ever been.

The painting was a perfect recreation of their room, yes, even with all the shadows and the flames, it was still *their* room, exactly as it had been whilst Jasper was painting. It had *every* last detail. It even had a visage of Gavin, peering around the doorway. But what caused Gavin's great distress were the two red dots looming above his head and the terrible, black shape towering over him in the doorway. The horrifying countenance of this monster was stretched unnaturally wide. It was prepared to devour him right where he stood.

Tickets?

'What do you mean you don't have the tickets? You were supposed to get them *weeks* ago, Keith.'

'Look, it's not that big of a deal, alright. So what I didn't get any of them online? We'll just go to the show, and they'll have tickets there.'

Keith looked around at his friends, they didn't have a lot of faith in his idea, but there wasn't much else they could do.

Keith, Vincent, Eliza, and Jeremy had been friends since primary school, and since Vincent's—the youngest's—eighteenth, they've always gone to the local music festival, Mooving the Groove, *every. year.* From their times wearing ripped jeans, coloured hair, and enough piercings to make magnets a real concern, now to their button-up shirts, khaki pants, and covered-up tattoos, they hadn't missed a show for over ten years. None of them had any intentions to start ... which they should've thought about before leaving Keith in charge of getting the tickets.

Currently, the friends were in Keith's flat, having met up before Mooving started, so they could catch up over coffee.

'This is the *one* thing we can rely on. Every year we do this,' Eliza said.

'Yeah, and I'm not about to miss Mooving cause you fucked up, Keith,' Vincent said.

'Alright, calm down Vinny. Fuck me for making a mistake. I already apologised. Anyway, you're not gonna miss out, I'm telling ya, it's gonna be fine.'

The friend group piled into Eliza's minivan and hurried to the festival, wanting to sort this mess out as quickly as possible. Thankfully, it wasn't a long drive to reach the local showgrounds where the festival was held. Despite being early, the group saw the parking lot opposite the showgrounds was nearly full. Whilst they hoped there would still be *some* tickets available, the massive "Sold Out" sign above the entry booth, said otherwise.

Keith didn't say anything as they pulled into the car park and found a space. He was racking his brain trying to come up with a way to avoid his friends murdering him.

'You've really gone and done it now, mate.'

'Thank you, Jeremy. Very helpful, mate.'

'And what have you done with our money? Seeing as you didn't buy the fucking tickets with it,' Vincent asked.

'Alright I might be an asshat, but I'm not a thief, I've still got your money.' Keith flashed his wallet. 'I can give it back to you right now if you want. That is only if you don't want me to still buy your ticket with it.'

'And how the fuck are you going to do that? Can't you read? They're sold out.'

Keith grinned. 'Ahh, yes, but there are always those who buy tickets just to sell them off at a slightly higher price.'

'Scalpers, that's your solution?' Eliza said.

'Do you have a better one?'

The others looked at each other but said nothing.

Having not found any scalpers in the car park, the group trudged across the short, arching bridge to the showgrounds.

'I am *not* paying extra for scalped tickets,' Jeremy said.

'Yeah, this is all coming out of your pocket, Keith,' Vincent added.

'I wouldn't have expected anything else, guys. But, when I get you these tickets, will you stop fucking complaining?'

Standing atop the bridge offered a perfect view into the festival grounds, not that the wire fence obscured much. The stage was huge and extravagant, plenty of shelter had been set up, each performer had a stall where you could buy their merch, and there were a few drinks stations sprinkled throughout. Even though things were just getting warmed up, the place was swarming with people. The weather was amazing too, it wasn't overcast or windy, but there was still enough cloud coverage on this sweet spring day that the sun wouldn't become overbearing.

Seeing the grounds only made the group's anger towards Keith and his fuck up even greater.

'How are you even going to find a scalper?' Eliza asked.

Keith shrugged. 'Just ask around, I guess. And look for someone shady.'

Vincent rolled his eyes. 'Great.'

After they stepped off the bridge, Keith started walking in the direction opposite the ticket booth and began asking each person they passed if they were willing to sell their tickets. Meanwhile, the rest of his friends were trying their best to act like they didn't know him even while following him—at a reasonable distance.

Luckily, it didn't take long to find a scalper. They were leaning against the fence, smoking a cigarette. Everything from their sleeves of tattoos, their dark, baggy clothes, and the thick brown stubble covering their jaw and neck screamed "shady". 'Just the four of ya?' the scalper said, stamping out their cigarette.

'Yep, how much?' Keith said. He was the only one of the group who had stepped up to greet the man.

'Mmm ... two-fifty.'

'What? The bloody tickets are a hundred bucks normally.'

The scalper shrugged. 'Should've bought those tickets then.'

Keith felt eyes boring into the back of his head. 'Look, can't we just say, five hundred for us all, that's fair, ain't it?'

'Not even close, brother. One thousand. Take it or leave it.'

'Fine, I'll just find someone else selling tickets, I'm sure they'll be happy to take the money. You're the one missing out.'

The scalper laughed. 'Yeah, good luck with that.'

Keith stomped off, huffing. His friends awkwardly hurried after him, not making eye contact with the scalper.

Tickets?

Unfortunately, they didn't find anyone else offering tickets.

'I'm not fucking paying one grand for some tickets, especially not to that asshole. I don't even have that much on me,' Keith said.

'No chance he'd take an IOU?' Eliza said, but she was the only one who chuckled at her "joke".

'What are we gonna do? I think we're out of options here,' Jeremy said.

'We never should've left this cunt in charge of things. I say we don't even bring him next year,' Vincent said.

'Alright, Vinny, tell us how you really feel. There's no need to give up hope just yet, there's still other ways.'

'And what's your next genius idea, dickhead?'

Keith looked away, needing a moment to think. A grin slowly spread across his face. 'I know what we'll do.' He marched towards the ticket booth.

'What?' Eliza hurried after him. The boys eventually tagged along.

'Simple. We'll tell them we've lost our tickets.'

The boys stopped in their tracks. '*That's* your big idea?' Jeremy said.

Keith looked back at him, still marching onward. 'Have you got a better one?'

Jeremy and Vincent exchanged looks. They both wondered which terrible choice in their life caused them to end up following an idiot like Keith. But no one offered another idea, so the group soon found themselves lined up at the ticket booth.

'Tickets, please,' the collector said. Her ticket puncher was at the ready, her gloved hand squeezed the contraption and set it off in anticipation. *Clack.*

Keith was a little put off by how the woman's smile seemed to consume her entire face, but he stepped up to the booth and leaned close to the open window anyway. 'Uhh, about that, I was hoping you could help us out, uh, ma'am. See, my friends and I, somehow, we must've misplaced our tickets, and now we don't know what to do?'

'No tickets?' the collector's smile lessened.

'Uhh, no, we lost them. But we did have them, we just lost them, though if you could let us in—'

Her smile vanished. 'No ticket, no entry.' Her dull, grey eyes stared through Keith.

'R-Right... of course.' Keith backed away and turned to his friends, retreating with them.

'Well that was a brilliant idea, *how* didn't it work? I'm shocked!' Vincent said.

'Shut up, will you? It was worth a shot, wasn't it? Anyway, did you see that lady in the booth?' Keith didn't dare look over his shoulder.

'Yeah, she was ... weird. I don't know what it was, but just looking at her—' Eliza shuddered. '—gave me the chills.'

'Her smile *was* kinda weird.' Jeremy said. '...Still doesn't take away from how dumb your plan was.'

'Yes I heard you the first time ... but, lucky for you, I've got one last idea that's fool-proof.'

'Well it better be if *you're* the one coming up with it,' Vincent said.

Eliza groaned. 'Maybe we should just call it quits this year, it's not the end of the world.'

'Nah nah, we don't need to give up, trust me, this one *can't* fail. Honestly, I should've led with this, I don't know why it took me so long to remember.'

Even despite Keith's repeated failings, he sure was talking this idea up a lot; the others began to believe he had a miracle plan.

'What now?' Jeremy said.

Keith grinned like his idea was worth a million bucks. 'We jump the fence.'

Their eyes slowly turned from Keith to the fence. It wasn't high, around four metres they guesstimated; there wasn't any barbed wire at the top, it was just the showgrounds, not a prison; and there were some decent grassy patches amongst the dirt, evidently the groundskeeper didn't care too much about keeping it neat near the outskirts.

'You know what. I think that's the only smart thing you've said all day. Took you long enough,' Vincent said and gave Keith a pat on the shoulder.

'I mean, we're the stupid ones to not think of that right away. Just jump the fence, I bet tons of people do it every year,' Eliza said.

Tickets?

'Shit, and we better do it quick, I think they're starting,' Jeremy said.

Music flew out from the stage. Even from the sidewalk, they heard the opening act begin and the festivities kick off crystal clear. Hearing it wasn't enough, they needed to be *in there*, amongst the crowd, soaking in that electric atmosphere.

'We better fucking hurry then, come on, down this way, no one will see,' Keith said before leading them away from the entrance.

The group returned to where they had met the smoking scalper. He wasn't there anymore.

The first song was wrapping up and transitioning into the next. Keith gestured to the fence, smiling at Eliza. 'Ladies first.'

She giggled and grabbed on. Vincent rolled his eyes and started climbing beside her, soon Jeremy was scaling the fence too.

'Such undignified brutes,' Keith scoffed.

Eliza giggled more. After Keith boosted her up, he started climbing as well. The first three clambered over at roughly the same time. When they landed, they froze.

'Watch out,' Keith said, coming down after them. They didn't move.

'Keith...? Something's wrong.' Eliza looked up at him, eyes full of confused terror.

'The hell are you talking—' He jumped down in front of her and the world vanished. A new one replaced it as quickly as it had disappeared. This one was just ... *wrong*. '... about.'

They looked around. Everything was the "same", they were still in the showgrounds; they could still hear the music—even if it sounded like the speakers were underwater, slowed down, everything was out of tune, and it was reversed—but it was *different* too. Everything was covered in a purple haze and wobbly. The ground, which had been perfectly flat, was now bumpy and hilly, with no grass at all, only rocks and dirt. Even the clouds were twisted into dark spirals, like mini cyclones. The nearest tent was now shaped like a snail's shell. And the fence had transformed from a simple wire mesh to a gnarled, and twisted thing. Forget the absence of barbed wire across the top, now it was made from the stuff. Looking closely, bits of skin were clinging to the razor-sharp barbs, but most worryingly of all, it was so tall it disappeared into the sky. Despite the nightmarish landscape and alterations, the world outside the fence hadn't changed one bit, it was still a peaceful, perfect day, and cars continued driving past.

'What the *fuck* is going on?' Eliza said.

'What the hell is this shit?' Jermey said.

'Is this some kind of sick joke, Keith?!' Vincent asked, getting in Keith's face.

'Don't look at me! I don't know what the fuck is going on. How could I even do something like this? This is... we just... its... I don't know what the fuck it is! But ... let's just find somebody, okay? There's gotta be someone around here, they can, they'll explain.'

'Explain *what*?! We're in some kind of fucking ... some fucking hell or shit, *God*! I hope we're in hell cause I really wanna kill you right now, Keith.'

'How the fuck is this *my* fault, Vinny?'

'If you had just bought the damn tickets when you were supposed to none of this would've fucking happened!'

'Jeremy, I swear, if you spiked our drinks... oh god please tell me you spiked us!' Eliza paced back and forth.

'Liza, as much as I'd like to say yes, I didn't spike your shit, and that was *one* fucking time ... and trips don't look like... *this*.'

Keith ignored Vincent's shouting long enough to formulate a new plan. The snap of his fingers attracted the group's attention. 'The ticket booth. We go to the ticket booth, that lady will be there, she'll know what's going on, she'll help us. This is... just, smoke, or an optical illusion, part of the show, it has to be. What else could it be?'

'The fence was electrified and we all died?' Jeremy suggested.

Keith was already walking away. Eliza, Jeremy, and even Vincent followed him.

They walked with urgency and soon the booth was in sight. It looked normal enough on the outside, maybe a bit bigger than they remembered, and with a pointier roof, but it was completely normal compared to the rest of the strange, topsy-turvy surroundings. However, black metal spikes barred the gates. Eliza expressed her newfound doubt in the idea, but Keith pressed on, undeterred by the developments. Keith marched up to the side window and knocked on the wall beside it to grab The Collector's attention.

The Collector turned their head; the rest of their body remained perfectly still. They looked at Keith and his friends as if they were a newly discovered species. Distressingly, the front window of the booth was blocked up with concrete, despite that, before Keith's knock, The Collector had been acting as if they were dealing with another festival-goer.

'Uhh, hey, can you explain what's—'

'Tickets?' The Collector interrupted.

Clack

They had that same, all-consuming smile.

'What? No, no we're not here to buy tickets we—'

'No. No buy.' *Clack.* 'Where tickets?' *Clack.* The smile faded. 'Inside.' *Clack.* 'Need tickets inside.' *Clack.* 'Where tickets?' *Clack.*

'Uhh...' Keith backed off as the clacking continued.

'If inside, need ticket. If no ticket, can't be inside. Why inside? Where tickets?' They continued to punch holes into nothing, squeezing the device like it was a stress ball.

Vincent walked up to the window, slamming his hand down on its sill. 'Listen you crazy bitch, what the hell is going on here? You better start explaining right fucking now.'

The Collector stared at Vincent's hand, the whites of their eyes darkened to that same, lifeless grey. 'Ticket?' The Collector punched a hole through Vincent's hand.

He screamed and fell back, grasping his injured hand as blood squirted from the perfectly round hole through his hand. 'Wh-What the fuck?! You fucking psycho what the fuck do you think—'

The friends watched, stricken with fear, as The Collector stood from their seat and raised to their full height, a height that was beyond humanly possible. They stretched taller, the booth and its little window stretched with them to encapsulate their gigantic form. As their body grew, it was as if their skin stayed the same size, and the result gave them a gaunt, almost transparent look, as if their skin would rip right off. They were gangly and crooked. Their bones bent out of shape as they made rigid bumps along their skin. Their lips were dragged away from their smile, revealing a toothless grin.

'Tickets?' The clack of their hole puncher sprung the friends into motion again. Eliza shrieked as she led the pack in their flight away from The Collector.

The Collector's long, scythe-like arm snatched Vincent's ankle. They squeezed through the window.

'*Helllllp!*' Vincent cried. Keith and Jeremy looked back. They watched Vincent hopelessly flail at The Collector as they brought him up to their face. 'Get the fuck off me!'

'Tickets?' Even their hole puncher had grown. They jammed it around Vincent's torso and squeezed tight, punching a hole right through the side of his stomach, blood burst forth like juice from a squished grape. Vincent writhed in agony, stuck in their grasp, he looked back to his friends and watched them leave him behind.

Keith dragged Jeremy along, chasing after Eliza who hadn't stopped running. 'We can't help him! We gotta get the fuck outta here!' Keith shouted, trying to convince himself rather than Jeremy.

Screams punctuated each new gaping wound that was punched into Vincent's body. When Jeremey looked back, he saw half a dozen holes, all along Vincent's body, blood pouring from them like a fully powered faucet. The Collector muttered "tickets" over and over as they continued their search. They brought their hole puncher to Vincent's head.

He felt the metal graze his pupil. '*Wait wait wait! No no no! Noooo—!*'

His screams were silenced as a crater was smashed into his skull where his eye used to be.

Once he stopped squirming and thrashing, The Collector dropped him. Their head turned to Jeremy and Keith. 'Tickets?' *Clack.*

Jeremy almost tripped as he sped after Eliza.

The boys caught Eliza when she was stopped by the fence. She'd run across the entire showgrounds, and was now at the side fence. She crashed against it. Clinging to the sharp wire she shook it in a half-hearted attempt to tear it down, even as the wire cut into her palms. '*Heeeeeeellllp!*' she squealed.

Keith placed a hand on her back. 'Eliza! Calm down, fuck, we gotta... shit!' He looked around, panting heavily. He couldn't see The Collector, but he had heard the clacking of her hole puncher chasing after them while they were running.

'Heeeellllppp! Pleeeeeasse!' Eliza sobbed, slowly letting the fence go as she dropped to the floor. Her hands spread her blood through her hair as her tears rained on the dirt.

'There's gotta be a way out. It can't go on forever. This is, it's fake, this is all fake. Just a trick,' Jeremy said as he stared at the sky. He grabbed a firm hold of the fence then pulled himself up. He winced every time he dragged himself higher.

'Jeremy! Get down from there, you idiot, you're gonna get yourself fucking killed. ... Shit!' Keith looked around, pacing in a circle. On the other side of the fence was a dirt path that ran alongside the showgrounds. Then it was just trees as far as he could see. Maybe, someone was out there. He cupped his hands around his mouth. '*Heeeeeeeeey*! Can somebody hear me!? We need help!'

In between sobs, Eliza joined Keith in calling for help, and like a blessing from god, a couple showed up, wandering from the main road, bewildered by the shouting.

The young man and woman held hands as they cautiously approached the group. 'H-Hello? What's the matter?' the woman said, she looked concerned, eyes darting between the three, whilst the man looked spooked, trying to pull her away.

Eliza sprung to her feet, fresh tears pouring down her face. 'Ohhh thank god! Please, please you have to help us! We're stuck in here and the ticket lady turned into a monster and is trying to kill us! She killed Vinnyyy!' she broke down into sobs.

'Please! Call the cops, there's some fucking monster in here killing people, and we're trapped inside, this fence goes on forever!' Keith pleaded with them, speaking over the top of Eliza.

'Hey!' Jeremy shouted. He'd already climbed twice the normal height of the fence. 'Thank fuck! Please, you've gotta help us! We don't know what the fuck happened but this place is fucked up.'

The woman covered her mouth, tearing up as she looked at the group. 'O-Okay, I-I'll call help.' But as she reached for her phone, the man tore her away from the fence.

'Don't! Let's get out of here and leave these junkies alone. They're just freaking out over nothing,' he said.

'Wh-What!? No no no, we're not on drugs!' The group continued to plead and cry with the couple.

The woman was pulled further away. 'B-But Deion, look at them. They're so scared and they're bleeding, can't we call an ambulance for them?'

'We're already late! And then you want us to sit here and babysit some druggies who are off their head? Fuck that. It's a festival, babe, this shit happens. Just ignore them, it's only a bad trip, nothing'll happen. Come on!'

'B-But...'

Deion dragged her back down the path, stomping away from the group.

'Nononono, *please!*' Eliza begged, following the couple.

The woman looked back at Eliza, met her eyes, and then turned away. The couple hurried away faster. Eliza fell to her knees.

'Fuck you assholes! I hope you fucking die!' Keith screamed and kicked the fence.

'Tickets?'

Keith's heart started beating so fast it was like it had stopped. He turned his head and saw The Collector standing ten metres away, just out of her arm's reach. She had a gaping grin. Blood dripped from her hole puncher after every *clack*.

He bolted to Eliza and yanked her onto her feet. '*Run!*' He pulled her along, giving her no choice in the matter as they fled again.

The Collector watched them go, then her eyes crawled to the shaking fence. She dragged her gaze up to Jeremy who was ten metres in the air and still scrambling higher. 'There's gotta be a top, there's gotta be a top. It can't go on forever,' he muttered to himself.

The fence sagged and rattled, shaking like a spider's web. Jeremy looked down and pissed himself as he saw The Collector scuttling after him, undeterred by the yellow stream dribbling out of Jeremy's pants.

Jeremy climbed as fast as he could, ignoring the stinging pain in his hands as the wire cut deeper and deeper. But still, he wasn't fast enough.

Tickets?

'Ticket?' The Collector said before she punched a hole right through Jeremy's ankle.

'Aarghhh!' Jeremy screamed. He tried to pull himself higher but his legs fell limp in the air after The Collector took out his second ankle. He clung on desperately. He was so pale he was almost translucent when The Collector appeared beside him, Her grin turning to a frown.

'No ticket? ...' She looked at his nearest hand. 'Ticket?' A hole stabbed his hand and even cut through a link of the fence.

His hand fell away with another cry of pain. He weakly swiped at her but could do nothing to stop her as she brought the hole puncher over to his other hand.

Clack.

They were fifteen metres high. Jeremy screamed until he splatted against the ground.

Keith and Eliza had circled back, going away from the main road, and instead towards the stage and the sound of the distorted music. 'There has to be other people in here,' Keith said. 'They can help.'

'What the fuck is happening?' Eliza cried as she stumbled behind Keith. 'Why didn't they help us?'

'Forget them!' Kieth pulled her around in front of him, gripping her shoulders tightly. 'Focus, Liza, we need to get out of here. We need to *survive.*' He urged her towards the music, though as the swarming crowd of people came into sight, he hesitated and slowed down. Something was off.

The stage was empty despite music blaring from its speakers, and the people, they weren't distorted like everything else ... but, they were cold and strange. They swayed to the music, almost in unison, but that's all they did, back and forth they tottered, like buoys.

'Keith? I don't like this... w-we should go back to the booth, we can leave there, can't we? Let's just leave!'

Keith ignored Eliza and pressed forward. He grabbed the nearest person's shoulder. 'H-Hey buddy can you he—' Keith almost fell on his ass when they turned around.

Their skin was perfectly smooth and grey where their face should've been. They had no eyes, no mouth, no nose, nothing.

'You're not supposed to be here,' the blank-faced ghoul "said". Their "face" hadn't moved a muscle, but the voice came out as clearly as if they had spoken right into Keith's ear.

Keith backed up. Eliza screamed and he whirled around. He expected The Collector, but came face to blank face with more ghouls who had surrounded them. He wasn't sure if this was any better. Somehow, they were in the middle of the crowd, and every ghoul was "looking" at them.

'You're not supposed to be here,' they chanted. It was a wall of noise as the same monotonous voice spoke a thousand times at once, even the music started to morph and change into something that sounded like the chant.

Eliza and Keith covered their ears, cowering before the sea of ghouls that pressed in around them. Keith gasped, feeling the air grow lighter and colder as the lifeless, dense bodies closed in. He grabbed Eliza by the hand and started to drag her through the crowd. She followed close behind him, repeatedly muttering, 'I wanna go home,' as they went.

Then she screamed again. She was wrenched from Keith's grasp. He looked back and saw Eliza flung into the air, waving about like a flag as The Collector drew her up high.

Clack!

Eliza screamed and blood splashed down upon the faceless ghouls, turning them from grey to crimson. Keith turned away, forcing his way through the crowd frantically. The screams and clacks both faded into the distance.

Keith burst free from the crowd and almost tumbled over. His hands scratched against the dirt and gravel as he pushed himself into a standing position and kept running. He had one destination in mind—the ticket booth, or more importantly, the gate it was connected to. Even if it was blocked up, there had to be a way to get through. Maybe it was an illusion, maybe there was a button in the booth that could open the gate, it was the only idea he had.

He couldn't hear The Collector behind him, but it didn't matter, he didn't slow down or think he was safe. He dodged around leaning tents and soon the booth was in sight. He gained a burst of speed when he saw it, and another when he heard the faint, echoing voice of The Collector behind him, saying: 'Ticket?'

He dove through the booth window, which looked smaller and narrower than ever. He got caught on the counter and had to squeeze through, struggling like a worm.

'Ticket?' The Collector's icy hand gripped his leg and pain shot through his calf. He bit back his scream and wrenched himself free, collapsing to the ground inside the booth. The Collector's face peered into the room as Keith scrambled away from the window and looked for *anything* of use; something to fend off The Collector with, or a way to open the gates and unblock the front window. He ducked away from The Collector's swiping arm as it flailed inside the booth. 'Ticket? Ticket?! *Ticket*?!' The hand retreated and The Collector gripped the top and bottom of the window, stretching it apart. Once again the booth grew. Keith heard The Collector climb into the room, felt their hand on his leg again. He clawed at the floor as he was dragged into the air. He spotted something white against the grainy green carpet and snatched it up. It was a wrinkled slip of paper, a hole already punched through it. It was a ticket!

'Ticket?' He felt the hole puncher against his thigh.

'*Wait*! I have a ticket!' He shoved his fist out, the ticket crushed in his grip. The Collector's eyes snapped to the slip of paper, and they dropped Keith. Landing on his head dazed him. He slowly sat up and watched The Collector inspect the ticket, their eyes widening as they smoothed the paper and held it close to their face.

Keith couldn't help but smile as he caught his breath. He'd been saved.

'Not ... your ... ticket.'

His smile shattered. They crumbled the slip of paper in their ghastly hand, their eyes darkened. Their ticket puncher gleamed in Keith's eyes as they swooped in.

'Wait wait wait, *waaaiit*!' Keith's back pressed against the wall. He raised a hand in front of his face.

Clack!

M.P. Seipolt

The Hunt

The beat-up, old truck rattles along the bumpy dirt road. Young Wayne looks forlorn out the window at the trees as they rapidly pass by; he can't recall how long ago the smooth tarmac changed into this mess of dirt and rock.

The radio is barely audible over the chatter of the other occupants. His uncle, Dan, and dad, Leo, sit up front. Both of them have a can of beer already cracked open. Occasionally, Dan's son, Jordan, pesters the two men for a sip. Jordan's almost fully out of his seat, leaning more into the front of the cabin as he listens to Leo and Dan share their stories of first hunting trips, first kills, and other shenanigans.

'What's the biggest thing you've ever shot, pa?' Jordan asks.

'It'd have to be that moose we killed up in Ontario, right Leo?' He turns to look at his brother.

Leo has one hand on the wheel, the other cupping his can as he's nursing his beer. 'I can't think of anything else that could've been bigger. Damn things were bigger than horses.'

Dan nods. 'Hey, wasn't it durin' that same Canada trip, where I heard you pissin' outside the tent at night and thought a damn bear was out to get us?'

Leo laughs and grins. 'Oh man, you were spooked as bad as I've ever seen. Came out jumping, waving your damn rifle about. I almost sprayed my piss on *you*.'

The two share a laugh, while Wayne scrunches up his face. Blocking the noise out is proving to be impossible. Jordan's elbow jutting into him every time they hit one of the bumps along the road, isn't helping matters. *Surely we're nearly there.*

'How much longer until we get there?' he asks his dad.

Leo turns his head. 'Twenty minutes, give or take a few. Why? You need to piss now?'

'No. Was just asking.'

'Well I do,' Dan says. 'Pull over, would ya?'

Leo pulls over and stops the car. Dan hops out, and ambles over to the nearest tree to relieve himself.

Trees. It had been nothing but a sea of trees that stretched on as far as Wayne could see for hours and hours.

Birds scatter from the treetops, taking to the skies before rushing towards the car. They capture the attention of all the car's occupants, and even Dan as he leans back, head swivelling to follow their flight over the car and then back down the road, the exact way the fathers and their sons had come from. Dan finishes up, but instead of returning to the car, he steps around the tree, peering further through the woodline, at something deeper inside the forest.

'What's he doing now?' Leo beeps the horn, startling Dan. Dan quickly returns, slamming the door as he sits down.

'Geez, don't get Yer panties in a bunch,' Dan says.

'What the hell were you looking at, anyway?'

Dan shrugs. 'I don't know, just felt like there was somethin' out there.'

'There's probably a million things out there, it's a damn forest.'

As they start driving off again, both Jordan and Wayne look out the right-side window, heads side by side as they peer through the trees as best they can. 'I don't see nothin',' Jordan says.

Wayne can't see anything either, but he a knot festers in his gut. He feels something watching them.

The drive doesn't continue much longer after that. They turn off the dirt road and head further into the trees on an even less defined path. Shortly, they pull up before the wood cabin they'll be spending the week at.

The cabin looks small, and feels even smaller. There are only two bedrooms, one obviously intended as the master bedroom for the parental couple with a single king-sized bed, and the other for the children with bunk beds. Wayne drags his bag inside the room, staring at the beds.

Jordan pushes past him and dumps his own bag on the floor. 'Shotgun the top bunk.' He throws himself up onto it before Wayne can even object.

Wayne frowns slightly but places his bag on the bottom bunk. 'Fine. It's not like I care.'

The cabin's walls are rather thin, and they can hear their dads in a small argument about who gets the other bedroom. Apart from the two bedrooms, there's a small bathroom, and the main room is open-planned, a mixture of a kitchen and a sitting room, with a large couch and a grand fireplace. Plenty of trophies are strewn over the mantle and along the walls. Wayne isn't certain if the trophies are real or fake.

Leo's voice comes through the walls. 'I should get the bed because I'm the oldest.'

'Bullshit,' Dan answers, 'I always had to give you everythin' when we were kids, it's my time to enjoy some privileges for once.'

There's a pause, then Leo speaks again. 'Alright. Rock, paper, scissors, how about that?'

'You're on.'

Again, neither boy hears anything for a few moments before Dan suddenly curses. It seems the little brother would still have to settle for the couch this time.

It isn't long after the game of rock, paper, scissors that the four hear another car pulling up outside of the cabin. While they are still in the process of getting set up, everyone stops and turns towards their doors, unsure if their ears were playing tricks on them or not. A short and sharp knock at the door, told them they were not.

Dan moves first, being the closest, he's the one to answer the door. A uniformed Ranger stands outside.

'Howdy,' the Ranger says.

'Evenin',' Dan replies.

The boys emerge from their room, staying back as they look past Dan and watch the proceedings. Leo steps up beside his brother. 'What can we do for you tonight, sir?'

'Oh, there isn't anything that I need from you folks. I was just checking in to make sure that you've made it all right and that you're getting settled in without any issues.'

'We are,' Leo says.

'That's good. There was one other reason for my visit tonight. I needed to ask you if you'd heard anything about the recent trouble we've been having with a wild boar. It's a rather nasty beast this one, been terrorising the wildlife and raiding some camp sites.'

'Hell yeah. Heard y'all needed someone to come shoot that big sonuva bitch,' Dan says.

Leo frowns, turning to his brother. 'You didn't mention any boar, the boys aren't ready for boar hunting. How long has this been going on?' Turning to the Ranger, he says, 'I'm sorry, thank you for warning us. My brother and I have brought our sons along on their first hunting trip to go out and find some deer.'

'Hmm.' The Ranger looks over their shoulders at the boys further inside. Jordan stands with his chest puffed out and his head held high. Wayne's eyes drift downwards to the rug covering the wooden floor. 'I think it'd be a bad idea for you to go after the boar, especially with any who are inexperienced. I was just coming to warn you, not ask for any help. But don't worry, us park Rangers have got everything under control. If you could just radio us and let us know if you spot the pig, that'd be great. I'll give you the frequency, and you can tell them that Ranger Edson spoke with you before.'

'We can certainly do that,' Leo says.

Dan nods. 'Alright, alright. We won't go lookin' for it, but if we come across that big beauty, we'll shoot it all the same.'

'I appreciate the help. As long as you all stay safe, that's what's most important.'

Ranger Edson exchanges the radio frequency needed to contact the Parkland Rangers' HQ with the fathers.

'It was nice meeting you, Edson,' Leo says, reaching out to shake the Ranger's hand.

Edson shakes Leo's hand, then Dan's. 'Nice meeting the both of you. You have a fun time now, and if you need anything, don't hesitate to radio.'

With that, he gets back into his truck, and left. The sun is setting as he drives back out down the only path leading from the cabin towards the main road.

Bologne sandwiches are all the family have for dinner that night, and the two father's urge their boys to get into bed for an early night's sleep, warning the boys that they'll be up at dawn to begin hunting in the morning; they'll need all the energy they can muster.

Wayne crawls into bed, staring up at the bottom of Jordan's bunk. Not that he knows much about hunting or the protocols surrounding it in places like this, but he worries about how serious the danger of the boar might be, if the Rangers think it's important enough to let them know about it.

'I wonder what it's like, hunting pig. I bet they go down just as easy as deer, if ya shoot 'em 'tween the eyes,' Jordan mutters to himself.

Wayne sighs and turns onto his side, staring out the curtainless window. He doesn't want to be here, but he feels like he doesn't have a choice in the matter. His father's words echo in his head.

'You're gonna have to be a man one day. It's time you grew up! Your uncle and I are going hunting, and you're coming with us. I won't let my son grow up to be a spineless sissy.'

He shuts his eyes tightly, trying to silence the memory of his father's voice. He can't do the same for Jordan's.

'Hmm... nah. I bet they got a thick skull them big fuckers. Might have to shoot 'em straight through the eye instead.'

Listening to his cousin's ramblings, Wayne slowly drifts to sleep.

The rising sun peering through the trees and shining right into the uncovered window, wakes Wayne early, even so, he hears his father and uncle moving about in the other room. He silently slips out of bed and trudges to the door. Stepping out, he's hit with the smell of cooking meat, both men in the small kitchen, preparing breakfast.

Leo turns his head. 'Go wake your cousin. After breakfast, we're heading out.'

Without a word, Wayne turns around and reenters the bedroom, shambling over to the bunk bed again. He jostles Jordan. 'Jordan, wake up. Breakfast's almost ready.'

Jordan shrugs him off and grumbles, pulling the blanket over his head more.

'Come on, we're going hunting after we eat.'

There's a pause before Jordan's head emerges, his short hair messy and his eyes crusted with sleep. 'We are?'

Wayne nods.

The two boys venture to the small table and join their fathers for breakfast which consisted of: a plate of eggs, sausages, and bacon, with glasses of orange juice to wash it down.

Midway through the quiet breakfast, Uncle Dan gestures at the boys with his knife. 'Now you boys enjoy that there meal. It's the last y'all get unless you can kill something out there. A man's gotta provide for himself.'

'Don't worry pa, I bet ya by the end of the night, we'll be stuffed full of the pig I shot,' Jordan says through a mouthful of food.

'Heh, that's my boy.' Dan smiles, patting his son on the shoulder.

'Now now, you can eat pig any time. You're eating it right now.' Leo waves a piece of bacon in Jordan's face. 'Besides, we're not here to hunt that boar I didn't even know anything about.' He glares in his brother's direction. 'We're here to hunt some elk... trust me. You'll want to try some venison if you've never had it before.'

Jordan looks down at his plate, muttering, 'I don't care 'bout no goddamn elk...'

After the four finish their breakfast, the boys change. Once they gather their equipment, they set out into the woods. The men lead the way, while the kids follow behind. Each man and boy carries a Winchester rifle with them. Tthe men have slightly larger rifles loaded with .270 calibre bullets. The boys carry smaller versions, stocked with .243s.

As they travel deeper into the dense forest, Wayne can't help but look around in wonder. Sure, they'd gone camping before, but nothing as out there as this. These woods are so different compared to what he's used to back home, even to those other camping trips, let alone his usual suburban life. There's a warmth that comes from being closer to nature, but at the same time, a coldness that comes from being alone, the two feelings swirl around inside him. The smell is the biggest shift to him. The air out here is so much crisper, cleaner, but it carries a strong, woodland scent of oak and cinnamon, along with the musky smell of dirt and dead leaves underfoot. Speaking of those leaves, each step, no matter how careful, has a distinct crunch and weight to it as his foot dips into the soil slightly, leaving his irrefutable mark in his wake. Their footsteps are not the only sounds they hear as they wander ever deeper into this isolated patch of land. The occasional bird cries out from the trees. Any rustle of leaves or bushes causes every head to turn towards the disturbance, and the unmistakable hum of insects surrounds them. The deeper they go, the more alone Wayne feels.

As they get deeper, the men become more focused. After an hour of walking, they start pointing out hoofprints and signs of deer, teaching the boys how to properly track such beasts. Always look for water, they say. Droppings too are an important sign, once you find their grazing areas and watering holes, you'll be sure to run into one soon.

Wayne does his best to absorb the lessons, crouching low next to his father whenever the man points something out. If he's going to do this, he'll do it right. While Wayne's an upstanding student, Jordan's more jittery and less focused. He's a bundle of energy, one who needs to get to the good stuff already, a loose cannon that needs to be pointed in the right direction before he misfires.

After another hour of tracking, Leo throws his hand out and brings the party to a halt. He gets low and crawls forward. Parting some bushes, he beckons Wayne forward. Wayne lies flat to mimic his father, inching forward, he peers through the gap. His breath hitches in his throat. Standing before them is a beautiful, slender deer, grazing in the grass. She's no more than twenty metres away from them, completely oblivious to their presence.

Dan gestures for Jordan to be quiet as they edge forward to inspect the deer. Jordan gets down and trudges toward the bush, poking his head around the side of it. He frowns upon seeing the young elk. 'It's just a stupid deer, big whoop,' he whispers.

'Quiet, boy,' Dan chastises.

Leo turns to his son. 'Go on Wayne, she's all yours.'

Wayne looks at his father, dumbfounded, but of course, why else are they here?

'If that's alright with you, Dan?' Leo looks at his brother.

'Be my quest. Don't think Jordy's too interested in this one anyway.'

Jordan isn't even facing the deer anymore, he's scanning the rest of the forest, looking for any sign of his desired prey.

Wayne swallows a lump in his throat and unslings his rifle from his shoulder. Under instruction from his father, he lies under the bush, his head buried in the shrubbery but still with a clean line of sight. His barrel sticks out from one end of the bushes, his body the other.

His father crouches close to him, watching the deer. 'Take it nice and easy. Line it up, steady your breathing. It's just like shooting at the range. Keep your eyes on the target, and hit that bullseye. You've done it dozens of times, I know you can hit this shot.' A comforting hand on the middle of Wayne's back does little to calm the boy.

Wayne's heart races. His cheek rests against the side of his rifle, the stock firmly against his shoulder. With one eye he stares at the magnified image of the elk, watching the innocent creature graze, unaware that its life is in his hands; in his index finger. *It's another living being. It couldn't be further from the paper targets at the range.* His breathes heavily, he tries to get it under control along with his pounding heart, and his skull throbs with his panicked heartbeat. He struggles to will himself to take another life.

'It's not going to just stand there forever, son,' his father urges him. 'Take the shot. Before it's too late. Wayne, take the shot.'

Wayne steels himself, holding his breath. His world goes still, he zeroes in on his target, and his finger begins to squeeze the trigger.

But then it moves. The deer's head shoots up, alerted by something. It snaps to the side, staring at something beyond the trees that way. Then it scrambles, hooves skidding and kicking at the dirt as it clumsily bolts out of the little clearing and races away from whatever it saw.

'What in the hell?' Dan stands up, frowning as he looks towards the right, trying to peer through the trees and see what might've spooked the deer.

'Nice one, lil cus,' Jordan says smugly, standing up.

Wayne emerges from the bush, a frown on his face. 'But I didn't do anything.'

'No. That was something else. Something spooked it... don't know what.' Leo pats Wayne on the back, reassuring his son.

'Do you think it was the boar?' Jordan sounds excited by his own prospect.

'Whatever it was, we shouldn't let it get in the way. C'mon, the deer can't have gotten far, let's get after it,' Dan says.

'Right.' Leo gets up and moves out into the clearing. It proves easy to pick up the deer's erratic trail out of the clearing, and the group quickly gives chase, following after it.

As they chase after it, the men take the lead once more. Dan turns to his brother. 'I ain't ever seen one get *that* spooked before. Goddamn thing nearly tripped over itself trying to get outta there.'

'Whatever spooked it must've given it one hell of a fright,' Leo added.

'It must've been the boar then, right?'

Glares from both men are all it takes to shut Jordan up.

As they continue tracking the fleeing deer, a horrible, growling squeal echoes around the woods, seemingly coming from all around them. The group stops in their tracks, looking all around with widened eyes.

'Maybe it really was that damned boar...' Leo mutters.

'I ain't ever heard a boar sound like *that* before either,' Dan says.

A skull-piercing shriek comes from ahead—the agonising cries of the deer spread throughout the forest. The men look at one another, then back at the boys. 'Come on!' Leo says and breaks into a run, rushing towards the source of the pained cries. The boys chase after him and Dan as they disregard any form of stealth, noisily sprinting through the woods.

After several minutes, they stop, coming to the scene of the slaughter. Leo gasps and backs up, bumping into Wayne who peers around his body. Jordan steps around his uncle and slowly creeps forward, standing beside his dad who's gawping down at the mutilated corpse of the deer. 'Oh, sweet Jesus...' Dan makes a quick cross over his chest. Both boys stare silently.

The deer had at least been put out of its misery. It lays dead in the dirt, its guts spilt onto the ground; a large portion of them missing. The soil underneath it is almost sanguine-coloured mud. Its body is nearly split in two, its chest cracked open, bloody ribs sticking out in the air, hardly any meat left clinging to the bones. Its throat is ripped out so badly that there are only a few ligaments and flaps of skin keeping its head attached to the rest of its body.

'Oh, God... what could've done something like *this*?' Leo stares, unable to take his eyes off the bloody aftermath. Wayne grips his hand, and he squeezes back.

'I-I ain't... I ain't seen a boar do something like *this* before... just what kinda monster pig are they dealin' with out here?' Dan finally turns away, and pulls an enraptured Jordan with him.

'How big would a pig have to be to do that?' Jordan says. Wayne swears he sees a sparkle of amazement in his eyes as Jordan imagines taking down such a dangerous predator.

Wayne's silent. What can he say about such a horrid scene? All he knows is that he *really* wants to go back home now, and he hopes his father sees sense and realises they have to go home too. How can they hunt with something capable of *this* lurking about?

'We have to radio this in. The Rangers have to know about this.' Leo fumbles with his bag and pulls the radio out, adjusting it to the right frequency.

'H-Hello? Ranger HQ, do you read me? Over.'

After a moment's silence, a feminine voice answers. 'I read you, this is Wanda at Parkland Ranger HQ, who am I speaking with? Over.'

Leo collects himself with a deep breath. 'My name's Leo Stafford. I'm here renting a cabin in the park to do some hunting with my brother and our sons, and, and I spoke with Ranger Edson last night when we arrived. He gave me this frequency. He told us about a wild boar that has been causing trouble lately, and asked us to report any signs we find of it, and I'm radioing now to tell you that we just found a damn big sign of the thing. ... Over.'

'You spoke with Ranger Edson last night? Over.'

'Yes! And he didn't tell us that this damn boar can rip a deer in half! What I'm looking at here, a normal boar shouldn't be capable of doing. You need to get your people to...' He looks around, his eyes falling on his brother.

'Uhh, I think we're two hours... east-northeast from the cabin.'

'We're roughly two hours directly east-northeast from the Parkland Hunting Cabin. Over.'

'Thank you, we'll note that down but, Ranger Edson spoke with you at your cabin, and then he left? Around what time did he leave? Over.'

'I-I don't know the exact time. It was at sunset. Look, what are all these questions for? Maybe you don't understand the severity of things out here, but this deer the boar killed looks like it's been mutilated by a fucking dinosaur or something! ... Over.'

Wayne had never heard his father swear like that before.

'I understand, sir, and we're taking it very seriously, but right now we have a more pressing issue. Ranger Edson didn't return to HQ last night and we haven't been able to contact with since. We've just started a search party. I suggest you head back to your cabin for today and we'll send someone over to check up on things when we have more information. Over and out.'

Leo lowers the transponder, looking around at the others, his mouth slightly agape.

'Y-You don't think the boar got him ... do you, dad?' Wayne stares at his father.

'Don't be ridiculous, it's just a goddamn pig, even if it can tear up a deer... he was in his truck. He must've just gone home without telling anybody ... and left his radio in the truck,' Dan says.

'Right... y-yeah, I'm sure he's fine.' Leo nods. 'But, it won't hurt to check. We should head on back to the cabin anyway, and we're the closest to the road. If something happened to him, he'll be right there, and if he isn't, then we know he's fine. It won't take long to check.'

Dan agrees with the plan, not seeing any harm in searching.

'We'll take the boys back to the cabin first.'

'Nuh-uh, I'm searchin' too! What if the boar's still around,' Jordan says with more excitement than fear.

'I-I'm not leaving you, Dad... I'm staying with you.'

Leo sighs.

'You can't lock us in the cabin anyway, so you can't stop us from comin'.'

'Well, at least we don't have to go back to the cabin then, and can just start searching now.' Dan acquiesced to the boys' demands fairly quickly.

Leo sighs louder but doesn't say anything. He turns back to the direction of the cabin and starts off towards it. He keeps his rifle at the ready, firmly grasped in his hands as they hurry back the way they had came, making greater time now that they weren't worrying about being quiet, or tracking down any potential prey.

It's a tense journey. It takes them over an hour to make it back to the area surrounding their cabin. Throughout their return, every sound that permeates the forest has their heads on a swivel. Could that be the boar? Do we need to run? Should we stand and fight? Will the two of us be able to handle it? Leo and Dan are experienced enough to know the smaller calibres won't have any effect on a beast capable of that kind of carnage. They hope their two rifles will be enough if it comes down to that.

Once they are near enough to their cabin, the tensions ease slightly, and they veer towards the direction of the path heading out of the forest and back onto the main road. They urge their boys to keep close, both men hold their rifles at the ready. Travelling over the softer, dirt that has been smoothed down into a distinct path thanks to its constant usage by trucks and cars, their footsteps are silent. Once again, they slow their pace, now looking for any sign of Ranger Edson or his truck. Backtracking along the path, it doesn't take them long to find the first and only sign they need. The Ranger's truck lies abandoned in the middle of the road. One door opened as far as it can be.

'Dad?' Wayne calls tentatively.

'Shh.' Leo holds out a hand, then places it back into position on his weapon, shouldering the rifle as he approaches the vehicle carefully. His eyes dart across to Dan as the men split away from one another to cover different sides of the truck.

'You in there, Ranger?' Dan shouts.

Nothing.

'Stay back,' Leo warns the boys. He moves forward briskly and swings around, looking inside the open door. The truck's empty. The radio spits forth chatter from the other Rangers. Leo leaves it for now.

'Christ. Leo, look at this. What the hell do you think he could've run into to make a dent like that?' Dan had moved to the front of the car, staring in horrified awe at the bonnet of the truck that had crumpled inwards.

Leo looks around. 'I don't even think one of those damn moose would've been big enough to make a crater like that, and he didn't run into no damn tree in the middle of the road. ... Ranger Edson!?'

Jordan creeps up to check on the damage done to the truck, his eyes widen at the sight of the totalled vehicle. Wayne's pulled along in Jordan's wake. 'Whoa... do you think it was the boar? Maybe he killed it ... it'd have to be dead if it got hit that hard,' Jordan whispers.

'Dan!' Leo shouts before scrambling off the road and crouching down near a disturbed part of the undergrowth. 'He must've gone this way, chasing after whatever he hit.'

Dan inspects the tracks, pulling up a fallen leaf smeared with blood. 'It's bleedin' bad, whatever it is.'

'Stay with the truck,' Leo commands the boys. He and Dan follow the tracks deeper into the woods. Of course, the boys quietly shadow their fathers, their curiosity taking control.

They follow a path of destruction as if whatever had run through the forest had smashed through as many trees as it could. Many branches are snapped off, bushes trampled, bark scraped off, and some trees are even tipping over. Blood stains everything.

'He must've got that big pig good!' Jordan whispers excitedly.

The Hunt

Wayne frowns. He wants to turn back, but something propels his feet forward. Every step feels worse than the last, but he can't leave his family. One thought runs through his mind—if the Ranger killed the boar, then where is he?

It isn't long before Wayne gets his answer, and they find Ranger Edson ... or what's left of him.

'Jesus fuckin' christ...' Dan says.

'Holy shit,' Jordan exclaims.

'I told you both to wait by the truck.' Leo hurries over and tries to shield the boys from the scene. But nothing can stop it from infesting Wayne's mind.

Ranger Edson is dead. The forest surrounding him is bathed in crimson. The Ranger's torso is propped up against the base of a tree trunk. His jaw set in an eternal scream, his lifeless eyes trapped in a perpetual state of fear. Blood, streaming from a crack in the crown of his skull, caked his face. His arms were gone, only bloody stumps remained near his shoulders, and there were no signs of the limbs nearby. His legs... his legs were only connected to his body by a strewn-out line of intestines, his guts splayed open for display. A crow pecks at the viscera, eating its fill from the corpse.

'It's the boar. The boar got him,' Jordan says.

Leo drags the boys away from the gory scene. 'Dammit, Dan! We're leaving. Radio the HQ and...and tell them we found him.'

Dan tears his eyes from the corpse. Gripping his rifle tighter, he backs away, eyes constantly scanning the forest around him. The monster's out there, he knows it's close. When the bloodshed is out of sight, Dan radios the HQ and lets them know what they'd found.

Wayne sits on his bunk bed, hugging his knees. Jordan sits by the door, it's cracked open just enough for one watchful eye. Though he doesn't need to see to hear his father and uncle arguing.

'I don't care what the Rangers say, they clearly don't have the situation under control. We need to leave and get the boys away from here. We'll go hunting a different time, but I won't take them out there while that... *thing* is still out there.'

'Jesus Leo I...I know where yer comin' from, but these things happen in the wild. The Rangers say they know where the boar's territory is thanks to all the sightings, and we can just hunt in the opposite side of the park. We'll be prepared anyway, why do you think we've got these damn guns if we ain't gonna use 'em? 'Sides, we ain't drivin' anywhere tonight. It's too damn dark.'

'Fuck!' Leo turns away, retreating to the window. He scans the dark forest that surrounds them. 'I don't like this, Danny. In the morning, we're leaving. Soon as the sun's up.'

Dan sighs. 'If that's how you feel after sleepin' on it, fine.'

Leo looks back at his brother. 'This isn't normal. We just need to get out of here and let the Rangers handle it.'

'We can agree on that, at least.'

The argument ends, and the two turn in for the night. Jordan closes the door and climbs onto his bunk, a frown on his face. 'What are they gettin' so worked up about? It's just a dumb pig... why does it have to ruin our huntin'?'

Wayne doesn't say anything other than goodnight as he lies down and closes his eyes. Sleep would be hard to come by that night, as the images of the carnage won't leave him.

Wayne's jostled awake, his cousin's face barely an inch from his own. 'Wake up. We're fixin' this ourselves.'

'Wh-Wha?' Foggy from sleep Wayne sits up. Jordan slinks over to the door and peeks out. It isn't even light out, yet the boy is already dressed in his gear and boots. 'What are you doing?'

'We're goin' huntin'. We're gonna kill that fuckin' pig.' Jordan leaves the room and disappears down the hall.

A chill that no amount of blankets can warm runs through Wayne. He gets out of bed and carefully follows Jordan. Jordan's at the coffee table in the sitting room. His father's rifle lies across it, his father across the couch, empty beer bottles across the floor.

Jordan takes the rifle, then looks for the bullets. Taking those too, and loading the gun, he moves to the door and quietly unlocks it. Wayne follows him before the door swings closed, shutting it gently. 'What are you doing?' Wayne repeats.

'Are you dumb? I already told you. Somebody's gotta take care of that pig, and if no one's gonna do it, I will. 'Sides, you should be mad too. Don't you wanna kill it? It already stole your first kill. You need to get revenge.'

No such desire struck Wayne. 'I-I think we should just leave it alone and head home like my dad said.'

'Tch. Stop bein' such a pussy. When are you gonna grow up?' Jordan shakes his head. 'You can stay here for all I care, but I'M killin' that pig. I *have* to. Then we won't have to leave, and we can keep huntin' like normal, and Dad'll see that I'm not just a little kid any more.' He storms off into the forest, heading down the driven path, going to where they'd last seen signs of the boar—where Ranger Edson had been mutilated.

Wayne closes his eyes. His heart drums loudly in his chest. He wants to run back into the cabin and wake his father and uncle. He wants to scream at Jordan and tell him he's being an immature asshole, and that he's going to get himself hurt. But he doesn't do any of that. Instead, he does what he always did, and he gets swept along by Jordan, silently following him, keeping all his complaints and his worries inside. It always ends up like this, even back when they were younger. Jordan always leads the way and Wayne gets dragged along on whatever adventure the brasher, more confident cousin wants. Usually, it ends up with them getting in a lot of trouble, getting yelled at by their parents and grounded for a day or a week. Usually, not always. Even now, Wayne can't stand up for himself and make his opinion heard. All he can do is follow Jordan as they journey into the unknown.

Eventually, they reach Ranger Edson's abandoned truck. No one had found the keys for it, and the tow truck couldn't make it out last night, so it remains in the middle of the road, a haunting reminder of the Ranger's fate. However, this time, Jordan doesn't directly follow the obvious tracks shooting off into the forest. Instead, he looks on the outskirts of the tracks, and around the site of Edson's murder, looking for more signs of the boar and where it can be.

Wayne doesn't search much, he just meanders behind Jordan, constantly looking over his own shoulder. He shudders every time his eyes wander in the direction where Edson's remains had been found. He can't see it, but Wayne knows there are only a few thin lines of trees and bushes blocking the grizzly scene. 'W-We can't find anything... it's too dark. We should go back.'

'No way. I ain't goin' back 'til I kill that pig.' Jordan squats low to the ground. 'Ah-ha!' He rushes over to a broken branch, looking ahead. 'This way.'

Wayne looks back. They can still turn back. It's getting brighter, but if they turned back now, their parents wouldn't even know they'd left. Jordan doesn't care, he's already pushing on, and Wayne follows. They travel further into the woods, Jordan chases after whatever signs he can find, pulling Wayne along faster and faster. The sun rises over the horizon, illuminating the tracks. The increased light and ease with which they find the ensuing tracks do nothing to ease Wayne's fears.

'J-Jordan... we really need to get back. Come on. Let's just go back to the cabin.'

Jordan growls and whirls around, stomping over to his cousin stopping inches before his face. 'If you want to run back to your mama and cry like a little pussy, go ahead! I don't care. I'm sick of always havin' to hold your hand. I won't let you hold me down anymore. You need to grow up, but I'm not gonna be the one who does it for you, not anymore! I'm a real man now and I'll prove it, to all of you. I don't need to be lookin' after a little baby while I'm huntin'.'

Wayne's mouth drops open, then closes again.

'That's what I thought.' Jordan turns away and returns to the trail again. Wayne can only stare. Neither of them hear the boar.

It blindsides them. Jordan never sees it until it hits him, goring him right through the side with a massive tusk. Wayne only sees a huge, dark blur pass by, the wind almost knocking him off his feet. Blood splashes his chest. The beast crashes into a tree, but that hardly slows it, it brushes by and continues running, carrying Jordan with it. Jordan's high-pitched screams are the thing that finally unfreezes Wayne. He hears the rampaging beast smashing its way through the woods as Jordan keeps squealing. Wayne steps forward, his whole body trembling.

That is *not* a pig. Not like any he'd seen.

Jordan's screams stab Wayne's skull. A gunshot booms. Wayne steps back. He can't see the "boar" and Jordan. It vanished as quickly as it appeared. Wayne needs to get help. Yes. He has to get help. That's why he turns and runs. He's running to get help. Not because every fibre of his body is screaming just as powerfully as Jordan, telling him to get as far away from that monster as possible.

The screams fade, but they still torment Wayne, endlessly. He covers his ears, clutching at his head. Another gunshot echoes through the trees, then all is quiet. He can't hear anything except his heavy panting, the thumping of his heart, and the sound of his feet crashing against the forest floor as he races back to the cabin.

That ... boar, It isn't normal. He saw it, and it isn't normal. It might have the head and the tough, bristly hide of a wild pig, it might be bigger than any he had ever seen but... its body isn't normal. He swears it has a large hump in its back, and that its forelegs are much thicker and longer than its hind legs.

Leo and Dan are already outside of the cabin when Wayne returns. They look as if they'd just thrown on their clothes and are about to head out searching. Wayne had run non-stop. He leans against his father's truck, panting still. Tears stream down his face as the two men rush forward. His father expresses how worried he was, and how happy he is to know that Wayne's safe. Dan's concerned about Jordan and bombards Wayne with questions about the other boy's whereabouts, what they were doing, and what those gunshots were.

When Wayne catches his breath, controls his sobbing, he explains what had happened as calmly as he can, right from the moment that Jordan woke him up, to the point where the boar attacked them, and Wayne fled. All throughout the explanation, Dan's face is a mess of emotions. Starting with anger and concern that his boy is foolish enough to venture into the woods, and at himself that he let it happen. Fear creeps in, then disbelief. 'You... are you lyin' to me? Are the both of you tryin' to play a trick on us? Well it ain't funny! Jordan! Get yer ass out here right now! Or yer in for a world of hurt.'

Wayne shakes his head profusely. 'I-I wish I was lying Uncle Dan... I-I'm sorry I...I tried to get him to come back... I really did! I kept begging him to go back but he-he just wouldn't listen.'

As suddenly as the boar had taken his son, Dan's expression shifts to one of dismay and anguish. His legs wobble and Leo has to support him to keep him standing. Tears fall from the man's face and dampen the ground. He wails—Wayne's heart almost breaks at the sound. Leo puts an arm around his brother's shoulders, hugging him close, pressing his head against him. Dan shoves Leo aside and wipes his face, his despair quickly replaced with burning, vehement hatred. He storms back into the cabin, and swiftly reemerges with Leo's rifle in hand.

'Danny... what are you doing?' Leo asks.

Dan marches past. 'I'm findin' my son, and killin' that god-forsaken monster. I won't let my son's death go unpunished!'

'Danny! Don't be... we need to tell the Rangers and we can go find him together. Danny!'

Dan doesn't stop. He marches through the trees, making his way straight to where Wayne says the boar attack happened.

'God fucking dammit.' Leo shakes his head then hurries after his brother.

'D-Dad?' Wayne starts after them.

Leo looks back but doesn't stop. 'Just wait at the cabin! Tell the Rangers and tell them to get here, *now*.'

'No! I-I'm not leaving you, Dad. A-And I don't want to be alone.'

'Shit.' Leo shakes his head again. Dan hasn't strayed from his revenge-fueled path. Leo can't leave his brother behind, but he can't leave Wayne either. So they all venture back into the woods in search of Jordan ... and the beast.

Dan's frantic march leads the way. It doesn't take long to reach the gruesome scene of the latest attack. However, unlike Ranger Edson's attack, they don't find a body. The only thing they find is blood painting the forest floor, and the shattered remnants of Jordan's rifle.

Dan fires into the air, roaring at the trees. '*You sonuva bitch! I'll kill you! Where's my son!?*'

Leo steps forward, placing a hand on Dan's shoulder. 'Let's go back.'

Dan shrugs off the hand, shaking his head. 'No! I ain't goin' back without him. He's all alone out there. A boy needs his father.'

Leo sighs but relents. 'Alright... it...it can't be far. There must be tracks, a blood trail, something.'

Indeed there is a blood trail and tracks, they aren't hard to find with the sun overhead, luminous rays shining through the cracks of the canopy above. The trail goes on for a few dozen metres, leading to a small creek. Then it just ... ends. It leads to the water, then there are no tracks coming out on the other side.

'Where is it?' Dan searches madly. He stalks up and down the creek's bank, looking for any further sign of the monster or his boy, but finds nothing.

'Dan... we need to turn back. We'll get lost. Let's ask the Rangers for help, then we'll keep searching with them.'

'*No!*' Dan barks, glaring at Leo. 'I bet you wouldn't turn back if it was Wayne out there. So don't you tell me when I can stop lookin' for *my* son.'

Leo winces but holds his tongue. Dan splashes across the creek, figuring that the monster must've crossed over in an attempt to lose any pursuers.

The search continues long into the night, without any sign of Jordan, or the beast. Wayne stumbles along behind his father, stopping and leaning against a tree whenever Dan stoops down to inspect a patch of the ground more closely than the rest. It's hopeless, it's all the same. They hadn't found anything, and with the sun having set, it's unlikely they will find anything. They hadn't eaten or drunk anything, and they'd been running around the woods since sunrise—even earlier for Wayne—Leo's concern for his brother grows the longer this farce of a search drags on. *He's probably already delirious thanks to his heightened, emotional state, and lack of food and water wouldn't be helping.*

'Dan! We *need* to go back.' Wayne can't help but compare how his father's acting now, to how he was with Jordan this morning. He shudders and looks at his Uncle Dan, hoping he isn't marching to his doom as well.

Dan just ignores Leo this time and continues onward, scanning every bit of every little clearing, checking every tree and every bush, literally leaving no stone unturned before moving on.

'We all need rest, you especially. It's doing us no good continuing on like this. Let's just go back. First thing in the morning, we'll head back out with the Rangers, and we'll find him. But we need to rest, we need to eat, and we need light. Please.'

Dan continues as if he's deaf. After a few more paces he stops. He doesn't face Leo and Wayne, but they both hear the tears in his voice. 'I can't... you can't ask me to go back. How can I? How can I go back to that cabin, lay down, and rest? How can I sleep, when I know he's out here? My boy. He's my baby boy, Leo. I can't abandon him. I won't be able to rest 'til I've found him. I'll starve if I have to, and I'll stay up all night. I'll search for as long as it takes 'til I find him. You'd do the same for Wayne. I don't care if you leave me out here with him, you can turn back and rest, you need to look after Wayne. But please, let me do this.'

Leo looks at Wayne, tears shimmering in his eyes, but a faint smile on his lips. 'Looks like we're gonna be searching for a little bit longer, Wayne. You just hold out for a little while more, then we'll be heading back to the cabin real soon.'

Wayne steps back, eyes looking beyond his father, horror overcoming his features.

A gunshot goes off before Leo's head whips around. He turns just in time to see the boar charging towards Dan who stands his ground and unloads another shot at the monster. It doesn't slow down in the slightest, and rams straight into him, piercing his stomach. The impact lifts Dan off his feet and knocks the rifle from his grip; it lands by Leo's feet. The multi-pronged tusk rips through Dan's back, piercing him fully. The monster continues its charge, slamming into a tree. The mighty pine shudders heavily and nearly collapses from the thunderous crash. The boar rears back on its hind legs, lifting Dan higher as he sinks deeper onto the tusk. His screams are muffled by the blood overflowing from his mouth down his chin. With a shake of its humongous head, it flings him from its tusk and sends him crashing to the ground with a sickening thud and a nauseating crack as Dan lands right on his head, snapping his neck.

Leo falls to his knees, staring into his brother's lifeless eyes.

As if the monster doesn't even notice the others there, it prowls over to the fresh corpse, holds its legs down, and rips its guts open with its tusks, further tearing the hole it had already created when it gored Dan. Then, it began to feast.

'*Get the fuck off my baby brother!*' Enraged, Leo grabs the fallen rifle and rises to his feet. He fires, hitting the monster square on the shoulder, but it doesn't react, and keeps feasting, gorging itself on Dan's intestines.

Leo trembles as he chambers the next bullet. He fires once more, this time hitting the monster directly on top of its head. It flinches, and the feast stops. It raises its head, staring at Leo and Wayne, staring with eyes that are all too human. Its jaws ply open unnaturally, the lower jaw splits in the middle, revealing a cavernous mouth filled with a thorny tongue and jagged teeth.

It roars.

It's an unnatural shriek, something no creature on earth should be able to create. Wayne covers his ears. The noise grows louder the more it bounces around his skull. It shakes his bones and sets his heart into overdrive. An image of his own bloody death at the *hands* of this monster fills his vision.

Leo almost drops his rifle as he staggers. He reaches for Wayne and shoves the boy away, soon turning and springing into a sprint. They have to get away. He has to get Wayne away from that thing and keep him safe no matter what. 'Don't look back, just run!' His voice is weak as if the shriek had drained all strength from him. He's pale too, but he runs as fast as legs will carry him, stumbling over himself at times but keeping his feet. Wayne runs with him, their feet pounding the ground in sync, their hearts pumping in sync as well, even each panting breath comes in unison.

A heavy *woosh* passes above them. Leo's eyes widen as Dan's body flies through the air and smashes into a tree, rattling the trunk before breaking apart into two misshapen halves. Blood and gore splash onto father and son as they run. Leo pushes Wayne's head down. 'Don't look! Just run!' He holds Wayne's head. Wayne shuts his eyes tightly.

Another unnatural shriek pierces the air and pierces their hearts. Wayne stumbles but is held up by Leo who forcefully pulls him along. Leo's colder than he ever has been, even as sweat pours down his face. For the second time that day, Wayne runs all the way to the cabin without stopping.

Father and son slam against the side of their truck, only then did Leo let Wayne go. Leo rushes inside the cabin, soon sprinting back out with keys in hand. 'Get in!' He yanks the door open and throws himself into the driver's seat. Wayne jumps in next to him as Leo fumbles with the ignition. 'C'mon, C'mon, C'mon!' He shoves the key inside and twists—the engine roars to life and he stomps on the acceleration. They speed down the bumpy, dirt road, both of them scanning the treeline surrounding either side, looking for the monster, but they see no sign of it.

'Fuck...' Leo breathes heavily, he can't rest easy just yet. He wipes sweat from his brow, his bones still ice cold.

'Uncle Dan's dead... Jordan's dead too... I couldn't stop him.' Wayne curls up on his seat, his head in his hands.

Leo reaches over with one hand, holding onto his son, trying to comfort him somehow. 'It's okay. We're okay. We're gonna be okay.' He suddenly slams on the brakes, the truck screeching to a halt. Ranger Edson's truck is still in the middle of the road. 'Shit!' He looks around, then steers to the side of the road, skirting along the edge to pass the truck and continue down the road. There's a slight decline as they leave the driven path and push through the thickets along its edge. They crawl past the Ranger's truck, just about to right themselves when the boar smashes into their side.

The chassis caves in, and the car tips over like it weighs nothing. The car rolls sideways then pummels a tree. Leo tries to hold onto Wayne as they bounce around the cabin, his seatbelt keeps him mostly secure, but prevents him from stretching out and protecting Wayne who was unbuckled. Wayne slams into his door, bouncing wildly during the roll. He hits his head. His world darkens.

Wayne isn't sure how long he had blacked out for, but when he wakes, his skull is pounding and inky shapes cloud his vision. He's awkwardly lying at the bottom of the wreckage, the truck resting on its side.

'...ne ... Wayne!' A high-pitched drone shoots through Wayne's ears as his hearing returns. He looks up to see his father looking down at him from the top of the car. 'Wayne. You're awake.' Relief washes over Leo's face. 'Just, stay calm, stay still. It's going to be alright.'

'What?' Wayne shifts around, grimacing and hissing as pain flares from his ankle. Touching it, it's already swollen, moving it at all caused sharp pains to run up his leg. *Is it broken?*

'Wayne. Take the gun.' Leo passes the rifle down by its sling.

'Dad... what are you—'

'Just take it. Hurry.'

Wayne grabs a hold of it.

Leo lets go, smiling. 'When it's safe, you get out of there. Head to the road, don't stop.' Tears roll down his cheeks. 'I love you. I've always been proud of you, son. Tell your mother I love her too, and I'll miss her... and that I'm sorry... I'm so sorry.'

Before this trip, Wayne had never seen his father cry, and now here he is, tears flowing freely for the second time that day. Before Wayne can ask what's happening, Leo drops from the car and staggers into the woods, clutching his side.

'Dad... no... don't leave me.' Wayne tries to pull himself out of the truck, but the pain is unbearable and he slumps back down. Where's Leo going? Why had he left the gun? Why didn't he take him? Wayne settles on the answer that his dad must be going for help, and he'll be back soon with others. That answer satisfies Wayne for a moment, and he lies his head back, closing his eyes, content to fall back asleep and wake only when someone comes to rescue him. His eyes burst open when he hears the monster's cry in the distance. It came from the direction his father had run towards.

His father won't be returning.

Wayne's last tear drips down his face. Again, he pulls himself up, pushing through the pain this time as he drags himself free from the wreckage. He tumbles off the car and lands on his side with a heavy thud followed by a loud groan. He slowly stands. With one last look towards the last place he had seen his father, he closes his eyes and silently says goodbye to the man he had loved all his life. He knows he has to survive, for everyone's sake. He turns away from the way his father had run, and limps into the forest. He can barely tell where he's going. Each step brings agony, and his vision hasn't cleared. He's exhausted and cold. He walks for as long as he can, but eventually, he trips, and no matter how hard he tries, he can't pick himself up.

Am I going to die?... Am I dying now? He pants weakly. He looks around wearily and finds some exposed roots that had grown overground and created a small arch by the base of a tree. He crawls towards it, nestling himself under the leafy roots. He slumps down fully, his body relaxing. He closes his eyes again.

It's daylight when he wakes. He has no idea what time it is, but it's warm and sunny, and miraculously, he's alive. He might wish for death his head aches that painfully, and his ankle and foot feel as if they were aflame, the swelling has only gotten worse. It's definitely broken. Still, he pulls himself out from under the roots and back onto his feet. He takes in his surroundings but has no idea where he is. He can't give up though, and picking a direction, he walks as best he can on one leg. He prays he chose correctly.

His stomach gnaws at him. It feels as if it's eating itself. His throat is drier than a desert and he's dizzier than he's ever been, having to constantly steady himself against the trees just so he stays in a straight line. After walking for what felt like an entire day, he finally spots the road. Freedom! Safety. He hobbles towards it with renewed vigour, hurrying to the edge of the treeline, however, just before he steps out, he freezes. The road is deathly quiet, and nothing is in sight. But still he does not step out from the safety of the trees and expose himself on that open strip of road. It's there. He can *feel* it. The boar is watching, waiting. Waiting for him to run away and expose himself.

He doesn't know how, but every part of his body, even his very soul warns him not to step foot on that road. *Don't be crazy. If it...it would've already killed me if it's nearby. How could it know? Why would it be watching the road? It's just a dumb animal; a stupid pig. Just like Jordan said.*

He clutches his chest and leans against the tree. He can't stop the dying screams of his loved ones from replaying in his ears, nor can he block out the events of Uncle Dan's death, and imagined visions of scenes of Jordan's and his father's grizzly ends. Then his own mutilated body pops into his mind's eye, his gutless corpse splayed out on the road, the tarmac painted red with his blood. He steps away from the treeline and creeps further back into the forest.

He can't run away.

Not while that thing's still out there. He has to put a stop to it. For his family, and his peace. So he can be free.

He turns his back on the road and shambles through the woods again, throwing himself deeper into the monster's territory.

He needs water, badly. He wanders through the trees until he finds a stream, collapsing by it. He drinks greedily, as if he wants to drink it dry. His face is drenched when he sits up. His mind is clearer with one of his needs met. His ankle still burns and throbs, only getting worse the longer he's out here, and his stomach continues to cannibalise itself. He needs to act fast.

But how can he find the boar, and how can he ensure *he* found *it* and not the other way around? There's no way he'd survive if it got the jump on him like it had everyone else. Then he saw it, an elk just across from him. It stoops its graceful head and begins to drink from the same stream, as if it hadn't even noticed him. Perhaps he's in such a sorry state it thought he's some strange, harmless part of nature.

'Bait... I have to use a trap.'

He waits until the deer drinks its fill, then stands and crosses to the other side of the stream. He carefully studies the ground, searching by rocks and roots until he finds what he's looking for. He crouches down and carefully scoops up a handful of manure. The small pile of deer shit is still fresh, and still has a sour stench. With the manure in hand, Wayne travels further away from the stream until he finds a large clearing. He checks there's plenty of cover from the brush surrounding the clearing, then he sets the manure down in the middle of it.

Taking up a fist-sized rock, Wayne crushes the manure, releasing an even fouler stench that burns his nostrils. If he had anything in his stomach, he most likely would've puked it up at that moment. He tosses the shit-smeared rock down next to the crushed dung and then scrambles back to the brush. He lies in the thicket, covering himself with it, only the barrel of his rifle and the scope pokes out from it as he keeps a close eye on the clearing.

He hopes the boar comes, though trusts it would; it's a hunter too, and it won't be able to resist the pungent aroma of its prey. He waits and waits, unmoving from his spot. Hours pass, he hasn't moved a muscle since dropping into his hiding spot.

Then it arrives. Without a sound, it steps into the clearing. The silence with which such a massive monster moves horrifies him, but Wayne doesn't allow himself to shudder. He keeps perfectly still, his sights trained on the boar.

It sniffs around the clearing, and Wayne gets a perfect look at the monster. Demonic is the only way to describe it. Its thick snout is covered in blood both old and new. Chunks of flesh still cling to its many tusks. Each huff of its nose sucks a pile of leaves into the air, and sounds like the growl of an engine.

Its snout brushes the stone Wayne had used to crush the shit. It snarls and smacks the rock aside, casually puncturing a tree. It looks right at Wayne's hiding spot.

Wayne holds his breath, staring into the eye of the boar as it stares back. Those eyes are too human; the same shade of brown as his own. They don't belong on such a monstrous face, yet at the same time, anything else would been even more out of place.

Wayne pulls the trigger.

The gunshot reverberates around the silent forest. It's as if time stands still. Not even the air moves as Wayne stares at the boar. And then the boar falls like a crumbling tower, crashing into the earth with a boom that shook the forest. It never rises.

It's dead.

The Hunt

Wayne stands. He can't take his eyes off the lifeless monster. His first kill. He feels nothing as he stares at the corpse. His father, uncle, and cousin are avenged, but nothing can bring them back.

He leaves his kill behind. He is no more of a man than before he pulled the trigger, but it doesn't matter. He returns to the road, the sun setting on the final day of his hunt.

This time, he steps out onto the road and doesn't look back. He leaves the forest—everything—behind.

www.ingramcontent.com/pod-product-compliance
Lightning Source LLC
LaVergne TN
LVHW021701060526
838200LV00050B/2459